SANTA CUTIE
A SPICY HOLIDAY ROM-COM

CHERRYVILLE
BOOK ONE

JENNY ALEXANDRA

A NOTE FROM THE AUTHORS

While this book is a fun and (hopefully) hilarious rom-com, it also touches on subject matter that may be difficult for some readers. If you're worried that trigger warnings might spoil the story for you, please skip the following paragraph and enjoy the book.

This book includes depictions of religious-cult abuse, family estrangement, references to past sexual harassment, a narcissistic parent, and a parent living with dementia. These topics are handled with care and are informed by the authors' real-life experiences.

For the deconstruction girlies

CHAPTER 1

I have a problem.

Not the kind of problem people have with alcohol, drugs, or having sex with an ex when Mercury is retrograde.

This problem is taller, sparklier, and slightly pricklier.

"You hoard Christmas trees!" my best friend Allison shouts across Home Depot's parking lot as we wrestle to push the floor model onto one of those rickety orange carts. We're breathless, sweaty, and sound like we're pushing out a baby—not a seven-foot fake Norway spruce.

She's right.

Hello, my name is Melody, and I am a Christmas tree addict.

I'd cue the chorus of "Hi, Melody," but let's be honest: no one else has this problem.

Ally stops to catch her breath. "Whatever happened to the 'every time we buy something, we get rid of something else' rule?"

"First," I huff, pushing the cart (are these wheels rusty?), "I live in a home, not a library. I don't have to return shit to justify getting new shit."

I'm really hoping she doesn't bring up the storage unit.

"What about the storage unit?"

Goddamnit.

The storage unit is the mysterious abyss where all my Christmas trees go at the end of each season—

"I've seen Christmas trees go in, but never come out," Ally says. Her tone has the accusatory edge of a *Dateline* narrator.

"That is because I buy a new one every year. I don't need the old ones—yet."

I have flocked trees, white trees, berry-and-pinecone real-touch evergreens, trees with multi-colored lights, and trees that barely light up at all. Each one is different. And each one is necessary.

Definitely, absolutely *necessary*.

The cart veers off course, and it takes every muscle fiber I've gained in my 30-day wall Pilates program to steer this bitch back toward my car. So far, we've hit one Chevy van and two Mercedes with our Christmas spirit.

Ally stops again to make a point.

"You know, Fitz was a starving kitten before my parents rescued him. For years, they had to check every bag of cat food before it went in the pantry, just to make sure he wasn't ass-up in a bag of Meow Mix."

Fantastic. We've reached the point where I'm being compared to Ally's ancient childhood cat.

I sigh.

Yes, I was deprived of Christmas. Now, I'm the one ass-up in a bag of Santa's cookies.

As an ex-member of Heaven's Heralds (that's a religious cult, not a children's choir), you'd think they'd be all about the baby Jesus' birthday celebration, but no. Growing up under their roof meant creepy pre-recorded hymns on CD instead of live Christmas carols, the scent of Lemon Pledge instead of gingerbread or pine, and the haunting absence of illuminated trees in deep December. Just as my luck would have it, I was born into the one cult that considers itself Christian, but also feels superior to all the other Christians because they refuse to engage in anything with "pagan" origins.

So basically? That's everything under the sun (or should I say Ra?).

In that world, birthdays were the most offensive to God (and God is very easily offended, apparently). Frolicking beneath a tree used in ancient solstice celebrations to honor the Big J's birthday? Big no-no.

So were the Pledge of Allegiance, the Easter bunny, and my own birthday, which I still struggle to celebrate just because of all those times I had to turn down birthday party invites and buttercream cupcakes. The year I finally left, I bought a dozen cupcakes on my birthday and ate them all in one sitting. I puked them all back up the next morning (worth it), but I digress.

Back to Christmas.

While some kids relished telling others Santa wasn't real, I got to break the news that neither was Jesus' birthday—he was actually born in the spring. Birthdays weren't really his vibe anyway since his bestie, John the Baptist, was murdered and his head was served on a silver platter as a birthday gift. Nice visual for my fellow six-year-olds, right?

Luckily, I only divulged this information when hounded—and usually, while I was stuck sitting in the hall, watching all the other kids (even the ones in in-school suspension!) eat Christmas goodies before break. You know what's worse than a six-year-old with FOMO? A hangry and humiliated six-year-old with FOMO.

Now the payback for that FOMO is a storage unit packed with Christmas trees and a bank account that bleeds red and green—every December.

3

Cue the world's smallest jingle bells.

"It's not gonna fit," Allison says as we try to wedge the box in the backseat of my tiny silver Honda Civic.

"It'll fit," I say, using the Gucci boots I'm paying off with buy-now-pay-later at 20% interest to jam the box into the car. (They must be good for *something* besides debt.)

"Mel," Allison says, wiping a bead of sweat from her brow.

I decided to switch tactics.

"You're going to break your car!" Allison presses her hands to her cheeks, watching me body-slam the door—my dogged persistence in action (often to my own detriment).

"It… will… fit… Goddamn it!" I swear I hear an artery pop in my neck, but it's just the door clicking shut. A satisfied grin spreads across my face as I dust off my hands.

"It's not latched," she says, grimacing.

"It's fine," I say, turning my back on her. "Get in the car."

WHEN I GET HOME, Ally helps me carry the (now slightly crunched) box up to my apartment. I hand her a Tupperware full of freshly baked red-and-green M&M cookies (her payment), and she squeals with delight, skipping off to share them with her fiancé. And by share, I mean she'll let him have one and then hoard the rest.

Now the real work begins.

I drag the box to my living room, slice it open with a box cutter, and take a breath before pulling out the tree, section by section. First, I unfold the base and then slide each section into the next, fluffing branches as I go. I'm an expert tree builder at this point. I fish the top from the box, grab a ladder, and crown her. Finally, I give the branches a quick spruce, making sure the tree is full and symmetrical.

Now for my favorite part.

I get on all fours and crawl under the tree. I find the cord and plug my seven-foot fake spruce into the wall.

When I crawl back out, she's like a shiny beacon of hope. Big, fat, colorful LED globe lights—I simply *had* to have her. Never mind that she was $500. Never mind that I already have at least four other trees with colorful LEDs. This tree is different. This tree is unique. This tree is *special*.

Something I've said about all of my trees. And the truth is, I feel that way about every single one of them.

I love them so much, I give them all names. I think I'll call this one Elsa, on account of her being modeled after a Norway spruce.

(*Frozen* was set in Norway, right? I only saw the movie once because I thought it was Pixar and instead got accosted with singing and ice-princess makeovers.)

My new baby is colorful and gorgeous, but bare—time to doll Elsa up. My gaze drifts to the tiny closet tucked between my living room and kitchen. Ah, yes, the Closet of Doom.

The Closet of Doom is my "junk drawer" closet. Since the storage unit is completely jam-packed with Christmas trees, everything else I've collected in thirty years of life is stuffed inside this postage-stamp-sized cave. Once, as a semi-joke, Ally taped a hand-written sign to the door: "Open at your own risk." Fair, considering she once opened it without permission and got pummeled in the head by a box of books I've been hoarding since sixth grade. Turns out *The Baby-Sitters Club* and *Sweet Valley High* are as good a weapon as any.

Allison had a sizable goose egg for two weeks, and I was so freaked out that I left the sign up for at least ten months.

That closet has it all: winter jackets, boxes of childhood memorabilia from my parents' house after they kicked me out, shoes I don't feel like putting away when company comes over, and, of course, Christmas ornaments.

It's always been my dream to have so many ornaments that I'd have a true collection. Enough to be a picky bitch when choosing the tree's aesthetic each year. And yes, people disorganized enough to nearly kill their best friends with the contents of their closets can still have a fabulous aesthetic. No one sees the inside of the closet anyway—and when it comes to home organization, my motto is, "it's what's on the outside that counts."

I brace myself, crack the door, and stick one foot out in case any of the three dozen Amazon boxes decide to stage a coup. After some careful rooting around, I find two red storage bins full of ornaments. One look at Elsa's multicolored globes, and it's clear this Norwegian girly needs a vintage vibe. I dig through the tissue paper in search of this year's lewk and settle on *White Christmas* meets *Home Alone* (the first one—obviously).

Dragging the boxes into the living room, it occurs to me—I decorate my tree alone every year. I could invite Allison, I guess, but tree decorating has always been my personal reaffirmation ritual. Reaffirming that my life outside the cult—outside of my family—was worth celebrating. The lights, the trees, the tinsel aren't just sparkly, pretty things. They're my freedom.

My parents think I started rebelling at 17, but it was actually middle school. I was tired of being sent into the hallway, tired of parroting Biblical interpretations I could barely recite (much less understand) to prepubescent classmates, who used everything as ammunition to make me an outcast. Tired of knowing how to spell "righteousness" before I could spell "Mississippi." I was a social pariah, ripe for bullying. Darwin—another thing the Heralds don't believe in—could've seen this one coming and taken that bet to Vegas.

By high school, I was fighting with my parents every weekend. The only thing worse than kids picking on you is adults profiting from a cult picking on you. My anxiety was at an all-time high. I was "disciplined" for failing to stay out of "worldly" things—like wanting higher education, having opinions about political candidates, and caring about women's rights.

I hang a sparkling green present-shaped ornament on Elsa and sigh. As much as I'd love the company (and Allison would never say no to a good Chardonnay), this process is my religion now.

The phone rings. An unknown number with an area code I know all too well. It's that time of year, and there's one person I do regret leaving behind. I send her to voicemail, like I do every year. I know in my heart it will never change—she will never actually leave the cult—and because of that, I wish she'd just stop calling.

In true T. S. Elliot fashion, I didn't leave the cult with a bang —I left gradually, with a whisper. And when my parents realized I wasn't coming back, it broke their hearts. I'm not sure they would have cut me off on their own, but the pressure to "do what's right"—to abandon your daughter in the name of God— is intense. Especially when you're hounded every day, and told your eldest, most rebellious kid will lead the younger ones astray. Oh, and probably get into drugs. To be fair, I've never been into drugs (maybe the occasional special gummy before bed), but I can see how that threat would be a powerful, last-ditch bid for control.

In the end, it was easier to cut me loose in God's name than to stand up to an organization and uproot an entire life and belief system.

My mom has been to my apartment exactly once in the last six years—ironically, in December—and when she saw the Christmas tree (that year it was Cindy Lou Who), she had a flash of lucid sentimentality. She said, "You remind me so much of your grandmother." A cult-free, Italian woman who obsessed all year round over Christmas and started baking her famous cookie spreads in September. When I took it as a compliment, my mom's brain seemed to short-circuit—probably from the strain of thinking for herself and the reality of the estrangement —and she told me I'd chosen Christmas over her.

I haven't seen her since.

Luckily, I had Ally and her fiancé Teddy to get me through the pain of it. Plus, my job as a senior interior decorator for an online home-decorating app keeps me busy, if not broke. The pay is crap, but at least I can work from home. Like I said, I value my freedom above all else.

I spend a good three hours hanging ornaments on the tree before the colorful bulbs start forming little halos, and I can barely keep my eyes open. I change into candy-cane pajamas and crawl into my big comfy bed alone—always alone.

Tomorrow is Saturday, and I start my new weekly volunteer gig at a local nursing home. Volunteering is something my therapist suggested a few years back when I was struggling to come to terms with the living loss of my family. I've worked in soup kitchens feeding the unhoused, read books to under-resourced kids, and walked dogs at the animal shelter. But my favorite by far has been delivering meals to seniors. They're truly forgotten over the holidays, and visiting them reminds me of being with my grandma on Christmas—the only holiday tradition I was allowed (a little secret my parents kept from their meddling cult).

This year, I scoured Craigslist and landed an opportunity to play Mrs. Claus once a week at Forest Park Assisted Living. I've never been more excited for a volunteer shift, but they want me there at eight a.m. (apparently, that's lunch time for some of these early birds). I set my alarm and smother my face in an assortment of creams before drifting off.

I dream of an entire forest of Christmas trees of all shapes and sizes—some with starry twinkling lights, others with colorful blinking lights.

In the distance, I hear the deep, barrel-chested laugh of the man who skipped my house year after year, even after I set out

8

secret glasses of milk and whatever cookies I could scavenge in my parents' pantry.

I try to catch a glimpse of red among the sea of trees, but there are too many, and the lights are too bright and blinding. Eventually, the sound of laughter and jingling bells fades. I collapse in the middle of the forest. I don't hear him anymore.

The trees loom large and lovely around me.

I am alone. Always alone.

CHAPTER 2

$\mathcal{M}$y alarm goes off with the same jingling bells from my dream. Disoriented, I smack the snooze button without thinking. When I finally come to, I've overslept by a solid twenty minutes.

I rocket into the Mrs. Claus red velvet dress with faux fur trim, slip on my jingle bell shoes, and cinch a shiny black belt around my waist. With my teeth—so help me, God—I rip open the Amazon package that arrived yesterday, revealing a white, synthetic wig gathered into a messy bun. I pin up my long, auburn waves and pull the wig over my head. Mangled ringlets fall around my face and ears, and I do my best to fluff them out.

No time for a real face, so I grab my makeup bag and go. While trying not to swerve, I tap a circle of rouge onto the apples of my cheeks; at a stoplight, I swipe on a vibrant red lip. In the Forest Park lot, I rummage through my purse until I find a pair of oval spectacles—and just like that, Santa's sweetie is complete.

I grab the giant plastic-wrapped platter of cookies (the other half of the same batch I made for Ally) and bound inside.

The middle-aged receptionist greets me with a frown. Her

boxy cable-knit sweater sports a name tag in giant, easy-to-read letters: MISSY.

"You're late." She eyes me up and down, lingering on the shortness of my dress. "And a little young."

"I'm an old soul," I say, swallowing an eye roll and ignoring the late part—late is the price of free labor. I glance around. "Where's hubby?"

Missy points through an open doorway to where a crowd of old ladies giggle. I peel the wrap off my tray and offer it to Missy (she takes two cookies) before skipping off to the community living room.

It's a rippling ocean of white hair as the ladies cling to a tall, bearded man in a cranberry-red suit like he's Elvis. He throws his head back in laughter, hands on a pillow-stuffed belly, and the old ladies' squeals could register on the Richter scale.

A smile spreads across my face as his gaze lifts from his admirers to meet mine. My heart nearly falls out of my chest when I lock eyes with the most piercing blue I've ever seen. I'd assumed the Santa they chose for this gig would be much older, but there's only a light crinkling under his eyes when he smiles. Even behind the fake snow-white beard, I can tell he has a beautiful smile.

I fear I may swoon.

"Mrs. Claus!" he booms in a deep baritone that is probably an octave lower than his natural voice. It's charming—and goofy enough to snap me out of my hot-for-Santa haze.

"Yes, dear?" I answer without missing a beat, and I swear I catch a few disappointed glances from Santa's aged harem. Luckily, the ice here melts fast; the glares thaw, which is great, because I haven't been glared at over a boy since high school. Or, honestly, maybe ever.

I push toward the center of the elderly mosh pit, and he hooks an arm around my waist, pulling me to his side with surprising confidence.

Goddamn, he's strong. Never thought I'd get manhandled by Santa Claus, but I don't hate it. My eyes skim down his chest—ogling the outline of defined pectorals under thick red velvet.

"There she is." He winks. "My beautiful bride, the Queen of Christmas, who doesn't look a day over..." He leans in, squinting at me beneath my slightly lopsided, Dollar-Tree specs. "Twenty-eight."

I'm positive my face is now redder than Rudolph's schnozz.

The women sigh in unison, but I don't break eye contact.

"You don't look a day over... thirty-two yourself, Mr. Claus," I mutter, as flustered as the senior sirens pushing and shoving to rub up against Kris Kringle.

He smirks, still holding my gaze—until an elderly woman cuts in, shattering the spell.

"You're hogging him, toots!"

"Yeah," another grey-haired babe pouts. "And *you* get to have him all year!"

I can't help but laugh. Horny-for-Santa senior ladies were not on my bingo card for today.

Without breaking character, Santa eyes my cookies (the actual cookies, on my tray) and motions everyone toward the center of the activity room.

"How about some cookies and punch for all you good girls?"

Giggles all around. Someone stage-whispers, "Only if there's rum!"

"From your lips to God's ears, Grandma," I murmur, following my holly-jolly husband and his white-haired harem to the refreshments table.

Looking around the room, it's obvious that Forest Park didn't have much coinage to spend on Christmas this year. A sad strand of battery lights droops across the mantel; several bulbs are burned out. A few plastic berries and a wilted faux-pine sprig have been haphazardly hot-glued to the garland. A row of stockings—some festive and some, well, literal socks—

hangs unevenly, seams a little frayed. An ancient artificial tree slumps in a corner, strung with a few bulbs and beat-up hand-made ornaments, likely from residents' grandchildren. The overall effect is less "holiday magic" and more "what we could scrounge."

Missy comes in behind me with a cheap plastic punch bowl and catches me staring at the stockings.

"Do you fill those with bingo cards or something?" I ask.

Missy scoffs as if I've asked the dumbest question on earth and arranges the punch bowl on the plaid tablecloth beside my reindeer cookie tray. From beneath the table, she produces a half-empty bottle of rum, twists off the cap, and pours it gener-ously into the bowl. She stirs the punch vigorously as if it's more for her than the residents, ladles some into a small cup for her to "taste," and then tucks the bottle back out of sight.

"We do what we can," she says, throwing back the cup and ladling herself another.

She clocks my face, lifts a brow. "Studies show that seniors in nursing homes or palliative care benefit from a daily happy hour."

I nod. I'd love to see that study.

I'm pro-libation, but it's not even nine o'clock in the morn-ing. And as far as I can tell, Missy is not an ailing senior—just an ailing member of the admin staff, which I can certainly empathize with.

She registers my shock, ladles a third helping, and heads back to the front desk.

"Time isn't real when you're old," she calls over her shoulder.

Well, I can't argue with that.

The elderly smell the rum like sharks smell blood. In a flash, both the women and the men—who have been sulking in the corner while their 85-year-old girlfriends fawn over Chippendale Santa—leap up (bad hips be damned) and shuffle toward the punch bowl. I step back to avoid the stampede.

A few old men give me the up-and-down. I hear one of them say "knockers," and I pray to God he's talking about my knees.

Maybe I will have some punch after all.

I scan the room to see what Hot Santa is up to and find him helping a woman in a wheelchair. He fixes her a plate and wheels her to a table before he turns to help another woman with a walker into her chair.

Santa sits, and I grip my snowman cup a little tighter. Totally normal to go over and talk to him, right? I mean, we're volunteering together, and I'm sure the residents want us to stay in character as husband and wife. Also, I want a better view of those velvet red pants. They're lightweight—giving "gray sweatpants"—and I'm melting faster than the ice in my drink.

"Been a while, sugar?" A raspy voice cuts through my fantasy. I jolt, totally mortified.

I look down at a woman in a wheelchair. She has tightly permed white hair and a face full of personality—laugh lines, bright red lipstick bleeding just past her lip line, and mischievous green eyes that sparkle like she's up to something. She's dressed to impress, in an oversized Christmas-tree sweater and dangling ornament earrings. Even her wheelchair is wrapped in tinsel.

She grins up at me, a tiny smudge of lipstick on her teeth—adds character.

"You've got a little drool, honey." The woman taps the corner of her mouth. I feel a flush rise up my neck. "Don't feel bad, we all do. And no, it's not because we're missing teeth. Well, maybe for Maude. She's had shitty dental work this year."

"That's… too bad," I manage.

She breezes on, unfazed. "They bring Eben every year because he is so sweet to us old geezers and has a very big… heart." She times the wink perfectly, and suddenly, I want to relocate to the North Pole out of secondhand embarrassment.

"Oh, you know," is all I can muster. I take a very loud sip from my nine a.m. rum punch.

The woman extends a wrinkled hand, flashing crooked candy-cane nails. "I'm Edna."

"I'm Mrs—" I start, but she levels me with a look. "Melody."

"Well, Melody, get in line," she cackles, then wheels away.

I sigh, wishing my partner were a little troll man. I feel like a dog in heat.

Eben's table is filling fast. Ladies jockey for seats, dragging chairs over as he ho-ho-hos with these elderly (and hilarious) ho-ho-hos. I'm pretty sure I just witnessed one woman trip another with a rose-gold cane.

Thinking of Edna's wink, my stomach tightens. Apparently, it's so obvious that even someone with cataracts can spot it: I haven't been dicked down since RBG was alive.

My mom used to say older people know everything. I figured dementia and potent opioids would spare me from public humiliation among the older set. Still, I'm starting to think that while this crowd might not remember your name, they'll absolutely clock if you haven't boned anyone in half a decade.

I pull myself together and shoulder my way toward the party table, where Eben dusts crumbs off a woman's sweater. She coos, and the woman on the other side of him deliberately drops half her cookie into her own lap. I haven't seen fangirling this intense since my first and only One Direction concert.

I drag a chair through the crowd and claim my rightful place beside him. I eye the plate of my homemade cookies on the table in front of him—a few have already been nibbled. I smile. "Which one do you like best?"

Eben gives a jolly, performative chuckle. "Well, Mrs. Claus, they're all good, of course."

Leaning in, I whisper, "I'm Melody, by the way."

His glacier-blue gaze meets mine—unreadable. Maybe I

shouldn't have broken character; I didn't mean to throw him off his game.

As if on cue, a bell rings, and I'm saved by it.

Missy stands in the doorway with a giant cowbell, signaling it's time to move on to the next activity. The men file out like a drill team; the women linger, blowing dramatic kisses at Eben. He soaks it up, pretending to catch each one and pocket it, waiting until the room is empty to yank off his hat.

"They're a rowdy bunch," I say, relieved to use my normal chest voice again.

He rips off his wig and beard in one swift motion. I nearly spray a mouthful of rum punch all over him and his plate of half-eaten cookies. Underneath the Santa costume is the *hottest* man I've ever seen in real life: ashy blonde hair, mussed from wig wearing, full lips, high cheekbones, a jawline that could cut glass. A face card that would never decline—even at Saks. Who knew those pretty blue eyes were just the cherry on top of the Sexy Santa sundae?

Then I realize that icy blue has gone glacial. He drops the beard onto the table.

"Fuck Christmas."

CHAPTER 3

I feel like I just got hit with a stun gun. A shock wave rolls through me, but I'm frozen in place. Hates Christmas? But he's Santa Claus!

Okay, he's not really Santa Claus, you idiot. Get it together.

I down the rest of my rum punch in one gulp.

"What's wrong with Christmas?" is all I can manage to squeak out. Considering it's my favorite time of year—

Something I was deprived of year after year, as a kid—

And may or may not be the reason I'm no longer speaking to my immediate family—

His comment lands like a literal shock to my system.

I don't know why I assumed anyone outside a religious cult would love Christmas the way I do—maybe all the songs, like "It's the Most Wonderful Time of the Year" and "Joy to the World." This poser is my first true Scrooge born outside Heaven's Heralds (and, I guess, *The Muppet Christmas Carol*).

Eben plants his hands on his knees and stands. He's well above six feet tall, which two minutes ago would've added to the sex appeal. But I've never had a jingle-bell boner dissolve faster than when a man tells me he hates Christmas.

Then it occurs to me: maybe he's Jewish? Or aggressively Atheist? He can't be a Herald—donning a Santa suit, even to bring cheer to the infirm, is strictly a no-no. Maybe another religion allows Christmas-adjacent activities. Or perhaps this is community service for a DUI. Who am I to judge his yuletide affliction?

"Sorry, it's none of my business," I say as he yanks the pillow from his suit and tosses it onto a floral couch.

"Damn right it's not," he says, stripping down to a plain white tee and the kind of chiseled torso that inspires wet panties.

Not me. I'm as dry as an old fruitcake.

Fuck you, dude. Okay, now it's official. I hate nursing home Santa's guts.

Unfortunately, I don't have a change of clothes. So I stomp across the room in my jingle-bell shoes, grab my now-empty cookie tray, and make for the door.

I'm about as intimidating as a mouse that wasn't stirring in *Twas the Night Before Christmas.*

Before I can beeline out of there and never look back (I'm sure Meals on Wheels would still have me), Missy breezes in.

"Great work today, Mr. and Mrs. Claus!" she trills, cheeks flushed—spirits clearly lifting her spirits. "The girls can't stop talking about what a cute couple you are. The guys—well, I won't repeat what they said about you, Mrs. Claus, but it's clear you're both a big hit with our Forest Park family."

Eben and I exchange a look. I try to make mine sizzle with contempt. No idea if he notices.

"I'm so glad they enjoyed it, but I—" I start to say this Saturday is my first and last day—on account of Saint Dick-bag over here—but she barrels on.

"Is Wednesday at seven good for you both for pageant planning?" Missy asks, then adds: "It's the highlight of my year!" She does a little clap and shakes her fists to punctuate her excitement.

Um.

"I'm sorry, what?" I ask. There's a noticeable edge to my voice. Both sets of eyes flick to me. I must look pissed, because Missy's jubilee fades back to stoic.

"It was on the listing that you agreed to. A Mrs. Claus to pass out Christmas cookies and cheer and plan the Fifth Annual Forest Park Christmas Pageant."

Oh, cute. They've been doing this since the last time I got laid.

Curse me and my inability to read an entire ad before responding.

"Is Mr. Claus... going to be involved with the planning too?" I ask.

"He sure is!" Missy beams. Apparently, everyone here thinks Eben is a real headliner—everyone except me. I'm the lucky gal who gets to see the darker, yuletide-yucking side of Santa Claus.

Merry Christmas to me.

"Fine," I sigh, clutching the empty silver tray to my chest without thinking. Cookie crumbs shower my dress; a rogue smear of chocolate streaks the velvet.

When I look up, Missy and Eben are blinking like I'm either on the verge of a breakdown or a cornered wild animal about to bite.

Lucky for them, I was raised in a cult. Even under scrutiny, I'm the picture of calm, cool, and collected. My cards are glued to my chest; I will never show my hand—even under duress.

Maybe why I can't catch a dick, I don't know.

"Well, it was nice meeting you," I lie. "See you Wednesday!"

(Unless I hurl myself off a cliff first.)

My jingle bell shoes only add to my humiliation as I walk across the room like a merry maraca. I don't give Eben a second glance, but I feel his eyes on me all the way out.

Inside my head, I rip off my jingle-hell shoes and hurl them at his pretty, stupid face.

On the way home, I swing by the Toasted Cherry—Cherryville's cozy neighborhood roastery known for its seasonal drinks—to pick up my comfort beverage: a large Toasted Cherry Nog Latte with extra foam. It's got espresso (obviously), eggnog, and a sweet kick of toasted-cherry reduction. Basically, a hug in a mug (well, red paper cup).

Living in Cherryville, Ohio, you learn to embrace the cherry of it all: cherry pie, cherry sundaes, cherry soda, cherry cocktails, even cherry chicken (don't ask). The town was founded by a Quaker man named John Cherry, and although I don't think he had a particular affinity for cherries, the people of northeast Ohio are nothing if not literal. Stick around for the annual Cherry Festival in mid-summer—just be prepared to park far away and walk miles in the muggy Midwest heat for melted ice cream covered in—you guessed it—cherries.

By the time I pull into the parking lot of my apartment complex, my giant coffee is just a pile of foam at the bottom. Doesn't stop me from sucking down every last drop.

I jingle all the way up the stairs and get a few double takes from kids trying to scrape up what's left of a recent snowfall, building the tiniest dirty snowman I've ever seen. I should snap a photo for the Guinness Book of World Records (is that still a thing?).

My front door is a Christmas explosion I can't even stand to look at right now. I unlock it and head straight for the bathroom, which is Christmas-decor free, except for a bottle of vanilla-cinnamon hand soap with a full-body vintage Santa on the label. I turn the bottle so he faces the wall—I can't let him see me like this.

I strip out of this Godforsaken Mother Christmas getup and hop in the shower, scrubbing off Bad Santa's anti-Christmas ectoplasm.

It's okay to like Christmas, it's okay to like Christmas.

Nothing a little Christmas-cookie shower gel can't fix.

After I feel thoroughly cleansed of the shame of my anti-Christmas past, I dig around in my closet for the most explosively holiday-themed loungewear I own: a bright pink set with giant winking Santa heads that Ally gifted me two years ago. They're not exactly my taste—I'm more of a classic-red, monogrammed-pocket kind of gal—but they're perfect for the moment I'm in.

I plop down on the couch with a cup of microwaved cocoa and text Ally.

Me: *I hate Santa Claus.*

It's only seconds before bubbles pop up on my screen.

Ally: *Uh oh. Trouble in paradise?*

I hit "Call."

"Don't tell me your scene partner is a perv," she answers, already growling. "If he copped a feel, I swear to God..."

"No, no, nothing like that," I say, trying to calm her down before she finds out his full name and address and drives to his house with her boxing gloves on. "But he has no business donning that sacred Santa suit."

"Uh... Okay?" My love for Christmas far surpasses hers; she's a casual Christmas celebrator. I don't think she'd bat an eyelash if we decided to celebrate the winter solstice instead (although if you ask the Heralds, same diff).

"He's a total Grinch," I whine. (Sexy Grinch—I leave that part out.)

"Uh oh," she says, humoring me. "Tell me what happened."

And I do. I tell Ally about Eben (minus the tall-drink-of-water bit), how mean he was about Christmas, how it pinged all my family stuff, and the old guilt. I tell her about the jingle bell shoe, the horny senior citizens who think we're adorable, and the tipsy receptionist who's forcing me to collaborate with this man on Wednesday at seven.

"That is... a lot," she exhales, like she's been holding her breath.

"Sorry to dump on you at..." I check the clock. "God, it's only noon. I feel like I've lived a lifetime in four hours."

"That's why we sleep in on weekends," Ally yawns, "instead of volunteering at nursing homes."

That's when I get the *best* idea.

"You could come with me," I say.

"I'm sorry, what?" She's suddenly *very* awake.

"You love planning parties!" I say.

"For people under eighty," she snaps. "And for *pay.*"

Ally is the youngest senior publicist at Cherry Haus Media, Cherryville's most highly reviewed PR firm on Google. She can make the driest accounting firm sound sexy, regularly lands local cookie shops and breweries in national magazines, and once pulled off a Hometown Hero fundraiser with a Guardians star pitcher, which I will never stop being jealous of. I did, however, come away with a signed baseball, so—fist pump.

She does all of this for a sizable six-figure salary and generous benefits, so convincing her to volunteer for free will undoubtedly be an uphill battle.

Except, my secret weapon for getting Ally to do anything: dessert.

"I'll make you your favorite..."

I can practically hear her eyes go glossy over the phone.

"Dirt cake?" her voice goes up a hopeful octave.

"Mmmhmmm."

"But, but... that's a summer treat!"

"I can add red and green food coloring."

"It's not even my birthday!"

"Do you want the damn dirt cake or not?"

"If there's peppermint in my dirt cake, Melody, I swear—"

"Cross my heart."

I hear Ally sigh on the other end. "I guess I'll start scouring Etsy for printable holiday bingo cards."

I flop back on the couch, kick my feet in the air, and let out a tiny, triumphant squeak.

Ally is in.

CHAPTER 4

*O*nce you get past the old, musty smell, this place really isn't so bad.

There are a few decent food stands; the coffee tastes like mud, but everyone really just comes for the antiques.

No, I'm not talking about the nursing home—*ahem*, I mean *Retirement Community*. I'm talking about the Cherry Bowl, an indoor-outdoor flea market open every Saturday and Sunday from nine a.m. to five p.m. Proudly the second biggest flea market in the Midwest, it's home to more priceless junk than every grandma's basement in the county, Power-Rangered together.

The Cherry Bowl boasts the kind of crap that either makes you want to immediately burn your skin off with rubbing alcohol, or spend at least two weeks' salary on Romanov-era china and 17th-century English silver tea sets—depending on what kind of person you are. One look at my apartment—and my 1940s German Christmas ornaments that I was forced to buy as a set of twelve because the seller insisted that "they are a family" —and you can guess which category I belong in.

Now I'm here, scouring the market for cheap-but-pretty

baubles to spruce up the community room's shoddy decorating. I wish I could say Forest Park's sad holiday décor at Forest Park sparked a warm, charitable feeling in me—but the truth is I can't tolerate bad design. It's nails-on-a-chalkboard every time I see it, and apparently, I'm going to be staring at a lot of it in the coming weeks. So, here I am at the flea market, about to spend money I don't have to jazz up decorations for seniors, who are either too horny or tipsy to notice.

Also, I can't resist a good treasure hunt.

Ally, on the other hand, was not planning on attending the Cherry Bowl. Not today. Not a month from now. Not ever. I'm not sure she's owned anything more than five years old. Somehow, she donates more to Goodwill than she actually buys.

At this point, I've pumped her full of three coffees—two of them are gingerbread cappuccinos with extra whipped cream and extra cookie-crunch topping. We even swung through the MickeyD's drive-thru, but apparently it was all for naught, because she's been wearing the same scowl longer than the Led Zeppelin records over at stall five have been out of production.

"Why do I get roped into every hairbrained thing you do?" she asks.

"Because you love me."

"I do love you," she says, defeated. "But it's Sunday. A holy day of rotting. Instead, I'm here." She glances at a stall crammed with vintage toys. Well, some are vintage, and some are just… pre-loved. And a little bit dirty.

Ally wrinkles her nose.

"What do you think of this?" I beeline for a blue-and-white Chinoiserie Christmas tree.

Ally side-eyes it. "You already know what I think."

"Okay, let me rephrase. What will the seniors think of it?"

She takes the tiny tree out of my hand. "Didn't you say they were using old socks as Christmas stockings?"

"It's hard times for the elderly," I say defensively and yank the ceramic tree back.

She sighs. "Oh, just get it... *for the seniors.*" She does air quotes around the last three words.

I squeal and dig into my pockets for cash, ready to barter. There's nothing better than a friend who knows you so well— even if that means she knows how nuts you actually are.

By Wednesday, I'm hauling a trunk full of crusty treasures to Forest Park with Ally in tow.

I've spent the last three days trying to wrap an important (aka expensive) design project for Deb and Don, the co-founders of the home-design app I work for—people who fancy themselves "collectors who just happen to know tech." Translation: two retired interior designers sharing one outdated iPhone. Both are incredibly sweet with great taste—they're just hilariously bad at the tech part (despite the motto).

My clients are mostly thirty- and forty-somethings with trust funds or DINK lifestyles, trying to break out of the millennial-grey trance they've been stuck in since 2010. Don't even get me started on "farmhouse chic." As I tell clients: good taste is a marathon, not a sprint.

Ally thinks I should start looking for another job, but honestly, I can't do that to Deb and Don. Part of the reason I still have this job—even though it keeps me clipping virtual coupons—is that I love the work, and I love those two quirky nomads, who are currently on an exotic-fruit sampling retreat in Costa Rica. I'm amazed every Monday they've kept the "lights on" another week—but I wouldn't trade this job for anything (except, apparently, the poorhouse).

I didn't have time to eat between finishing the project and picking up Ally, so I'm shoveling a microwave burrito into my face while swerving down the two-lane.

"When's the last time you asked for a raise?" Ally asks, gripping the grab handle above her like it's a brake as I take a sharp turn into the parking lot. "The Dweedles need you, and you need a retirement fund. Or even a savings account."

Ally calls Deb and Don the "Dweedles"—after Tweedledee and Tweedledum. She was once in the room when they called me from a Hobbit tour in New Zealand. Somehow, their computer cord got chewed on by a rogue sheep, and I had to take a company call that Monday while they tracked down a new cord.

"I have a savings account," I say, biting my lip as I try to back into a parking space, where some asshole has mega-parked over the lines and well into my spot.

"I just keep having to use it." I inch backward. Thanks to this jerk, I've had to pull up and straighten so many times I've made myself carsick. Ally shudders—she's seen this before.

"Hey, why don't we stop trying to park like we're Dad of the Year and find a spot you can pull straight into?"

"No, I've got this! I'm not going to let this jackass ruin my perfect parking moment—"

"Mel, this is a monster truck and—"

A giant *crunch* and *scrrraaaape* finish her sentence. I freeze. Ally stares at me, and I don't want to look back. I know this look. I've seen it since kindergarten. A million times, in fact, since kindergarten. When you're estranged from your whole family, you get used to disappointing people, but disappointing Ally is tough, even if I pretend it's not.

The groan Ally makes sounds more like a wild rodent than a best friend.

"Damn it, Melody! You hit him!"

"I'm sure it's not that bad." I hold my breath. "But can you look, *pleeeeease?*"

Allison shakes her head. "Why do I always have to look at the casualties first –"

An aggressive rap on my window cuts her off.

"Christ," I mutter, turning to see who's trying to break my window.

It's Eben.

For a beat, the three of us—Eben, Ally, and I—stare at each other.

Then: "I think you hit my car," he says calmly.

"No, I don't think I did."

Ally smacks my shoulder. She doesn't take her eyes off Eben, who's clearly registering on her judgey (but accurate) hot-o-meter. Something I conveniently omitted when I regaled her with the horrors of Santa Jerk.

"I'm Allison—the one out of the two of us who has a moral compass. And yes, she did hit your car. We're so sorry."

"Ally, this is Santa Claus," I say, giving her *the look* only best friends can share, hoping she catches my drift.

She does.

"Oh! Santa. I mean—"

"Eben," he offers.

"Yes, this is Eben, who hates Christmas and also parks like a douche canoe," I add.

Eben ignores me and walks to his driver's side door, now sporting a gnarly scratch and a sizable dent. He inspects it and shrugs.

"Don't worry about it. I was in a hurry and definitely parked like an asshole." He runs his finger across the damage. "I think I can rub this one out pretty easily."

Ally snorts, stifling a laugh. I roll my eyes, leveling Ally with a glare. "Excuse my friend, she's a fucking pervert."

He smiles and waves it off. "Aren't we all?"

My face warms—and I'm instantly pissed at myself. It's one thing to blush for Santa; it's another to get hot and bothered for Krampus.

"Are you sure you don't want my insurance? The damage

looks kind of bad," I say, trying to deflect attention from the heat rising in my cheeks.

Ally looks at me like I've sprouted two heads—neither of which can afford my premium going up.

"Positive. But..." He nods at the front door, where Missy is standing with her hands on her hips, unimpressed that both of us are eight and a half minutes late.

"We should get in there before—"

"The meeting is in *here*, folks," Missy yells across the lot.

Eben sighs. "—before Missy starts yelling."

I pop the trunk, revealing a jumble of paper and plastic bags stuffed with holiday decorations.

"Here," I say, lifting the heaviest bag and holding it out to Eben. "Make yourself useful."

He huffs a laugh at my bossiness, and our fingers brush as he takes the bag. A jolt of electricity shoots through my fingers and up my arms; I wonder if he feels it too. His eyes widen in answer, and my cheeks betray me again, so I turn back to where Ally is loading her arms with bags.

"What's all this?" he asks, peeking into the bag.

"Your worst nightmare," I say, grabbing the last few bags and slamming my trunk.

"Ornaments are my worst nightmare?" he asks.

"Melody seems to be under the impression that Christmas is your kryptonite," Ally offers.

"Ah," he says. "She's not wrong."

I shoot them both a glare and head inside, the two of them trailing after me.

Just as we reach the door, a strong hand lands on my shoulder, gently holding me back. I turn and lock eyes with those baby blues. Maybe it's my imagination, but his eyes shine a shade warmer today—sky blue instead of Saturday's glacial chill.

I feel my resolve to be the biggest bitch in the North Pole

melting, too.

"Can I help you?" I ask, trying to sound tough. I turn fully to him, arms crossed.

"I think we got off on the wrong foot," Eben says. My perverted brain stops his sentence at *I think we got off*. My eyes start undressing him—slipping off the dark gray wool coat, tugging up his navy sweater. Is that cashmere?

He clears his throat, and my head snaps back so hard I worry it might pop off. When my eyes slide back to his face, he's grinning. A knowing, crooked grin. He's sexy and he knows it. Fuck my life.

"Jingle bell shoe," is all I can think to say.

He raises an eyebrow. "Pardon?"

"We got off on the wrong jingle bell shoe," I say, puffing my chest. It's a dumb joke. Too late to walk it back. Must own it.

"Sure," he says. The half-grin ticks higher, and his brows knit together for a split second. He thinks I'm weird. Well, join the club.

"I accept your apology," I say—preemptively. "And so does Father Christmas. The real one."

"Oh, I'm sorry for being rude," he says. "I'm not sorry for hating Christmas. That part stands."

My mouth drops.

My eyes narrow.

"Back on the naughty list," I say, pressing a finger to his chest. His rock-hard, cashmere-covered chest. My finger lingers too long. He glances down at it, surprised. I yank it back. It's like I touched a hot stove.

"That's a bad thing?" he asks, still grinning down at me. He waggles his eyebrows suggestively. I want to slap him—mostly to touch him again.

"Fuck you," is all I can muster as I yank the door open. Eben is right behind me; I feel the grin on my back.

Despite my rage at his non-apology apology, I make a pact

with myself as I hurry to catch up with Ally. (She's already deep in conversation with a much less scowly Missy—Ally has a way with difficult people.)

I will make Eben a nog-drinking, carol-singing, tinsel-stringing lover of Christmas.

Or my name isn't Mrs. Claus.

CHAPTER 5

I was right on the money.

Inviting Ally to the pageant-planning committee meeting (which consists of exactly four people: me, Eben, Ally, and Missy) was the best idea I've ever had. Mainly because, when Allison gets involved, she takes over, and I can sit back and space out. Or, in this case, hang the ornaments I bought from the flea market, plus a few things from home I thought might perk up their scraggly Charlie Brown tree.

I add gold, red, and green glass ornaments, a few strands of tinsel, and a red velvet ribbon. I drape pre-lit garland over the mantle and set out a few gold candleholders, though I hope to God no one lights them. I don't need to be responsible for burning the place down. When I'm done, I take a few steps back to admire my handiwork. It's not the Plaza Hotel, but I've definitely added some charm.

The tiny hairs at the back of my neck stand up.

I glance over—and catch Eben watching me.

He looks away fast, pretending to be fascinated by the peeling yellow wallpaper.

Interesting.

I smile to myself and wander back to the table, plopping down in the last open chair between him and Missy. His knee bumps mine and stays. I glance over—his eyes are closed.

Huh.

Ally's been talking for a solid twenty minutes straight. Hardly anyone else has gotten a word in, aside from occasional exuberant "ooh" or "ah" from Missy—she can scarcely believe her luck that a senior publicist showed up to her meeting pro bono.

It's one of the many reasons Ally and I became friends. Right now she's running this whole after-school project like the pro she is—hip-friendly party games, collabs with local businesses, and a neighborhood-backed cookie bake sale.

It takes me back to elementary school, when we were paired up for the fifth-grade science fair project. Allison titled it "Decomp Delight," and we studied how different foods decomposed over time. The kids went gaga for our project thanks to a McDonald's French fry and Big Mac combo that remained unscathed by the forces of nature for a full six weeks. We got an A (uncommon for me in science), and first place out of dozens of projects—something that had never happened before and would never happen again for me, not for Ally, who now works in public relations and regularly wins awards at her firm.

There were plenty of sleepovers during our science-fair era, and when the project ended, the sleepovers didn't—and never really have. It's rare to meet your best friend in elementary school and keep them into adulthood, but it's also rare to meet someone with whom you can be totally yourself—no pretending, no pretense. We share a sense of humor and a level of honesty we couldn't have with our parents or siblings. We are non-romantic soulmates—soul sisters, if you will.

I know, I know. Try not to gag.

That's why when I get a text from her that says:

WTF mel

I shoot her a glare from across the table. She glares back and keeps typing. I sink lower in my chair, paranoid Eben will see our texts, even though he's barely conscious.

u left out the part that santa claus is a sex bomb

I type back: *he hates xmas. talk about a boner killer.*

Ally: *you didn't celebrate christmas until you were 22.*

Me: *yeah and now I can't stop won't stop.*

Ally: *you don't have to like him to fuck him*

I sit up straight, glaring daggers at Ally. She shrugs and keeps typing.

Ally: *time to get your paws on that Claus.*

She makes a claw gesture and curls her lips in a silent growl.

"Ladies, are you listening?" Missy asks, eyes ping-ponging between us.

No.

"Yes," we both say in unison. Between us, Eben is slouched in his chair, eyes still closed. Why isn't she berating *him* for not paying attention?

"As I was saying," Missy snarks, "the ultimate goal of our Christmas pageant is to get enough donations to buy Christmas presents for all our seniors." She hands us printed copies of what appears to be Santa's list for the seniors. "This is their Christmas wishlist, and as of now, we don't have enough to cover it."

Well, that's depressing. Forest Park doesn't have enough funding to cover a few Christmas presents? I glance over the list. We're not talking diamonds and Cartier here—just a few simple presents per resident: board games, new pillows, and Netflix subscriptions. Also disturbing: these folks don't have families to bring them presents?

As if reading my mind, Missy says, "We only get enough funding to cover basic costs. Anything extra is extra." She shifts in her chair. "And not all our members have family close by. Or family at all."

Her eyes flick to Eben, still slouched, eyes half-mast, expression unreadable. Bored, even.

"Next up," she says. "The talent show—our biggest money-maker. The community turns out, and the seniors shine. Tomorrow the residents pick their talents, and then it's up to the staff—" She looks pointedly at the three of us. Ally and I trade a look. Um, we are not staff. "—to get everyone performance-ready."

Ally leans in and whispers, "This is a disaster waiting to happen."

"Speaking of waiting, do you at least have an ambulance waiting outside?" I cover a snort.

Missy shoots us daggers.

"We've been running this pageant for ten years and nothing bad has ever happened—in fact, when Eben's—"

Eben's eyes snap open, and he sits up straight. He and Missy share a look I can't decode. She clears her throat. "Five years running, and not a single mishap. Not even a snagged pair of pantyhose, let alone an ambulance call," she finally finishes.

While I'm busy clocking Missy and Eben's weird little exchange, Ally—the science freak/comms genius/math whiz—has been running numbers on her phone.

"So," she says, business pants on, "just looking at the wishlist, number of residents at Forest Park, and what the talent show earned last year—there isn't going to be enough to cover everything from the show alone."

Missy sighs. "I guess each senior can only get one thing."

My heart sinks. Isn't it bad enough to be stashed away in some overpriced raisin ranch—either a gazillion miles away from family, or worse, a mile away from family that just doesn't give a crap about you—and then on top of that, the home you pay eight grand a month to wait-to-die in can't even afford two Christmas presents from CVS? Not on my watch. I am fired up.

"I mean, we could set up a donation booth at the Cherry

Bowl," I offer, locking eyes with Ally. I'm there every other weekend anyway; might as well set up a table for a few hours and collect donations for a good cause.

Her face telegraphs that I've overstepped and forced her to overcommit. Whoops. Then I watch disgruntled turn to delighted. Her eyes sparkle. Her lips twist. Uh oh.

"Why, that's a great idea, Melody!" she chirps to Missy, with whom she's now thick as thieves. "Eben and Mel can play Mr. and Mrs. Claus for the children at the flea market."

"WHAT," I say it so loudly that an old lady walking by with a walker startles, and nearly tips. Missy bolts upright, ready to intervene. But the woman regains her footing and resumes inching along, but not before shooting me a dirty look.

Eben leans back in his chair and crosses his arms. "With all due respect, pretending to be Santa Claus for two days out of my weekend is my personal hell."

I open my mouth to agree, but Ally scrunches her face and scoffs at both of us. "*With all due respect,*" she says, mocking him, "it's like four hours each weekend for what, less than a month? You'll survive."

The smirk on her face is infuriating. She knows exactly what she's doing—trapping us in a situation with no easy exit.

"Think of the children," Ally intones.

"And of the seniors," Missy adds, unhelpfully. She makes meaningful eye contact with Eben. He exhales a long, weary breath.

"Fine," he says, dropping his arms and sinking lower like a deflated balloon.

"Seriously?" I look from face to face. They wait for my list of reasons Ally's idea is terrible. It doesn't come. Because I remember my secret goal: to convince Eben Claus (I still don't know his last name) that Christmas is indeed the most wonderful time of the year. And there's nowhere like the Cherry

Bowl at Christmastime. There's hot chocolate and carolers and Christmas booths selling antique ornaments.

Okay, you know what? This could be good.

Never mind that my partner in this endeavor happens to be one of the best-looking guys I've ever seen in person. I shove that part to the back of my brain.

"You know what? Fuck it, I'm in," I say. My eyes wander over to meet Eben's. The smile on his face is almost undetectable, but it's there. Ally claps gleefully.

She'll be getting an earful from me later.

THE RIDE HOME IS EXCRUCIATING. Not because I'm mad at Ally (I'm not), but because she will not stop going on and on about Hot Santa.

"Why didn't you tell me he's like ten feet of pure Adonis?"

I try not to throw up in my mouth.

"Okay, calm down, he's barely six-foot-three and he's good-ish looking, I guess," I lie.

Ally's jaw drops. "You're joking, right? He's objectively gorgeous. An absolute ten out of ten."

I shrug. "But he *hates* Christmas. Like, hates, hates, hates. So it's ten minus a hundred. He's a negative ninety."

Ally hits me with the *look*—the incredulous *you-have-got-to-be-kidding-me* look only a best friend can deliver.

"You are deeply lying to yourself," she says as I pull into her driveway. Ally and Teddy's little blue Craftsman is Midwest perfection: a low-pitched roof, tapered pillars squatting on chunky stone bases, and a wide porch that runs the length of the house, anchored by a white swing that creaks just enough to be charming. Boxy windows are framed in crisp white trim, and the front door—rich oak stained Charleston Toffee brown—wears a giant fall wreath Ally grabbed at Costco on a whim.

When you picture the middle-class American dream, this is the house that pops into your head like a Zillow ad.

They've poured almost all of their money into it, so it's a good thing they both have good jobs. Allison does her senior-publicist thing; Teddy crunches numbers for a major accounting firm.

Once inside, I know the drill: shoes off, lined neatly on the striped rug. I wouldn't call Allison a neat freak, but if I'd emptied a retirement account to gloss the cherry-stained hard-wood floors *and* restore original 1935 crown moulding, I'd make everyone take off their shoes (maybe even hose off their feet) too.

The only exception to Ally's neat, clean, don't-wreck-my-life-savings rule is Tidbit—her and Teddy's 175-pounds-of-pure-love Saint Bernard. Sometimes I can't tell if the floors shine from the topcoat or Tidbit's drool. Either way, these floors are glossy (and slick) as hell.

Tidbit takes a running leap at me, and luckily, I am obsessed with giant Muppets and grew up with brothers. I brace against the couch before he goes full cannonball.

"Bitty boy!" I laugh as I'm knocked back onto the Restoration Hardware cloud couch. (God, this couch even feels like falling backward into the piles of money you spent on it). I scratch behind his ears. Drool commences.

"Tidbit, get down." A deep voice with the slightest Southern lilt interrupts the slobber-fest.

"Teddy," Allison says with an exasperated edge. "Can you please let him out until he calms down?"

"Aww, honey, but he loves company!" Teddy says, defensive.

"He also loves squirrels." Allison's patience is fraying, and it'd be easier for all of us if Teddy just took the dog outside.

I jump in and grab Tidbit's collar. He's thrilled to go on a walk with Auntie Melody to the great picket-fenced-in backyard.

"Come on, baby, let's get some fresh air," I say, ruffling his jowls with my free hand. We detour through the kitchen and make a pit stop at the treat jar, where I snag him a chewbone the size of a human femur. I open the back door, toss the bone, and step the hell out of the way as Tidbit barrels out, nearly flattening me. I catch my balance just as my phone buzzes.

Big ol' knee-jerk eyeroll. The text is simple: *hey i need to talk to you.* I shove the phone deep in my back pocket and take a deeper breath. I cannot do Cassie disappointment this year. For years, she was my closest sister, my built-in best friend, but her loyalty to the Heralds means I have nothing left to give or say to her.

Back in the living room, Teddy and Ally are settled on the sofa—Ally with some sober-curious red-wine alternative she found on Instagram, Teddy with a Bud Light. They're the perfect mix of opposites and somehow totally in sync since high school: both wanting the same college, the same style house, the same number of kids, and the same safe, predictable kind of job. The difference is in the methods—fourteen to-do lists (Ally) versus a post-it and a prayer (Teddy).

Teddy flips on ESPN, and even though it's Wednesday night and Teddy is a huge sucker for women's basketball (which is entirely on brand for his personality), he respectfully mutes it. Even though I love some WNBA myself (just don't get me started on the pay discrepancies), there are *things* to discuss. Teddy is equal parts gentleman and Chatty Cathy—he'll never miss a chance to gossip with us, even if that means muting his favorite mid-week athletic showdown.

"So," he pries, handing me a matching Bud Light, "Allison texted that things are heating up down at the geriatric North Pole."

I groan and smack Allison's arm. "Damn, girl, you couldn't even wait 'til the car was in the driveway!"

They exchange *the* look—the happily-coupled look that says

their best friend has been single too long and they have the world's greatest plan to fix that.

"Teddy," I warn, "you'd hate his guts. Don't root for this."

Teddy's eyes drift to the screen, where the Las Vegas Aces (thanks to A'ja Wilson) are mercilessly laying into their opponent. "Ally said he didn't even get your insurance info or get pissed that you hit his car."

"And he shouldn't have!" Heat rises. "Did she also mention that he parked like a psycho?"

"Were there no other spots?" Teddy asks earnestly. I regret hanging out with people who know me this well.

Ally cuts in, "Of course, there were other spots, but you know how she likes to—"

"Back in." Teddy nods, finishing her sentence. They exchange that look again—the "how are we ever going to get Melody laid again" look.

"I'm just saying," Teddy continues, "you hit a good-looking guy's car in the parking lot of the senior community where you both volunteer. He sounds nice. And he meets your height criteria."

I shoot eye-missiles at Ally for sharing non-essential information. Yes, Eben is a whole foot taller (and better) than what's slopped together for women on those "dating" apps.

"I'm guessing Ally didn't tell you the worst part," I huff.

Here come those glances again. I'm going to slap them both into next Christmas.

"She told me he hates Christmas, but—"

"There are no *buts* at the end of that sentence!" I explode. "I cannot go out with someone who hates Christmas. You know this."

I look between them, and a very whiny voice I don't recognize emerges. "I gave up everything for this holiday."

Ally's look is sympathetic, but not having it. "That's not exactly how that went down, Mel."

She's right. If I claim I left a cult knowing I'd be cut off by my parents *simply for Christmas*, I'd be agreeing with my mom—and I can't let that happen.

"Honestly, the best thing I can do is convince him to like Christmas—for his own good." I sip my beer and sink into the cushions. This couch is eating me alive.

"Don't you think that feels kind of culty?" Ally asks. "I mean, ten years ago you were knocking on doors trying to get people *not* to celebrate Christmas, and now you want to do the same thing—for the opposite cause."

"This is not the same thing at all," I say. "Nobody's putting me up to this. This time, the genius idea is entirely my own."

Luckily, if something even borders on a social good time, Teddy is the first to party in my corner. Ally looks to him for help, but Party Teddy has already taken over; he's imagining all the ways to sell Christmas to my future Grinch, and, apparently, how their best friend needs to catch a dick. I'm not sure how I feel about this elevated level of desperation, but I do welcome help on Project Christmas-is-the-Fucking-Best.

Teddy starts pacing, voice two octaves higher, talking so fast it sounds like he's auctioning off the living room. "First, we take him to the Winter Wonderland pop-up bar. Get a couple of snowman sangrias into this boy and karaoke some jazzy holiday classics." He breaks into song. *"I'm... dreaming of a whiiite... Christmas!"*

Oh my God, he's singing.

"Honey," Allison tries...

Teddy can't stop, "Then ice skating and movies at Reagan Park. You get an hour of free skate, followed by a Christmas movie of the week, with free popcorn and hot chocolate. We could all go. I hope they're showing *Elf.*" He rubs his hands together, barely containing himself.

"Teddy—" I try, but he's a runaway train.

I glance at the TV as the Aces hit a three-pointer, and the

crowd erupts. Teddy is as gone as the rest of this game—deep in the never-gonna-happen fantasy of all the Christmas double dates the four of us will go on.

"Teddy!" I finally shout.

He startles out of his reverie about his new Christmastime bromance.

"Dude, do *you* want to date him or something? Because that's fine. But you're missing one thing—I hate this guy. And I'm pretty sure he hates me. So as fun as sipping snowman sangrias with real-life Scrooge sounds, it's never going to happen. I'm going to show him up and then show myself out. You know what I mean?"

"No," Ally says. "That's a weird thing to say. We don't know what that means. At all."

"It means save your breath. I'm in it to prove Eben wrong on principle. And even if he ends up 'liking' Christmas, it'll be because he was forced—and that's not sexy. I don't want Christmas at gunpoint. That's like Christmas communism."

I deliver the last line like I've really done something here.

Ally raises an eyebrow and sits up. "So, let me get this straight."

Uh-oh. I hate it when Allison starts a sentence (directed at me—it's fantastic when directed at someone else) with 'Let me get this straight.' It means I've said something that doesn't add up in her extremely logical, cross-referencing-the-news-for-a-living brain. She's about to point out all the flaws, and nine times out of ten, she's right. I brace.

"You meet a gorgeous guy who, like Teddy says, checks the height box, has the face card that could overdraw all the accounts, doesn't care that you basically Carrie Underwooded the side of this car, spends his free time working with old people and dealing with that Missy woman—for free. And you're telling me that if he finally comes around on the one hang-up you have—a weird but I guess, legit hang-up—you still aren't going to want to fuck his brains into the mattress?"

"No," I say defiantly, chin tipped to the sky.

Teddy laughs and looks at Ally. "Hey, hon, we should bet money on this. When we win, we can put it toward the new Viking fridge."

Good luck, buddy. Even if they win a bet against me, they're still getting one of those my-Sims-are-broke fridges.

Allison sighs. "Your problem isn't this man."

"Oh, yes, it is."

"Your problem is that you're completely emotionally unavailable."

Ouch.

Someone please hand me some aloe. Ally just took a flamethrower to my psyche.

"I'm very available!" I argue. (God, here comes that whiny voice again. Who is she?)

"Your calendar being free and your heart being open are two very different things," Teddy counters.

Every now and then, Teddy goes from a sports-loving social butterfly with wild hand gestures and an ice-cold brewsky to Teddy-fucking-Socrates.

I go quiet because I know he's right. To survive a cult, you keep everyone at arm's length—especially in Heaven's Heralds, where tattling wasn't just encouraged but rewarded. Letting people in always came with risks. Unfortunately, the skills that kept me relatively out of harm's way (and boyfriend-free) in the cult are the same ones that helped me survive the loss of my family once I got out.

"I'll work on the emotional-availability thing," I say, standing to leave.

I don't sound convincing, even to myself.

Ally and Teddy watch me with matching concern.

"No, you won't," Allison says with a sad smile. "But I love you anyway."

CHAPTER 6

$\mathcal{T}$he rest of the week flies by in a blur, and before I know it, I'm suiting up to play Mrs. Claus again. This time, I trade the jingle-bell shoes for something a little less, well, jingly—red platform booties with white faux-fur trim, a remnant from my community-choir phase a few years ago. My therapist back then swore that joining the Crooney Tunes would alleviate the creeping isolation I felt after leaving the Heralds and being cut off from my family.

So I did. We sang at hospitals, nursing homes (somehow skipping Forest Park), community centers, a minor-league baseball game, and even a corporate holiday party for a company that got busted a year later for money laundering. (Fa-la-la-la-fraud.)

My last great romantic disaster also occurred during that phase. The guy was funny, sweet, cute... and ghosted me after three weeks and one memorably awkward bedroom encounter. Cut to me, a year later, spotting him at the premiere of *Good Cheer*—a movie pitched as *Bring It On* meets *It's a Wonderful Life* (shocker: it wasn't good). He was holding hands with his new boyfriend.

I was genuinely happy for him (religious deconstruction buddies forever), but also... wow, okay, universe. After that, I decided to take a "brief" dating hiatus. Five years later, here I am: still in the world's longest dry spell.

So I did what I always do: buried my feelings six feet under my skin. The trauma lives somewhere between my stomach and small intestine with all the other repressed emotions—causing a little indigestion and IBS—but otherwise I'm coping just fine.

And at least I don't have to look at it.

I check myself in the full-length mirror. The shoes add a few inches to my height and somehow take a few *off* the skirt, adding just a touch of sex appeal to my Mrs. Claus look.

Not bad.

When I pull up to Forest Park, Eben's truck gleams neatly between the lines like nothing ever happened—my Wolverine scratches, gone. As for my car, there are more than a few scrapes that could use a buff out, maybe a little paint. An oil change. A new transmission.

Really, just tow the car and start fresh. But it's not in the budget for at least another decade.

My heels clack across the tile as I nod at Missy and head toward my fictional husband. The old ladies are already clustered around Eben, and now a few extra senior men have joined the fray. Eben spots me; his eyebrows shoot up. I put on my sparkliest smile and strut over.

"Hello, Mr. Claus," I purr, attempting my finest transatlantic accent. At some point, I decided Mrs. Claus should sound like Katharine Hepburn, apparently. Between the two of us, Ally is the real drama queen (literally—she was always a lead in a school play), but years of reenacting old films in my parents' basement gave me a talent for atrocious accents.

"No jingle bell shoes today, Mrs. Claus?" he rumbles. His gaze drifts down and lingers ever so briefly on my bare legs. I imagine wrapping them around his hips and—oh. Oh no. Bad brain. *Bad brain.*

"She's ho-ho-ho-ing it up for you, Santa!" a white-haired woman cackles from her wheelchair.

"Edna!" her friend bops her knee.

"What?" Edna shrugs, unapologetic. "I would too if I still had legs like that!"

The ladies chortle, and my face goes candy-cane red.

"Give us a spin!" an old man in plaid shouts from a table where he and another old man are hunched over a board playing checkers.

"Cram it, Bob!" Edna fires back. "This isn't Vegas, and she's not a stripper!" Then, stage whispering to the ladies: "Not that he could get it up anyway."

"I heard that!" Bob growls.

I have decided Edna is my favorite.

I catch Eben's gaze drift up my legs again, and a jolt zips through me. Of course, the second he realizes I've noticed, he looks away. Was he checking me out? Not that I'm into it—but since the last guy who made a pass at me is pushing ninety and has an Amazon subscription for Depends, I'd be lying if I said I wasn't just the tiniest bit thrilled.

The moment is cut short by the arrival of the walking cold shower, otherwise known as Missy, armed with a clipboard. You can always tell when Missy means business because that clipboard Houdinis out of thin air whenever there's a schedule to keep.

"All right, folks! Listen up!" she shouts over the chatter—loud enough for the seventy-five percent who either have hearing aids or forgot to wear them. "You all know what today is."

Edna leans toward her bestie and whispers at full volume, "Potluck Tuesday?"

I giggle. Around here, food and sex are the only two constants. Whoever said older people lose their *joie de vivre* clearly has never visited Forest Park.

From the back, someone else shouts, "Potluck Tuesday!" Missy's smile strains.

Why do I get the feeling Potluck Tuesday is a popular happening around here?

"No, folks, it's not Potluck Tuesday. Today is Saturday." A few groans. "It's actually better than PLT—it's talent-picking day!" A smattering of polite cheers. Not quite the PLT fervor.

She continues, "Mr. and Mrs. Claus will come around to each table with a clipboard. Write down your *own* name and talent—no signing up your exes for sword-swallowing."

She glares at Edna, who snickers; a few of the men scowl at her.

"And nothing profane or suggestive—this is a family event, for God's sake."

I swear I hear a few disappointed murmurs.

She presses the worn clipboard into Eben's hands and bails from the room.

He rakes through his blond hair, exasperated. "This is just a blank sheet of paper."

As he rules neat columns—Name, Talent, Notes—I'm rudely left to stare at his broad shoulders, the way his Santa suit pulls around his very well-developed biceps, the red velvet straining over strong thighs—wow, okay, stop imagining being pinned underneath him.

He glances up, and my gaze flicks skyward, the portrait of innocence.

"All right, who wants to go first?" Eben asks the room. My eyes drift back down to his hands, which are engulfing the clipboard. I imagine them gripping my waist while he—

"Me!" yelps a short man in plaid pants belted somewhere

near his sternum. Bless him for breaking my huge-hands hypnosis.

"I want to make sourdough bread."

Marilyn, a sassy, boxed-blonde who might be his wife or girlfriend, jumps in. "Roger, you gotta get off Pinterest. Sourdough isn't a talent! It's a Depression-era survival skill."

He looks defiantly at Eben. "Sourdough bread. Put it down."

"I can supervise in the kitchen," I offer. Eben shrugs and pencils Roger in for the very "white-woman" talent of making sourdough.

We make the rounds, jotting down talents: tap dancing, crooning, and even baton twirling (which worries me deeply). Finally, we land on my favorite spunky gal pals, Edna and her best friend, Millie.

"I'm going to dance," Edna says, matter-of-fact, fingers resting on the blanket draped over her knees.

"Okay," Eben says, smirking as he writes *dance* next to Edna's name.

"Dance?" Millie scoffs, eyeing Edna's wheelchair. "Are you nuts?"

"I sure am!" Edna grins. "What's your talent, Mill? Touching your knockers to your knees while standing up straight?"

Millie sticks out her tongue as Edna cackles at her own joke.

They remind me of me and Ally. May we still be razzing each other at eighty.

"Any kind of dance in particular?" Eben asks Edna. "Foxtrot, jazz, ballet…?"

Edna is deadpan, but mischief glints in her eyes, "Don't worry about it."

Eben jots down "don't worry about it" next to *dance*, and then side-eyes me while he adds "knee knockers" by Millie's name. I let out an involuntary snort-chuckle—a snortle, if you will.

49

"What's so funny?" Edna asks, so earnest and innocent that it only makes me laugh harder.

"Mrs. Claus," Eben elbows me, realizing he may not be as in on the joke as he thinks. "Pull yourself together."

This ridiculous moniker does nothing to help. I'm doubled over, wiping tears. Edna is playing him like a fiddle, and he has no idea.

"She's going to do something dirtyyyyy," I whisper in his ear between giggles, dabbing my eyes with my sleeve.

"Edna? She's like ninety," Eben protests.

"And horny as a teenager," I say. I waggle my brows. "Care to wager?"

We glance back just in time to see Edna's hand sliding up some old guy's trouser leg under the table.

He grimaces. "Yeah… I'm not taking that bet."

We dissolve into laughter. Eben abandons the Santa chortle for his natural laugh—higher-pitched and kind of hiccupy and adorable. His smile is filled with straight, white teeth and slightly pronounced incisors. I imagine them snagging on my lower lip as his tongue slips into my—

GODDAMNIT, ENOUGH.

I shake the thought out of my head, but his eyes have settled on my face—searching, almost soft. My skin flushes.

There's a tug on Eben's sleeve.

He turns—and freezes. Tugging on his sleeve is a woman— young for Forest Park, sixties maybe—with blonde hair streaked silver. She gazes up at him with big, uncertain eyes.

"Excuse me, Santa," she says. "Where am I?"

Something in his expression tilts. He lowers his voice. "You're at the North Pole. You're one of my helper elves. Think you could help me collect names for the talent show?"

His voice is tender, warm as cocoa—achingly sweet toward this woman who is clearly here for memory care.

She nods, and he passes her the clipboard and walks with her to the next table, patient and steady, letting her set the pace.

My heart thumps hard against my ribs.

I'm supposed to be breaking down his defenses, showing him the magic of Christmas.

But if he's the Grinch, why is my heart the one growing three sizes?

CHAPTER 7

"You look... festive," Teddy grunts from the backseat, leaning forward as far as the human-sized dog on his lap will allow to inspect my costume.

"You look great, Mel," Ally says, reaching back to give her dog scritches as he slowly suffocates her fiancé.

Once again, I've conscripted my best friend into flea-market duty. What is the point of a best friend if she can't be your plus-one to every event that wigs you out?

Only this morning, it's plus two and a half. Teddy decided to come too, and color me surprised when he piled into my Civic with that hulk of a dog. Tidbit occupies the entire backseat; Teddy rolls the window down so that Tids can drool outside the car, not in it.

"Thanks," I say. "I've been wearing it so much I'm worried it'll become glued to my skin."

"I'm sure Eben won't mind—"

Ally reaches back and swats Teddy on the leg.

"I was just thinking," I say, my shoes jingling as I brake at a stop sign, "he probably has a girlfriend."

"Are those...jingle bell shoes?" Teddy asks.

"He does not have a girlfriend," Ally says. "What happened to the North Pole-dancer heels from yesterday?"

I met Ally at our favorite brunch spot after my Mrs. Claus shift. One look at my "Mrs. Ho-ho-ho" shoes (her nickname) and she spent the rest of the meal sneaking R-rated holiday puns into the conversation. Highlights include jingle balls and Miracle on 69th Street.

"After an old geezer pretended to fall just so to look up my skirt, I decided to retire Santa's stripper shoes."

"Aww, let the old man live a little," Teddy says.

"Shut up, Ted," Ally says. "Wait, does Mrs. Claus even have a name?"

"It's disputed," I say, wistfully. "In the 1970s stop-motion animation, Mrs. Claus's name is Jessica, which is… interesting. I've also read Gertrude, Mary, and Carol."

"What about Crystal?" Teddy asks.

Silence from us girls in the front seat.

"Crystal Claus," he tests. "Has a nice ring."

Ally ignores him. "The point is, it sucks that she's this Santa sidekick with no name or identity other than 'wife.'" She's about to launch into a feminist tirade, and honestly, it's too early on a Sunday for that. I need two more gallons of coffee before I can join her in dismantling the Santa Claus myth.

"I'm fine with Mrs. Claus," I say, trying not to sound dismissive. "But since today is for the children, *Crystal Claus* needs to sit this one out."

"Heh," Teddy chuckles, beaming that I used his nickname.

"Fair enough," Ally says, throwing her hands up in surrender.

My phone rings—loud. I forgot to put it on silent. My ringtone through January 5—same as always— is Trans-Siberian Orchestra's "Carol of the Bells." Instant nervous-system shakedown.

"Who's that?" Allison's nosy as ever.

I kill the ringtone and just stare at Ally. "Guess."

She opens her mouth, but then takes one look at my face and zips it. I'm in no mood to talk about my family right now.

It takes four million years to find parking, but once we do, Teddy helps me haul our hastily thrown-together setup to our assigned booth while Ally takes the dog for a pee break—mainly to keep him from christening random objects. We dress the table: a red cloth, a white faux-fur runner. Donation box out. A clipboard with a signup sheet.

Allison returns, hands Tidbit to Teddy, then helps me hang the backdrop.

She somehow finagled a fireplace scene from her office—decorated trees on either side, stockings hung by the chimney with care, a window with Santa's sleigh sailing across the night sky (meaning two Santas per pic, but we're not here for logic). The kids will love it, and the parents will love skipping the mall line, paying what they can instead of mall-Santa prices—for a bad actor who probably smells like cigarettes anyway.

Eben eventually rolls up, looking every bit the tall drink of Santa he is.

"Sorry I'm late," he says, straightening his beard.

Teddy spins around from wrestling Tidbit away from the trash. His jaw drops.

"Wow," Teddy says, giving Mr. Eben Claus an unabashed once-over.

"Hello," Eben says, shifting from one foot to the other, uncomfortable.

"Uh, Eben, this is Teddy," I say. "Ally's fiancé. You'll have to excuse him—he's a, um, big fan of Santa Claus."

Ally elbows Teddy. "Dial it back, Rudolph."

Teddy steps forward with his free hand. Eben shakes it, confused.

"Nice to meet you, Bad Santa," Teddy says—his lack of filter backfiring instantly.

Eben blinks. I dip my head into my palm.

"Okay, that's enough," Ally says, corralling both Teddy *and* her dog (who is now trying to knock over the trash). "We're grabbing coffees—what can I get for you two?"

"Peppermint mocha," I say, not missing a beat. My eyes slide to Eben; he looks amused.

"Black for me, thanks," he says.

"That's the psycho coffee order, right?" Teddy stage-whispers, and Ally pushes him toward the coffee bar.

"They're cute," Eben says. "How long have they been together?"

"A little over a decade," I say. "They're tail-end-high-school-sweethearts."

"What does that mean?" he asks, tilting his head.

"They got together right at the very end of senior year and have been inseparable ever since," I say dreamily. I've never been envious of their relationship, but I've always loved their love story—straight out of a romance novel, minus the will-they-won't-they. It was obvious from day one they'd be together. Always.

"Isn't that just high school sweethearts?" Eben asks, slipping on his fake beard.

"I don't know, I think of high school sweethearts as people together all through high school who get married at nineteen," I say, tossing a few dollars into the donation box.

"They're not married?" he asks, fixing his hat.

"I mean, basically, but no." I turn to him and notice the beard is crooked. Without thinking, I reach up to adjust it. "They bought the house, got the dog, have the rings... just need to say the words."

"What about you?" he asks. The question vibrates beneath my fingers, and a chill sweeps my spine.

I freeze. "What about me?"

He clears his throat. "Are you... sweethearts with anyone?"

"Not unless you count my vibrator," I mutter. Eben's eyes

widen behind the spectacles. I drop my hands from his still-crooked beard and slap a hand over my mouth. Did I really just say that?

It's a wild thing to grow up without a Santa Claus and then confess to a man in a Santa suit that your boyfriend is a sex toy.

"Oh God," I groan, "I'm so sor—are you laughing at me?"

His "bowl full of jelly" (a pillow belted under the suit) jiggles along with his shoulders. He doubles over. His real laugh is higher-pitched than the Santa boom—a bright, boyish tenor. It's lovely. I savor it, even as my cheeks turn beet red.

"I'm sorry," he says, hands on his knees, wiping away tears. "I was not expecting that."

"Expect the unexpected," I say, blowing out a breath. I press my lips together, willing them not to smile. "Glad you think my pathetic, desert-dry love life is hilar–"

"Hey, wait," he says, sobering. "I didn't say that. I'm not laughing at that."

He steps closer and twirls a snow-white tendril of my Mrs. Claus wig around his finger. "You're just surprising, that's all," he says softly.

"Santa?"

Think of the most childlike voice imaginable saying "Santa," and that's the one that startles us out of our... whatever this is. Eben backs away so fast he nearly topples into the child staring up at us.

"Uh, hello..." He drops into the Santa voice and looks for a parent. He spots the boy's mom by the donation box, a dollar in hand.

"Peyton," she mouths, picking up the pen to sign in.

"Peyton!" Santa crows, tapping his temple. "See, I knew that."

"Wow," the kid breathes, eyes wide and sparkly.

"Santa, would you like to have a seat so Peyton can tell you what he wants for Christmas?" I ask. A Southern drawl slips out, deviating from yesterday's Mid-Atlantic—oops.

Eben shoots me an amused, bewildered look, one eyebrow dipping. I shrug.

They asked me if I could play Mrs. Claus, not if I could act.

"Of course! Good idea, Mrs. Claus," he booms. He's got that deep Santa voice down to a science. It's kind of sexy, not gonna lie.

Shut up, brain.

I guide Santa and Peyton toward the oversized chair draped in rich green velvet. Big, red poinsettias frame the scene, with all their glossy petals and glittery leaves. Santa settles in, waiting for Peyton's tiny nod before reaching out to pull him onto his lap.

"How old are you, Peyton?" Santa asks. Peyton counts on his fingers, then holds up the middle three.

"Wow, three! You've gotten so big!" Santa says. Peyton smiles shyly, humbled to be talking to Big Red himself.

"What do you want for Christmas?" Santa asks, eyes crinkling behind the beard.

Peyton lights up like a damn Christmas tree.

"Um, um, um..." He scrunches up his face, loading up his mental spreadsheet. "Pokémon, trampoline, dinosaurs, basketball..."

The kid goes on for a while. I grab Ally's Canon and snap a photo. I'm no photographer, but neither are the mall elves. I'm sure this one-dollar Santa visit will meet expectations.

Peyton's mom watches, proud. I tell her we'll email photos later today. She thanks me and coaxes Peyton away from Santa with the promise of hot cocoa with extra marshmallows.

"For someone who hates Christmas, you sure do have this Santa thing down," I tell him, still testing my drawl.

"Thanks, Paula Deen," he says with a playful wink. I shoot him a dirty look and toss a secret bird behind my back as I pivot back to the table, where a line is forming.

Am I flirting with Santa Claus?

"Are you flirting with Santa Claus?" Ally says just out of Eben's earshot. She hands me my peppermint mocha.

"No," I say, taking it. "We're just, you know, helping the children. And the old people."

"Ah, yes," Ally says dryly. "For the children and the old people. When did you become so damn altruistic, Mel?"

"Geez, it's not like I'm flirting with the Easter Bunny!" I whisper-scream.

Teddy has a knack for overhearing what shouldn't be repeated out loud. On cue, he hands Eben his psycho-black coffee and announces, "Wait—who's flirting with the Easter Bunny?"

I groan. Why are the people you love most also the ones guaranteed to embarrass you the worst?

"So, Santa Man," Teddy says. Eben eyes him with a hint of suspicion. "We're all headed to the Drunken Elf tonight. You wanna tag along?"

We are? Since when.

"Now," Teddy adds, teasing, "this is a pop-up Christmas bar —a Santa-speakeasy, you might say—and despite the red suit and pillow-stuffed gut, I've heard you're not a fan of the Big C?"

"Teddy," Eben says, "nobody is a fan of the Big C."

Great. Santa is hot enough to melt the whipped cream on my mocha, *and* deft enough to manage Teddy's enthusiasm and expectations—no easy task.

Teddy blinks. I lean and whisper: "He means cancer, ding-dong."

"Oh." His face falls, but in true Teddy style, he rebounds. He zeroes in on Eben. "Fine. You hate Christmas and cancer—what about beer?"

Eben laughs. "Beer, I love."

"Great. See you at nine?"

They launch into a double-dude handshake, sealing my fate.

I scan for Ally—she's supposed to rein Teddy in before he auctions off my glass slipper at midnight.

One look and I shut my mouth. Ally is balls-deep in a tug-of-war with the world's strongest, sweetest St. Bernard—and she's losing. Miserably.

Straining with all her plant-protein might, she yanks pointlessly on Tidbit, trying to keep him from crushing the five-year-old in Santa's chair, clutching a tattered Elmo and waiting (patiently-ish) for her photo with Discount Santa. I glance at the toy and pray she's asking for a new Elmo this year.

"Babe, drinks tonight?" Teddy hollers, blissfully unaware of the chaos and his impending murder.

Ally's face turns redder than my half-Irish ass on a Florida beach in mid-July.

"Can you please just help me with him?" she hisses.

Another thirty seconds and Tidbit's going to *Beethoven* our Santa set—and Ally—straight into the food court.

I throw my head back laughing as Teddy jumps in to wrestle his giant bear. When I turn to see Eben's reaction, he's staring at me. He looks away quickly, and I swear the faintest pink creeps across his cheekbones.

Interesting.

Behind Eben, a couple huffs and puffs, hauling a freshly cut Frasier fir tree toward the exit. Two kids in puffy jackets trail them, belting "O Christmas Tree." The parents pause to readjust their grip; the kids, maybe eight and ten, skip in a circle around them and then do a quick limbo under the trunk. Mom and Dad share a quick laugh, hoist the tree again, and the little parade disappears behind a tent toward the parking lot. A Grinchy pinch tugs at my chest before I can look away.

I wonder what it's like to grow up with Christmas—a family united in celebration and tradition. A real tree, cocoa by the fire, cookies in the oven, presents unwrapped on Christmas morning—all together. It's time I'll never get back. I'll never know the joy of being a kid on Christmas, only the ache of being left out.

And there it is—the sting of being without my family. Sure, I can certainly celebrate now, create new memories, and find fresh joy. I can do all the things I missed as a kid, on my own. But I'll always wonder what might have been—what a Hallmark Christmas might've felt like if my family hadn't been shackled to a cult.

"Are you going to take one home?" A soft, warm baritone interrupts my thoughts.

"Take one what?" I ask. Eben smiles down at me as another happy kid reunites with her mom after time with Discount Santa.

"A tree," he says, nodding toward the stand a few stalls down.

"Oh!" I touch my chin, considering. "I've always wanted a real tree. I'm afraid it would be dead in seconds."

"It's already dead," he points out.

"Right. Duh." I laugh, nervous—his brow furrows.

"You okay?" he asks, tilting his head. He touches my arm, and a shiver shoots through me. It's cold out, but suddenly I'm hot all over.

He's too close. It's too much. I step away.

"Fine!" I say, plastering on a bright smile. I turn to the next kid in line. "Who wants to see Santa?"

A chorus of tiny cheers screams "ME!" All I can feel is Eben's gaze on the back of my head.

Every time he touches me, it feels electric.

I wonder if he feels it, too.

CHAPTER 8

y closet is a catastrophic disappointment.
We're way past the "nothing to wear" phase
and deep into the "when did I stop caring what I look like?" era
—or maybe even the "should I be on SSRIs?" stage.

It's not that I don't love shopping. I did just bid on a vintage
set of Williams-Sonoma Santa salad plates on eBay last week.
But last I checked, I can't wear antique dinnerware to the bar.

I dig through the back of my closet and pull out a cold-
shoulder top. Hello, 2010. Now I'm genuinely curious—and
concerned—if that's really the last time I went to the mall. Or
ordered an article of clothing online. By the looks of this top, I
was still shopping exclusively by catalogue when it was
purchased.

Desperately, I rummage through my dresser drawers—a
graveyard of mismatched PJs and tangled underwear. Then—
hallelujah—I unearth a ruby-red cashmere sweater Ally gave me
last Christmas. God bless that woman—not just for her shopping skills, but for never leaving me behind in the fashion wars.

I cozy into the soft wool, and pair it with a black mini skirt I
found buried under a pile of old hats from a long-forgotten (and

deeply regretted) hat phase. Add sheer tights and black suede knee-high boots, and I'm officially ready to hate myself for loving that Eben is coming out tonight.

When Teddy first mentioned inviting Eben, I was too shocked to be pissed—though honestly, I shouldn't have been surprised. Teddy would invite the mailman out for drinks if it promised a good time and a potential new friend.

I guess Teddy butting into my life and inviting my arch-nemesis for holiday drinks is excellent for my plan to change Eben's mind about Christmas, but terrible for my plan not to sleep with him.

Not that I want to. Okay, let me revise: not that I want to *any more than any other woman partnered with a smokin' hot Santa during cuffing season would like to.*

I pop in my beloved hot rollers (thank you, *Seventeen* magazine circa 2009), coax a few going-out curls, swipe on lipstick—and I'm officially ready for a beer or three with Santa Claus at the Drunken Elf.

Ah, yes, the Drunken Elf. We go way back.

It's a little tavern that easily could pass for Snow White and the Seven Dwarves' favorite watering hole. A yearly pop-up just off the highway; it feels like the spot where overworked, blue-collar elves unwind after a long, thankless day hand-making wooden trains for kids who actually want iPads and Xbox consoles.

Fat, multi-colored Christmas lights are strung everywhere—inside, outside, and probably through the plumbing. Inside, a roaring fire crackles in a stone fireplace that always smells like chestnuts roasted by the fake elf-eared staff and handed out in nutcracker-printed paper bags.

Side note: those nutcracker-printed paper bags also make excellent barf bags if you accidentally go *ham* on some Buddy's Blazin' Bourbon.

Like I said, the Drunken Elf and I have history.

The first year I left the cult, this was *the* place I came to every Friday night. I was depressed, maybe drinking too much, but it was also my first time being allowed to celebrate a holiday—*any* holiday.

And celebrate, I did.

At twenty-two, I was finally free—no weird rules or restrictions. No one is spying on me or jumping out of the shadows to report my "sins" to the elders.

Yes, I lost my family, but I gained something else—myself. An identity. A "me" when no one else was telling me how to think or what to believe or who to be. And who is anyone without that?

I came here every Friday night that first Christmas, alone and free. This place is where I learned not just to love Christmas openly, but to love myself, despite everything and everyone I had lost.

But tonight, it's hard to think about everything I lost, not when I'm so dangerously close to feeling like I have something to gain.

Ally and Teddy snagged a cozy booth by the fireplace, within arm's reach of those delicious roasted chestnuts. The staff usually limits customers to two free bags a night—unless you're so wasted they consider the carbs a public service. But Ally and I learned long ago that the booth closest to the fireplace offers optimal access to chestnuts. From here, we can sneak as many bags as we want without having to be shitfaced to earn them.

Ally looks both comfy and glam in a fluffy white sweater and a red lip. I love her in winter white with a pop of red—welcome back, Marilyn Monroe! Cue the eyeroll when I say so.

Teddy looks at her like she's the sun, the moon, and the stars. No one's ever looked at me like that. A yearning stirs deep within me. I've always loved watching him love her; I've never thought of wanting that for myself.

"Where's your man?" Teddy teases, taking a sip of his Reindeer Ale.

"Don't get her flustered before he gets here," Ally warns. "If you make Melody nervous, she'll spill her drink all over the table within three minutes of him sitting down. And I'm wearing white."

"Oh, right." Teddy chuckles, remembering the last time we attempted a double date.

That was my first non-religion-affiliated date, and Teddy told me it was customary to *kiss the man's hand* when he arrived. Eager to fit in as a normal person, I took my Bumble date's hand as he sat down—and kissed it.

Very lovingly, as Ally likes to remind me.

The guy jerked his hand back so fast, I panicked and knocked my wine all over Teddy. Deservedly so.

"I swear on Santa's balls, I thought you knew I was joking," Teddy says now.

"You can't joke with social pariahs, Ted!" I clap back.

"I know, I know. I'm sorry!" He turns a little red, and that's how I know the apology is genuine.

"I, for one, thought it was a charming kiss," Ally adds, grinning.

"What kind of charming kiss are we talking about?" A deep, velvety voice enters the chat.

I look up to see Eben—tall, devastating, and very anti-Christmas in a black turtleneck sweater that is channeling Robert Redford in his prime.

Teddy opens his big mouth, and Ally and I kick him under the table at the same time.

Good lord, the yapper on this guy. He certainly puts some of those nursing home women to shame.

I scoot over so Eben can slide into the booth next to me. His hip brushes up against mine, and suddenly the fireplace feels like it's been turned up to *broil.*

Our elf server—her nametag reads Candy in curly peppermint font—approaches with a too-bright smile.

"What can I get for you?" she says, her voice dipping an octave lower than when she took the rest of our orders.

Beat it, Candy. I feel my face heating up. Good lord, am I getting jealous of a lady in fake elf ears?

"I'll just have a scotch and soda," Eben says.

"You got it," she purrs, tucking her pen behind a latex elf ear and sauntering off.

A knee brushes mine. I glance over. Eben's expression is stoic, but there's a hint of a smile as he sips his water. A drop clings to the corner of his mouth, and his tongue darts out to catch it.

Oh, lawdy.

"Scotch and soda, huh?" Teddy scans the menu. "Pretty sure you meant *Snowball Scotch.*"

Eben laughs. "Nope. Just a regular, boring scotch and soda."

It's nice having my friends here. My shoulders drop; my muscles relax. The Sleigh Bell Sour I'm drinking helps, too. Around Teddy and Ally, I can be myself. They can do some of the talking, while I solely focus on trying *not to be weird*—a full-time job if you're me.

Ally asks, "So, when you're not busy cosplaying as Kris Kringle, what do you do?"

Eben grins. "What do you mean? Being Santa is a 365-day-a-year job."

Teddy actually slaps his knee. "Dude, this guy is great."

Eben's eyes twinkle—*twinkle*, for God's sake—and my heart does something reckless. He's clearly having a good time with the two people I love most, which somehow makes me feel hopeful and sad at the same time. I'm not even halfway through the evening, and I'm already chalking this up as a lost cause.

"Well, the real gig isn't as glamorous," he continues. "I'm the media manager for Golding Home."

My heart stutters.

Ally kicks under the table, but misses her intended recipient —me. Instead, her pointed patent leather toe lands a blow squarely on Eben's ankle.

"Ouch," he mutters, massaging his ankle. "What, were you a soccer player in another life?"

"Varsity. State champ," Teddy says proudly. He slings an arm around Ally, whose eyes are doing wide-eyed Morse code at me. I cut her a look and clear my throat.

"So… you work for Golding Home?" I ask, taking a casual sip of my drink—the picture of cool, calm, and collected.

"Do you know it?" he asks, arm casually stretching over the back of the booth behind me.

Do I know it? *Do I know it?*

Golding Home is my *mecca*. The best and only Christmas décor store in Cherryville. Thousands of handmade ornaments. Miles of ribbons. And the best part: at least fifty top-to-bottom professionally-decorated trees.

It's my holy place. My sanctuary. My church of Christmas.

And Ebeneezer Scrooge himself works there.

"I've heard of it," I say, stirring my drink.

"Heard of it?" Teddy practically gasps. "She *lives* there during the holidays."

"Okay, Teddy."

"I swear to God, she'd set up a tent if they let her—"

"*Okay, Teddy.*"

Eben laughs. "I'll tell my dad you're a regular. He'll make sure you get a discount."

My drink freezes halfway to my lips. "Your dad?"

"Ronnie Golding," he says casually.

My jaw drops.

"Wait—the Christmas King is your *dad*?" Allison blurts.

Eben shifts in his seat. "That's correct."

Ronnie Golding is a Cherryville legend—the face of every

Golding Home commercial, all red suspenders and a booming laugh. He even inspires an unofficial Facebook page of thirsty middle-aged women salivating over his burly Santa shtick. The group—Ronnie's Naughty List—is private, and I shudder to think what goes on behind those digital curtains.

And that's Eben's *dad*.

No wonder Eben nails the Santa act. He s basically a Hot Santa nepo baby.

"You don't seem thrilled," Teddy says, earning an elbow from Ally.

"Let's just say, my dad's Christmas schtick gets old after a while."

Candy reappears with his drink, leaning *way* too close. "We've got food menus and free nuts—as long as you're drinking." She winks.

Teddy stands to grab a menu, jostling the table. Our drinks wobble dangerously, and we lunge to steady them. Candy backs off, momentarily distracted from her flirtation attempt, and I exhale, relieved.

Is it just me, or is it kind of ballsy to flirt with someone who's clearly on a date? Does this not *look* like a date to her? Or maybe it's not a date. What if I'm reading the vibes all wrong?

Good God, my brain is turning to mashed potatoes.

"Earth to Melody," Teddy waves the menu in front of my face. "You good with the Naughty Nachos?"

"Love 'em," I say, maybe too fast.

Candy walks off with our food order, and I turn to ask Eben how the hell the *King of Christmas* fathered a man whose heart is two sizes too small—when I feel the hair rise on the back of my neck.

"Melody?"

A shrill, unwelcome voice slices through the music. My mind blanks. Blood drains from my face.

Every bone in my body, every muscle, every cell—screams

run. I scan the room for an escape route, but every exit is framed with holly and twinkling lights.

The lights are too bright, the music is too merry, and the holiday magic I've grown to love so much is a noose around my neck, strangling me.

I'm trapped—surrounded by Christmas. Caught red-and-green-handed at the scene of a not-so-merry major crime against Heaven's Heralds.

And when I turn around, I'm face-to-face with the upturned nose of Heaven's biggest snitch.

CHAPTER 9

I can't tell if my pulse has slowed down or sped up, but my head is spinning. I can barely see Ally out of the corner of my eye, yet I can tell she's concerned by the way she sits up straighter.

"Courtney," I say—half greeting, half warning.

Eben's arm goes rigid behind me, and his chest puffs ever so slightly at the sound and feel of my discomfort.

"Man, Mel, it's been years," she says. Inside my head, her voice warps into something nefarious—almost reptilian. "Have you talked to your sister lately?"

She means Cassie. And she knows I haven't talked to Cass— or anyone in my family—for years. Every attempt ends the same: a campaign to drag me back to the church. I'd rather chew broken glass ornaments.

"You shouldn't be here." My voice comes out shaky, two octaves higher. I'm not a screamer—never have been—but that won't stop me from coming unglued. Trauma is a wild, uncontainable thing.

Luckily, with a best friend like Ally, I don't have to defend myself—especially being thrust face-to-face with my past stuns me silent. She knows exactly what's happening—because she had front-row seats to the worst thing that ever happened to me. A train wreck that ended with me leaving the cult—and my family—forever, with Courtney as the conductor who steered my life off the tracks.

Courtney was supposed to be my friend. Instead, she was my Judas.

A tiger friend to her marrow, Ally leaps to her feet.

"Hi there, *Courtney*, I'm going to give you exactly three seconds to walk away from our table before you're eternally sorry. I'm not religious. I don't believe in your God, or any god. But I do believe in karma—and ass beatings for loser bitches who fuck with my best friend. And trust me, an ass-kicking from a woman with eight soccer trophies, who doesn't believe in God, will put you in the motherfucking hospital."

The table is silent. Hell, the entire tavern goes silent.

Courtney stands behind me and blinks. I swear I can hear her eyelids scrape across her eyeballs. Allison has delivered a fatal blow. Courtney says nothing, turns, and stalks off—presumably to find the manager and claim verbal assault. Snitches get stitches, but they'll snitch till their dying breath.

"Let's get out of here," Allison says, tossing a few twenties on the table as she wriggles out of the booth. Teddy follows without a word. Eben looks down at me; I look up with a weak smile. He rises and waits for me to walk past before following, glancing back to make sure that Courtney is nowhere near our exit. Thank God, she's gone.

Outside, in the parking lot, Ally spins and hugs me.

"Are you okay?" she asks, squeezing tight.

"I'm fine," I say softly. I'm still shaking, but my pulse is settling.

"Trust me, I will cut that bitch if she even glances in your direction again," Ally says, pulling back to search my face.

"I know," I say, suddenly feeling like a wimp. I should've told

Courtney off myself. I should've told her to go to hell (even though the Heralds don't believe in Hell). I should've pretended I didn't know her. Now our night's ruined because I reacted like a lamb cornered by a lion.

"Don't beat yourself up," Ally says, reading my mind. "Did you drive?"

I shake my head. "Rideshare," I say, pulling out my phone.

"Do you want us to take you home?" Allison asks, darting a barely perceptible glance at Eben.

"I'll take her," Eben says, stepping closer. "If it's okay with you, Melody?"

It's the first time I've heard my name on his tongue. It sounds right there. My cheeks heat.

"Uh, sure," I say.

"Atta boy," Ally says with a wink at Eben. This time, *he* blushes.

"Glad you're okay," Teddy adds, still a little shell-shocked. Conflict isn't his thing. He's stiff as a board as they head for their car.

"This way," Eben says, motioning toward his truck.

My mouth goes dry. I've got to stop acting like a virginal schoolgirl, but this guy makes me nervous. I'm used to men who talk. Eben is the silent-and-mysterious type.

He helps me navigate the giant step up into his truck. Not easy in a mini skirt, but I trust he's a gentleman. He climbs in, hands me his phone to enter my address, the map pops up on the dash, and we're off.

"Sorry about that," I say, suddenly aware he probably has no idea what just happened—and bummed our night got cut short.

"Don't apologize," he says, pulling out of the lot. "Based on your friend's reaction, something terrible must've happened between you two."

"That's an understatement," I say with a snort. I uncross my arms and force my shoulders to loosen. Just thinking about Courtney ties my whole body in knots.

"Are you hungry?" Eben asks.

I sit up in my seat. I wasn't expecting that question. I was expecting *what happened?* Or *do you want to talk about it?* Not a hunger check.

"I could eat," I say.

"I know a place," he says, flicking off the map. "You like classic country?"

"I dabble," I say, trying to play it cool.

"COUNTRY ROOOOADS, TAKE ME HOOOOME, TO THE PLAAAACE I BELOOOOONG—" I scream with the windows down and heat blasting as we crest the hills toward the next town. The cold nips my cheeks and nose, but I don't care. Eben laughs.

"You just 'dabble', huh?" he side-eyes me, grinning.

I shrug and stick my head out the window like a golden retriever. The rural air is healing, and this sure beats telling him my sob story. He says it's a fifteen-minute drive to the place that's open this late (it's already after ten), but outside Cherryville, it's all countryside. We bump down a gravel driveway to a dive called Vinny's. A few beat-to-hell cars dot the lot.

I clutch the armrest. "Is this the second location?" I ask, deadpan—true-crime for "the part where the bad guy drives you somewhere remote."

A rough streak of dates a few years back sent me into a full *Dateline* spiral. Keith Morrison's voice has been narrating my inner monologue with men ever since.

"Only if second locations make the best pizza you've ever tasted," he says, grinning, windblown hair falls over one of his eyes.

Goddamn.

"Yum," I say, deciding he's too hot to be a serial killer (famous last words) and hop out.

"HOLY SHIT," I say, burning my mouth on a slice of extra-cheesy, perfectly crisp pepperoni.

Eben sits across from me, smug. "Told you. He folds his slice in half and takes a monstrous bite.

"How did you find this place? And why is it open this late?" I ask, wrestling a strand of molten cheese.

"College. They do a ton of late-night deliveries," he says. As if on cue, a delivery guy hustles past with ten pizzas and a mountain of breadsticks.

"It's Sunday," I say, double-checking my phone to be sure.

"Haven't you heard?" He leans in. "CSU's top-ten for party schools."

"Ew, you went to Cherryville State?" I wrinkle my nose.

"Go, Cardinals," he says, making a talking beak with his hand that somehow manages to be both ridiculous *and* charming.

"Oh, God. Don't tell me you joined a fraternity."

"Nope." He folds another slice. "I was working. I lived at home and commuted to school. No time to test-drive the party scene."

"No wonder you're single," I blurt. He freezes mid-bite. Open mouth, insert foot. "I mean—you look like you, so I figured you'd have married your college sweetheart, but now all of this makes sense because—oh, God."

I try to hide my face with my wrists; my hands are covered in pizza grease

He laughs, and his leg brushes mine under the table.

"What about you? Where'd you go to school?" he asks.

"Well, I... didn't," I say. I'm not apologetic—just factual.

"Oh!" he says, reacting to *how* I said it. "I'm sorry, I shouldn't have assumed..."

"No, it's fine. I..." Here goes nothing. "I was raised in a cult."

He doesn't rush to fill the silence. He just watches me—listening. Which is nice.

"A religious cult," I add. "They call themselves Heaven's Heralds."

"And you're out? You're safe?" His voice goes husky; his blue eyes turn puppy-dog sweet. The fact that his first instinct is to ask about my safety has me half feral. I could climb across the table and jump his bones right now.

"Yes. I'm fine." I smile. "Physically, anyway. Emotionally, they did some damage. As you've seen."

"That woman at the bar—she was one of them?" he asks. We've both stopped eating.

I sigh, buckle in, and tell him the whole story.

Four years before I left the cult, Courtney and I were "friends." We worked at the same mom-and-pop diner that loved hiring Heralders because we never needed holidays off, were "trustworthy" with the register, and generally had a grate-ful-for-scraps mentality.

Translation: we were easy to exploit.

One night, a manager—wannabe football star with a big nose and bigger ego—cornered me into staying late to help with dining room "repairs."

It felt off, but there were three other Herald girls in line for my job, and management loved reminding us how replaceable we were. So I stayed. Nothing happened—or so I thought.

The next day at work, no one would look at me. Imagine receiving the silent treatment from twenty people at once. Turns out, the scumbag manager told the entire restaurant staff we'd stayed late to hook up—bragging that he'd gotten the best blowjob of his life (flattered, but it didn't happen). I was barely eighteen. I stayed home the next day, humiliated. When Courtney called, I thought she was checking on me.

Instead, it was an ambush with the church elders. They harassed and punished me, and the story of my "misconduct" spread to every congregation in the state. The last conversation Courtney and I ever had was me sobbing, begging her to stop torturing me, and please, please, believe me.

"Jesus Christ," Eben swears, jaw slack.

"He wouldn't want anything to do with those people," I say, defiant. "That's what I realized when I left."

"What was she doing at a Christmas bar if she's not allowed to celebrate?" he asks.

"You know, I have no idea," I say. I had one lucid moment of telling Courtney she shouldn't be there—and then I blacked out.

"Maybe you should report her," he says, finishing off his Pepsi. "Give her a taste of her own medicine."

"I'd rather smash my favorite Christmas ornament and eat it than ever speak to any of them again," I say pushing my plate away.

"But your family?" he asks, accidentally poking the softest spot I have.

"Yeah. Of course I miss them," I say. Oh no—tears incoming. Knock it off, Mel. Change the subject.

I don't have to. I only notice Eben's leg touching mine when its warmth disappears. "I'm gonna go pay," he says, picking up the check. He squeezes my shoulder as he walks away.

We head back to Cherryville. It's below freezing now, too cold to roll the windows down. I shiver in the passenger seat, and Eben nudges the heat higher—no doubt roasting himself like one of those chestnuts from earlier. I know all the songs on his playlist, but I don't sing. I watch the winter stars—always the most vivid—glitter beyond the glass. Eben doesn't say anything. He doesn't have to. The pity hums between us.

At my apartment complex, he doesn't kill the engine, but he turns the music down.

"Thanks for the pizza," I say, opening the door.

"Wait a minute," he says, and my heart drops to my butt.

I turn. "Yes?"

"I still don't have your number," he says, tossing his phone onto the passenger seat.

"Oh." I pick it up and add my number as Mrs. Claus. He looks down, laughs.

On the stairs to my second-floor apartment, my phone dings.

Ho ho ho ;)

CHAPTER 10

My y job is excruciating this week. One of my clients was not satisfied with the final designs for her new house, and she happens to be a top executive at one of our major corporate partners.

A lot was riding on this one, and I botched it. In my defense, she said she loathed modern, so I opted for a classic French Provençal style—antique accents, a touch of shabby chic, and pretty pastels.

Her aversion to modern design was a seething animosity toward egg-shaped chairs.

In reality, she wanted modern farmhouse—like every other nouveau riche white woman I've had the pleasure of picking out barn doors for.

A rookie mistake. Let's face it.

Deb and Don were chill about it, despite their twin lobster tans after snorkeling the Great Barrier Reef. But now I'm balls-deep in a redesign of an 8,000-square-foot mansion that's making me want to gouge my eyes out with the wrong end of a wooden spoon.

So. Much. Beige.

My spare moments not spent drowning in *Interia* renderings (a program so slow and glitchy it makes me want to pull my hair out) are devoted to classic Christmas films and gorging on peppermint bark until I'm sick to my stomach.

I also obsessively keep checking my phone.

For no reason in particular.

Okay—so Eben hasn't said anything since our Sunday pseudo-date, and I desperately want to say hello, but I hate to be the first one to text. Call me old-fashioned, but if a guy is interested, he should be the Text-in-Chief, not me.

Right?

Just say hi, Ally texts. *You're so archaic it's almost anti-feminist.*

I hate to initiate, I text back while *White Christmas* dazzles on the TV. *If he's interested, he'll take initiative.*

Sounds like a line out of a bad female dating strategy book, Ally replies.

I hesitate and then start typing. *For your information, I've been flipping through* Never Chase Men *Again.*

Nooooo, God, she fires back.

Me: *What?*

Ally: *We do NOT under ANY circumstances read FDS books written by MEN.*

I bite down hard on a hunk of peppermint bark. The satisfying crunch is an addiction—an outlet for whatever repressed rage lurks deep inside me.

I sigh and stare at my phone for a long time before clicking on Xmas Hater (my contact name for Eben; "Santa Claus" was just too weird).

Hi, I type.

And immediately hate myself.

Goddammit, Ally, I text.

You did it, didn't you? You texted him. I can practically hear her giggling through the screen.

Now I'm going to obsess over this all night, I say, ready to pull my hair out.

My phone dings—and it's not Ally.

Eben: *Hey :)*

OMGOMGOMGOMGOMG, I type—triple-checking that it's going to Ally.

Ally: *He texted back?*

Me: *Yup :D*

Ally: *OMG YOU ARE FINALLY GOING TO GET LAID!!!!!!!!!!!*

Me: *Ok. Shut up.*

Ally: *Well, we've been worried.*

Me: *WHO IS WE.*

Ally: *Me and Teddy, ofc.*

Me: *A big FU to both of you.*

Ally: *We love you too. Gonna finish the dishes and hit the sack. Enjoy your new boy toy.*

She ends with a kissy face and a bunch of hearts with arrows —brief pause, then an eggplant and some water droplets. I send back a tongue-out emoji; she replies with an angel.

My phone dings again.

Eben: *How are you?*

Oooh, a *complete* sentence. No "r" and "u." Whew. Gets me all hot and bothered.

Me: *I'm good! Just eating peppermint bark and watching White Christmas. You?*

Him: *Oh, nothing. Just sipping hot chocolate out of an "I <3 Christmas" mug and singing carols by the fire, dressed in traditional Victorian garb.*

Me: *Can't resist a man in a frock coat.*

Him: *I'll have to remember that.*

I blush head to toe on the couch while Bing Crosby serenades Rosemary Clooney with "Count Your Blessings Instead of Sheep."

Him: *So what are you wearing?*

79

I nearly dump my entire box of chocolates—quick save. I frantically type.

Me: *Beg your pardon?*

Him: *I've made an internal bet that it's either candy cane pajamas or a nutcracker onesie.*

I look down at my red-and-white striped silk pajamas. I'm a walking candy cane.

I can't tell him the truth.

Me: *Just a T-shirt and some underwear.*

Him: *Is that right? Minimalist. I like it.*

Me: *That's how I roll.*

There's a long beat before my phone dings again.

Him: *It's a total lie, isn't it?*

Me: *How dare you.*

Him: *Thought so. See you tomorrow?*

I'd almost forgotten about tomorrow's pageant meeting. Ally already told me she can't go this week because of a work event. It's just me and Eben. Well, and Missy.

The thought of seeing him makes my stomach do flip-flops. Damn it.

Me: *I'll be there with (jingle) bells on.*

Him: *Ha. Goodnight, Mrs. Claus ;)*

Oh my God. For anyone else, being called Mrs. Claus by a potential suitor might be annoying—maybe even weird. For me, the Christmas-loving nutball? Hoo boy. I just had to cross my legs. That's dirty talk, baby.

I go back and forth on what to text back. Should I call him Santa? Just Eben? I settle on the obvious.

Me: *Goodnight, Mr. Claus <3*

WHEN I WAKE and glance at the ancient digital clock by my bed, it's three a.m. I swear I hear rustling in the living room—and the faint jingle of… bells?

I throw back the covers and stumble out.

In the dark, a flash of red catches my eye. I don't try to turn on any lights; no need to alert the intruder to my presence.

I tiptoe toward the Christmas tree. I don't remember having a fireplace, but a very tall man with a full beard rises to his full height. He looks right at me through oval spectacles, his eyes crinkling at the corners.

"Santa Claus?" I whisper. But he's too slim—and too deliciously sculpted beneath the thin red velvet—to be the real Santa. And even through the full beard, I can see plush lips, a straight nose, and twinkling blue eyes. There's something familiar about him—

"Honey, I'm home," he says with a big, sweet grin. He looks me up and down. "Wow."

I look down. I'm in a skimpy red teddy. A red Christmas bow ties over my chest.

"My little Christmas present—ready to be unwrapped." His hands skim my hips, slide to my waist, gripping and molding my curves. Heat pools low in my stomach. I brace my palms against a solid chest and look up—the beard, spectacles, and ridiculous hat are gone, revealing glacier-blue eyes, a clean, strong jawline, and soft, smiling lips.

"Eben?" I whisper.

"Shhh," he breathes, hands sliding down to cup my ass. I gasp as he lifts me until I'm straddling his waist, arms looped around his neck as he carries me to the bedroom.

He lays me on the bed and climbs over me. I'm breathing hard, my legs parting to make room for him. He smiles against my mouth.

"Shall I unwrap my gift now?" His fingers toy with the bow, and I feel the slow slip of silk as it loosens.

His gaze tracks his fingers as they trail from hips to waist to ribs to chest. His thumb ghosts over my nipple, and I buck.

"I'm going to make you scream, Mrs. Claus," he whispers in my ear before his head dips.

My eyes shoot open. I jolt upright in bed. The room is dark and tragically empty. I'm sweating, my whole body aching with desire.

I sit there, breathing, letting the dream dissolve—then open my bedside drawer and rummage for something to take the ache away.

CHAPTER 11

*O*hen my alarm goes off, I'm still reeling from my filthy Santa dream. It ranks among the weirdest dreams I've ever had—and is undoubtedly the most memorable. Who knew I had a Saint Nick kink? My subconscious, apparently.

No idea how I'm supposed to look Eben in the eyes today. Thank God we're not suiting up as Mr. and Mrs. Claus tonight —the thought alone makes me blush while I "get ready for work," a.k.a. brush my teeth, tame my hair, and throw a nice top over sweatpants for Zoom.

Business above; bed-rot below.

Ally texts on her lunch break.

Ally: *So?*

Me: *So...?*

Ally: *Bitch, what did he say?*

Patient, she is not.

Me: *Nothing, just asked me what I was wearing and then went to bed.*

Ally: *HE WHAT???????*

Me: *It's not what you think. He wanted to know if I was wearing Xmas PJs.*

Ally: *So he could jerk off while imagining it, clearly.*

Me: *You're gross.*

Ally: *You're the one with a Santa hat vibrator.*

Me: *I told you never to speak of it again!!!*

The Santa hat and I got friendly just this morning.

Ally: *Too late. Say, you should show Eben your toy collection...*

Me: *Not for all the snow in the North Pole.*

Ally: *I bet I know where he'd like to stick his North Pole...*

Me: *GOODBYE, ALLY.*

She sends an eggplant emoji sandwiched between Mr. and Mrs. Claus. I want to kill her for being able to read my mind and decipher my dirty little secrets. I decide not to mention the sexy dream, lest I be subjected to an onslaught of half-naked slutty Santa memes.

The rest of my day is spent agonizing over an excruciating 3D floor plan and trying not to think about seeing Eben later. I just know I'm going to turn head-to-toe tomato red when I see him.

THE SECOND I step into the nursing home, my filthy Santa brain wipes clean—a paper airplane knifes past my ear.

These seniors are feral.

Forget the Hallmark postcard of flour-dusted grandmas and porch-rocking grandpas spitting tobacco and folksy wisdom.

Rec hour here is Thunderdome.

The seniors at Forest Park could put any 2000s frat movie to shame. Even if it starred Seth Rogan. And Vince Vaughn. Hitting a bong. With Owen Wilson.

I could hear "activity" from the activity room over my car's engine when I pulled into the lot—and my car hasn't had an oil change in two years, so that's saying something.

Even from the hallways, the chaos is on an Olympic level. I don't know where to look first. Out of the corner of my eye, a hula hoop is spinning way too fast for someone who had a full hip replacement six months ago. Roger's hunched over a smoking contraption that sure as hell looks like a 1993 Easy-Bake Oven. And Edna and Millie are running a black-market lottery, selling tickets at the door. Well, Edna is selling. Millie is judging.

"Hi, Sugar, the jackpot is up to fifty mill. Wanna buy a scratcher?"

I stare blankly at Edna.

"Uh… where did you get those?"

Edna counts the cash stuffed in her bra alongside a wad of tattered Kleenex.

"I'm already up one cup size just in ones and fives!" Edna crows, still counting.

Millie crooks a finger at me and then shuffles away from her friend. She tugs my sleeve; I lean down out of pure curiosity. "Edna's son has a drinking-and-gambling problem—"

"He's a good boy!" Edna interrupts.

Millie rolls her eyes so hard it looks painful. "You spoiled him!" she shouts back, then lowers her voice to me. "That degenerate can't visit his mother once a year at Christmas without hitting the bottle or the ponies first, so he always brings a little something for his mom and her friends."

I watch Edna shove crumpled singles into her bra like a seasoned pro. "Why is she selling them?"

Apparently, her hearing aids are cranked all the way up, because Edna pipes in without even looking up from her stack of George Washingtons. "Because, sweetheart, I can't handle it if one of these geriatric losers wins on my dime. At least this way I get a couple of bucks out of the deal. You sure you don't want one, honey?"

"Sorry, Edna, I'm all out of ones," I say, tapping my purse.

I scan the mayhem—and realize something is missing. "Is Eben here yet?"

Millie scans the room. "Haven't seen him. Usually, he's glued to Anne, but she's MIA. Missy too. She's normally handing out coloring books and crayons during rec time—she treats us like toddlers just because some folks wear diapers. Not me. Three kids in three years; still got the steel trap."

Okay then.

Something whizzes past my head, and I duck.

Was that an *apple*?

"Sorry!" an old man shouts from across the room.

"Howard is reenacting the storming of Normandy for his talent," Millie explains.

"With apples?" I ask.

"Whaddaya want him to use—cannons?" She looks at me like I've got rocks for brains.

They're grown adults, sure, but this scene screams "needs supervision," not unlike the other diaper-wearing demographic. They're supposed to be practicing their talents, but Missy is supposed to be supervising while we plan the Christmas pageant.

God, I wish Ally were here. She'd better show next week or I'm TP-ing her house with tinsel.

I step out of the activity room and bump into someone at least ninety-five practicing the Lindy Hop. If you're unfamiliar, picture the human body right before it slips on a banana peel. That's essentially the Lindy Hop.

Please, God, let the floors be unwaxed.

I'm halfway down the hall, trying to remember where Missy's office is, when I hear voices—loud ones. I slow down.

Through the cracked door, I spot a tall figure pacing, gesturing wildly. Eben. His hair is a mess, jaw tight, voice raised. Across from him, Missy sits behind her desk, arms crossed like a kindergarten teacher about to hand out detention.

"You need to call your father," Missy says. "This is more than you can handle, Eben. You can't shoulder it alone."

"I'm not calling him." Eben's voice is rough. "He made his choice years ago. I'm not dragging him into my personal business."

Personal business? Why is Eben talking to Missy about his personal life? I know he's been volunteering here for years—maybe they're closer than I realized?

Missy exhales. "Eben, please, for her sake, let go of your pride—"

"It's not about *pride*." Eben snaps, cutting her off. "It's about what makes her happy."

Her?

Missy leans forward. "You need help. You know he'd—"

"No. I love her more than anything. I'm not doing that to her." Eben's voice cracks.

Love? Does he love someone?

More than... anything?

My stomach flips. Eben never mentioned a girlfriend. I've been assuming he's single like a complete dumbass. My knees go soft, and my microwave vegan pad thai starts rising like a bad omen.

"She's all I've got," Eben says, voice breaking. "We can make it work."

I take three slow steps back from the door, heart pounding.

This is ridiculous. Santa is obviously taken. And I'm apparently so emotionally stunted that I mistake basic kindness for chemistry. He listened to my cult sob story, and I turned it into foreplay. What a desperate, lonely loser I am.

My face burns. I spin around, desperate to escape before I melt into the linoleum.

I'm so caught up in my own humiliation. I don't even hear the door open behind me.

"Hi," Eben says, voice rough. "How long have you been standing there?"

"I just got here," I lie. "Nobody is overseeing the...activity... in the activity room, and it's, uh, complete chaos."

Eben sighs and stuffs his hands in his coat pockets. His face is flushed; he's trying to calm down. "Is Edna selling lottery tickets yet?"

"She has a bra full of ones like a Prohibition-era showgirl."

"Shit," Eben says, finally cracking a grin. I didn't return it. "We'd better get in there."

He doesn't move, though, and for a minute we linger awkwardly. He stares at me, expression softening but still hard to read. I want to burst into tears, but I'm not going to be a baby about a man who happened to be nice to me once. All right— twice.

"We'd better get in there, Mrs. Claus," he says at last.

"You can just call me *Melody*," I say, defiant. I pivot on one boot heel and walk toward the community room, adding a little extra swing to my hips.

Now I'm lobster red for a totally different reason. I had a sleazy sex dream with someone else's boyfriend. God, I'm dumb.

Missy finally emerges from her office looking worse for wear. Eben and I sit, silent. She collapses into her chair with a legal pad and, without missing a beat, starts listing roadblocks we've hit with the pageant planning. I don't hear a word. I hate that I'm this affected, but I really thought he was into me. It just sucks to have the rug yanked out, that's all.

Eben glances over a few times, but I don't look back. I stare at a corner of peeling wallpaper like I can glue it down with telekinetic powers. If I *did* have telekinetic powers, I'd also drop that giant, ugly fake plant over there on his head.

No. I mentally kick myself. *Knock it off.*

So what if he has a girlfriend? What am I twelve? I can be a mature adult about this.

His foot brushes mine under the table, and blood shoots to my groin as the touch catapults me back to my dream. I try to karate-kick the memory out of my head, but it won't budge. All I can feel are Eben's hands on my body, his breath on my face, his warmth pressed against me. Sure, it was just a dream—but it felt so real.

I want it to be real.

Wow. There it is. I finally admitted it to myself.

"I'm sorry, I can't do this," I say, standing. My chair nearly topples; Eben catches it.

"You can't hand out programs at the door?" Missy asks, face twisting with confusion.

"No," I say, panic rising. "I've gotta go."

I make a run for it. I know I'm making a fool of myself, but I don't care. I'm about to burst into tears, and I'll be damned if I do it in front of Missy, Eben, and a room full of unruly retirees.

I hear footsteps behind me. I don't look to see who they belong to. I just beeline for the door to the parking lot.

Not fast enough.

A gentle hand catches my wrist; I wrench it free. "Melody, wait," Eben says, so soft it hurts.

My body betrays me. I stop and spin, panting.

"What?" It comes out harsher than I intended. None of this is rational, but I can't help it. I'm a mess.

Eben looks taken aback, brow furrowed. "What's going on?"

"I just don't have time for this anymore," I say—half lie, half truth. "It's too big a commitment. I have a job. And a social life. I signed up to play Mrs. Claus once a week to bring happiness to neglected senior citizens.

"Then just do—"

"This is why I'm *tragically single*!" I shout at him. "I overcommit, and then I don't have time to meet people and go on dates and get laid!"

Oh, God, I'm really doing this. The shame train has left the station. Ain't no going back.

Choo choo.

"Dates?" Eben repeats, a hint of a smile tugging at his mouth. He's amused. I want to slap the smile right off his pretty face.

"Yes, dates! With hot men who want to fuck me! I need to be doing more of that and less of..." I gesture wildly. "Whatever *this* is!"

"If I ask you out, will you calm down?" he asks, clearly suppressing a laugh.

"What?" My voice jumps two octaves. What a simp I've become.

"I'll take you out Friday night." His grin is big and sweet. "Then we can put this whole quitting-the-pageant-planning-because-you-need-to-get-out thing behind us. Deal?"

If I wasn't cherry red before, I sure as hell am now.

What about the phone call? What about little Miss *"she's all I have"*? My brain spins inside my skull at NASA record-breaking speeds with questions I'm too embarrassed to ask.

Clearly, after my outburst, this is just a pity dinner for a new friend.

All I can do is nod like a bobblehead.

"Great," he says, grin stretches wider. "It's a date."

CHAPTER 12

"*F*or the love of God, Mel, it is not a pity date," Ally says, lounging against a clothing rack while I panic-shop for tomorrow. I've hit critical mass in the nothing-to-wear department, so I dragged her to the mall—her happy place, my ninth circle. She's already juggling three shopping bags for a wedding-date weekend with Teddy. Apparently, she *needs options.* "He wouldn't blatantly ask you out if there were a real-life Mrs. Eben Claus in the equation."

"I heard him say it," I say. "He loves someone. The ladies said he's always with someone named Anne."

"Grandma. Great-aunt. Hospice bestie. He volunteers at a nursing home for fun, remember?"

I groan, unconvinced.

"Fine, maybe he wants a throuple?" she deadpans.

I nearly choke. "A what? Ally!"

"What? Could be fun. Don't knock it till you've tried it."

"No, thank you," I gag. "I don't do throuples."

Ally shrugs, gleefully ruthless. "At this rate, babes, you don't do singles or doubles—you're not even picking up a racket."

"Whatever," I sigh, still unsure and slightly queasy. I hold up two red midi dresses that look almost identical. "Which one?"

"Uh…" She looks between them. "I like the brighter red one."

I hold it to my arm and frown. "Is it too orange?"

"Hmmm… okay, the darker red then?" She's out of her depth, and we both know it, but I still need her opinion.

"Does it have too much of a blue undertone?"

She just stares at me.

"You can't tell the difference, can you?"

She sighs, grabs both hangers, drapes both dresses over her arm, and heads to the register.

"Wait, what are you doing?" I ask, practically stepping on her heels.

"Getting them both for you," she says, setting them on the counter. "Santa's going to salivate over you in either dress, but your nerves are clouding your judgment."

"What?!" I say, alarmed. I reach for them; she knocks my hand away.

"It's an early Christmas gift," she says, pulling out her wallet. "The gift of getting laid."

"I'm not going to sleep with him on the *first date*!" I say it too loud, and heads swivel. An aggravated mother covers her daughter's ears and scowls at us. Ally rolls her eyes as the puritan escorts her child to safety.

"God, this isn't a Toys 'R' Us," Ally mutters, leaning on the counter. The cashier side-eyes us while ringing up the dresses. "You're at least going to make out with him, right?"

Do people make out on first dates? I wouldn't know. The last time I was in a "serious" relationship, I was still part of a strict purity culture—penetrative sex before marriage was sinful. Still, everything else somehow existed in a theological gray area (I'm not sure the elders would've agreed). We got great at dry-humping like fully clothed bunnies, eventually graduating to hands under clothes, then no clothes with mouths everywhere.

Needless to say, I can blow a guy like a porn star.

"If he even makes a move," I say, twirling a lock of my hair innocently as the cashier folds my dresses into a bag.

"Of course he will," Ally says, snatching the receipt and handing me the bag. "He's not a teenager in a sex-shaming cult."

The face that pops into my head has a dimpled smile and a floppy mop of hair—and it sends shudders down my spine for a very different reason than my cult nemesis, Courtney.

Jordan was the spindly ex everyone had in high school: the fast-food job, the car that barely started, the parents who hated me for not being church-perfect (I occasionally ducked out early to grab Wendy's—sue me). He was my first everything— first dance, first date, first kiss.

It was a slow burn, and when we finally did have sex, he cried afterward. No, not kidding. Then he turned around and blamed me for "leading him into temptation." He actually tried to pressure me to marry him and threatened to tell the Heralds if I didn't agree to it.

Thank God for Ally. When I told her, she threatened to show up at his house with a baseball bat. I broke up with him instead—so, technically, I saved his life. You're welcome, Jordan.

He married some other poor nineteen-year-old less than a year later, who, last I checked, has popped out at least four of his moppy-haired spawnlings. The circles under his wife's eyes are Grand Canyon-sized. I want to sneak over, nudge a window open, and set her free.

As for me, I was branded tainted goods—no one in Heaven's Heralds would touch me (what kind of cult would they be without a hefty dose of misogyny?). I tried dating outside the church, but I was too sheltered for that world, too. It's probably why I've avoided dating altogether—why I've mortared up stone walls around a stained-glass heart.

Subject change, stat.

"Why are you leaving me tomorrow?" I whine, clutching my bag to my chest.

"I'm not leaving *you*. I'm leaving the munchkin," Ally says with an excited skip. (The "munchkin" is her horse-sized dog, of course.)

Ally and Teddy booked a pet sitter for Tidbit while they road-trip to Chicago to attend Teddy's cousin's wedding. Teddy has approximately one million cousins, and I've met almost all of them, but this just happens to be a second cousin I've never met—so I'm not invited (boo). Unfortunate, since it's at the Ritz and I hear *Vogue* is covering it. (Apparently, the bride is the daughter of some famous fashion designer.) I've only ever seen them dance together at prom—the night their romance began— so yeah, I'm a little bummed I won't be there to recapture the magic.

But the timing couldn't be worse. Call Ally and Teddy my security blanket in human form, but I'd prefer the four of us go out together. Instead, I'm at the mall helping my best friend abandon me for the weekend.

"Having a Saint Bernard isn't that different from having a toddler," Ally explains, steering us toward the food court. "Except imagine your toddler—with all his new-to-the-world impulses—weighs 175 pounds. Teddy and I need this weekend."

The smell of freshly-baked pretzels permeates the air. We follow our noses to the royal blue-and-yellow temple of mall carbs: Auntie Anne's.

"I know, and I'm happy you two are going," I say, exhaling. It's… mostly true. "I just—I don't know, that's a weird way to ask someone out, right?" I know, I know, I can't stop ruminating. It's a disease. (Also: trauma.)

I'm losing Ally's attention (fair) to the intoxicating aroma of pepperoni pretzel bites and the hypnotic churn of the frozen lemonade machine. We stare at it, our mouths watering.

"It's also hard to get a read on people when you're eavesdropping and invading their privacy. You have no idea what he was talking about, and you're making a lot of assumptions." She shrugs. "Did you try—just asking him?"

I glare at her. She already knows the answer to that question. I would rather snack on roadkill than ask Eben point-blank about his conversation with Missy. Ally is much more confrontational than I am; she'd have barged in and demanded names.

Ally sighs. "No, of course you didn't."

I shrug, a little embarrassed.

"If I were you... Well, I'd ask," Ally continues, "But if you can't do that, assume that if he's asking you out, he's either available—or wants to add you to his ethically non-monogamous harem." She sticks her tongue out when my face contorts, then marches up to the Auntie Anne's counter. "Do you want to split—"

"Duh." I cut her off. In fifteen years, we have never not split Auntie Anne's at the mall.

Snacks secured, we park our butts firmly in the food court. With Ally's *hanger* (more like hungry aloofness) solved, she can focus on my anxiety again—critical, considering she's leaving town for three whole days.

"Listen, you were super weird first," Ally says with a mouthful of warm, salted pretzel goodness. "Which is fine. I think he kinda likes that."

"I wasn't that weird," I say defensively, fishing a bite from the bag. "I was upset."

Ally laughs. "You get weird when you're upset, and you get upset for weird reasons. And for the hundredth time, you shouldn't have been eavesdropping anyway."

"Okay, Mom," I say.

"Not because it's rude," Ally says, wagging a pretzel at me—salt flying. "Because you don't know who they were talking about."

I shrug and pop a pretzel in my mouth.

"So," she dusts her hands, "where's he taking you?"

As if Mr. Eben Claus and Ally are on the same wavelength, my phone vibrates. My whole body stiffens with simmering expectation. I keep my phone face down for a reason.

Ally smirks. "You gonna answer that?"

"Not sitting here with you," I say.

She gives me the look—the one that means I'm being a giant baby—and I crack. I flip the phone to see that Mr. Hates Christmas has indeed texted.

Pick you up at 7 tomorrow, Mrs. Claus?

Ally peers down. "He calls you Mrs. Claus outside of the nursing home?"

What a weird sentence to hear out loud, but... yes.

"It's just a joke," I say, flushing. My fingers fly over the keypad.

Perfect, where are we going? I text back with a Mother Christmas emoji.

Ally shakes her head, dismayed and amused. "Y'all have the same kink," she says.

I blush. Hard.

"No—"

"Yeah, yeah, I know. Santa hates Christmas, whatever. But he's getting off on this Mr. and Mrs. Claus thing. He clearly wants to fuck the Christmas right out of you."

"Let's see if he actually follows through," I say.

My phone vibrates again. Ally grins.

"That sounds a lot like follow-through to me."

I open our chat, trying (and failing) to shield the screen. Ally has the neck of a giraffe when she wants to see something on my phone.

It's a surprise.

What should I wear? I type, thumbs flying as I hit send.

He replies instantly. Ally opens her mouth to say something, and I cut her off—

"You'd better just be making room for another pizza bite," I warn.

Disappointed, she sighs, dips a chunk of pretzel-pizza into marinara, and lets me have a moment to flirt with the man I made a complete ass of myself in front of the other day—which somehow ended with him asking me out. I don't know. Whatever.

"Maybe you should embarrass yourself more often," Ally says between bites. "Seems to be working for you."

I swear it's like this bitch can read my mind.

The phone buzzes again. God, he's a fast texter. I mean, he *does* have a job. A very Christmas-y job, too, I swoon silently.

I flip the phone over.

A coat for sure. What's underneath is up to you ;)

His words catch in my chest.

"Are you okay? You're purple," Ally says, raising a brow.

I hand her my phone.

She scans Eben's text and looks up. "Girl, that man's going to make you limp."

I peg her in the forehead with a pretzel—but honestly? I hope to God he does.

CHAPTER 13

"One little hint?"

"No," Eben says with a smirk. His eyes radiate so much mischief and pride at keeping me on the edge of my seat that I can see those baby blues sparkle—even though the truck is dark and the road is even darker.

It's rude how dark it gets by 5 p.m. in the winter. Thank God for Christmas lights in late November and December; they keep me happy and sane. Mine stay up until February, purely to ward off the seasonal depression.

"You could be kidnapping me." I pout and slouch down in my seat.

"If I were kidnapping you, there would be definite signs."

"Like what?"

"Well," he says slowly, "it would be at night, I'd be very secretive about where I was taking you, the roads would be very dark so that nobody could see us, and I'd make sure our cell service was limited. Oh, wait." His smile turns wicked.

I glance down at my phone: one measly bar, barely hanging on.

"I don't see any rope in here," I say, a little breathless. I've

98

warmed him up—I can tell by the way his hips shift, trying to keep his eyes on the road. His knuckles tighten on the wheel, his breath stutters, and I have to resist the urge to lean in and whisper in his ear.

Eben clears his throat; his voice drops, huskier. "Santa always has some tinsel rope on him, doesn't he?"

I feel my soul leave my body. I cross my legs to keep from lunging across the console.

We drive in sizzling silence for a minute until he makes a sharp right turn off the rural road and into a parking lot.

My heart flutters. A huge backlit sign—"Celestial Gardens" in a swoopy cursive—glitters with stars.

My jaw drops.

"No way," I murmur.

By day, Celestial Gardens is a charming botanical garden featuring colorful daisy fields, lush rose beds, and a thick oak grove. During the holiday season, the gardens host a nightly botanical light show and art exhibit called GLOW. Gorgeous light installations by local artists are arranged throughout the grounds, turning the already beautiful rural oasis into a spectacular, fairy-tale forest. A miniature train station houses a small replica steam engine train that picks up guests on the hour, complete with a whistle and an "all aboard!" from the conductor (a.k.a. the herbalist who tends the indigenous plant garden).

Eben throws the truck in park, and I slip out of my seat belt, smiling.

"You picked a Christmas activity?" I squeal.

"Nope," he says, grinning, pleased with himself. "It's a secular art-and-light demonstration."

I glance toward the entrance—lights everywhere. Granted, they shine a full spectrum of colors, not just Christmas red and green. And no Bing Crosby or Mariah Carey—just eerie fever-dream soundscapes. But still!

He opens my door. (Who said chivalry is dead?)

"They sell hot chocolate," I argue. Eben holds out a hand to help me down.

"Everywhere sells hot chocolate. It's December. In Ohio." His brow furrows as I slip my bare hand into his. "Where are your gloves?"

The answer is somewhere under a pile of clothes in my closet, but I don't tell him that.

I zip my coat to my chin and then shove my hands into my coat pockets, ignoring his question. He shakes his head, and his hand settles at the small of my back, guiding us toward the entrance.

We walk side by side through the dirt lot, and his shoulder brushes mine. The warmth is a jolt to my system. Now I'm shivering for a very different reason. He searches his phone for our tickets.

As soon as we're through the gate, Eben reads my mind and beelines right to the concession stand.

In addition to the cutest gift shop in the world (which absolutely carries Christmas items—botanical ornaments, gingerbread candles, and snow globes, *thank you very much*), Celestial is home to my favorite hot chocolate of the season.

Though getting your hands on it is always an adventure.

The holiday staff is the same as the off-season garden staff, so the introverts who love talking to plants are suddenly forced to chat with holiday-loving extroverts in LED necklaces and light-up snowflake crowns. It's painfully obvious they'd rather be gossiping with a rhododendron.

I can hardly blame them.

We approach a little log cabin concession stand, where a chalkboard outlined with twinkle lights lists the limited menu. Hot chocolate or apple cider (spiked is optional), churros, caramel corn, candy apples—and pepperoni pizza, because Amurrica, I guess?

The two employees are deep in debate when we step up: a

middle-aged woman insisting winter jasmine blooms better than camellias in the snow, and her coworker—an awkward, acne-plagued teen—dying on the hill that snowdrops are the quintessential winter plant.

"Two hot chocolates, please," Eben says—to no response.

The botanical brawl escalates. Eben—towering at an impossible-to-miss six-foot-and-change—is being hard-ignored. He looks at me, stunned.

"Sorry." I laugh. "The face card doesn't work on plant people."

He snorts, but an adorable pink blooms over his cheekbones.

"Snowdrops bloom *through* snow. God, don't be dense," the teenager squawks, and the woman looks ready to confiscate his PlayStation and send him to his room.

I shoulder past Eben—shamelessly using our hot-chocolate crisis as an excuse to touch him. Even through his black puffer, I feel the curve of his bicep. For a split second, my dirty Santa dream flashes: his strong arms pinning me, the weight of his long, lean body pressing me into the mattress. The phantom memory triggers a gasp; I disguise it with a throat clear.

"Allow me," I say, stepping up to the counter. "Excuse me!"

Nothing but bickering.

I lean farther over the counter to get their attention, and the sleeve of my wool trench catches the chalkboard. With one smooth jerk, the whole thing comes crashing down.

That gets their attention.

"Oh my God, I'm so sorry," I say—only barely sorry. Not ideal to nuke the menu, but it worked. "We'd like two hot chocolates and a slice of pizza."

The teen shakes off the spat and rings us up while the woman tries, unsuccessfully, to prop up the chalkboard.

"Shit," she mutters as it crashes again and clips her foot. Eben leans over to help, and she thanks him with hearts in her eyes.

Really, who could blame her?

"Do you want anything else?" the kid asks, monotone, hoping for a no.

I clock Eben pulling out his credit card and melting a little. Oh, kid—that's the wrong question to ask me right now.

"Just one more thing," I say.

The kid hands Eben the hot chocolates and frowns. "Yeah?"

"You're both wrong. Christmas rose. *Helleborus niger.* Superior winter plant," I declare, nose in the air.

His pimply face twists into that barely-lived-and-knows-it-all scowl only a kid could pull off. The woman hands Eben the hot chocolates; I take the slice of pizza. "Look it up," I add with a shrug, take a hero's bite of my mediocre slice, and stroll away before he can muster a comeback.

I have a few more bites before offering Eben the rest. He happily swaps with me and polishes off what's left in two bites. There's something strangely intimate about sharing a slice of pizza. I wrap both hands around my hot chocolate, soaking up the warmth as blood rushes away from my extremities toward my cheeks—and other places.

The air is crisp, and though Eben's right—the colors reflected on the pond are very secular, lots of blues and pinks and yellows—holiday spirit still lingers.

At least half the crowd is sporting light-up Christmas sweaters or glass-bulb headbands (available at the gift shop for the low price of $25) and definitely didn't get the "secular" memo. Holiday or no holiday, it's cold as hell, and I really am kicking myself for not bringing gloves. I rotate: one hand toasty on the cup, the other jammed in my coat pocket.

I catch Eben eyeing my hands with interest every time I make the switch.

We pass the LED tulip field—a quarter-mile stretch of pixel-mapped flowers that ripple in synchronized waves, shifting from deep blue to purple to pink to crimson. I could watch for hours. It's hypnotic.

"How do you know so much about plants?" he murmurs in my ear, leaning down. The place has an art-museum hush—like you're supposed to whisper, take it in, observe.

I don't turn. Facing Eben head-on still makes me nervous, so I keep my eyes on the tulips.

"Oh, I don't. I just know a lot about Christmas. Flowers included," I laugh.

He inches closer. I can almost hear the sparks crackle between us; the tiny hairs on my neck rise. Heat rolls off him, and my arm tingles where it touches his through our coats. He smells like cinnamon and sandalwood, and I want to spray his cologne on my pillow.

"Why did you decide to volunteer at Forest Park?" he asks.

"Hey, it's my turn to ask a question," I pout.

His laugh is husky from the cold. His breath tickles my ear, and I can feel his eyes on the side of my face. I don't look up. "Fine—what do you want to know?"

I consider, lips pursed. "Why do you hate Christmas so much?"

He sighs and looks back at the shifting tulips. The colors glisten in his eyes. My heart aches at how pretty he is, even when he's sad. "For the first few years of my life, Christmas was a happy time. Both my parents loved the holidays. We did all the festive things—cookies, too many presents, decorating the tree, cocoa, classic movie marathons."

"Sounds idyllic," I say, almost choking on the words. I can't help feeling a stab of jealousy when people talk about their childhood holidays. How do you hate Christmas after all that?

"It was," he says. "Until one Christmas, everything changed."

Oh.

He takes a breath, gathering himself, then continues: "My dad wasn't around as much that year. My mom made excuses.

He was busy at the store. We did the festive things without him. And then on Christmas Eve, he didn't come home. He didn't show up on Christmas Day either. When I asked where he was, my mom burst into tears. The day after Christmas, he picked me up—and there was a woman in the car. Turns out, my dad found someone new. Younger. He spent Christmas with her, and every Christmas after. They had two kids—my half-siblings. And my mom was never the same."

He looks at me. Despite the cold, my free hand is clamped over my mouth in shock. "King of Christmas, my ass," he says, eyes sharp and sad all at once.

"Oh my God," is all I can whisper.

"I know you feel like you missed out," he says, jamming his hands into his pockets, "but for some of us, Christmas is an annual reminder of a very dark time."

I don't know what to say. I stand frozen, stunned.

"I'm sorry," I manage. My fingers twitch with the urge to take Eben's hand, touch his face, and slide my arms around his neck.

"Don't be," he says. He starts walking, turning down a dirt path that leads to the rose garden. I follow. "Being here with you is nice, even if it is a secular light display. Doesn't make it any less magical."

"I'm partial to a few Dickensian carolers myself, but the fear of being abducted by tiny snow fairies is a close second," I say, huffing into my freezing hand—the one not hugging a paper cup of lukewarm Swiss Miss (it was better last year, I swear).

"Are you cold?" he asks, side-eyeing my sad attempts to warm up.

"Always." I bury my free hand deeper in my pocket and shiver.

"Where are your gloves?" He asked once already, and I ignored him. This time, there's a hint of disappointed-dad vibes.

My chest puffs up. I am a grown woman, and I can forget my gloves if I want to.

"Where are yours?" I volley back.

"I don't need them. Here."

He plucks my hand from my coat pocket and tucks it into his coat. His warmth floods my fingers, then races up my face and, fine, other places. Good God, how is this man not married?

I love her more than anything.

I swat away the fear that he's already taken. That's just me being paranoid. I hope.

His thumb brushes my knuckles; my knees go soft. I will myself not to swoon. Collapsing on our first date is not ideal.

He leads me to a gazebo that shoots slow-moving, colorful lasers into fog. The music here is more ambient techno. Couples snuggle on benches with churros and spiked ciders, giggling and sneaking kisses with the illusion of privacy.

We claim the last empty bench, my hand still tucked safely in the warmth of his coat pocket. I look around. Eben leans over to whisper in my ear.

"This is weird," he says. I giggle. It is weird, but I like it. His breath skims my cheek, and a shiver shoots down my spine that isn't from the cold.

I look up; he's looking down. I flush, gulp down the last of my hot chocolate, and set the empty cup on the bench.

"Your turn," he murmurs near my ear. "To answer my question."

Why did you decide to volunteer at Forest Park?

I stare into the fog, not ready to meet his eyes, not even sure why his question hits so hard. There's a lot in my past I haven't shared with anyone—except maybe Ally. My heart ticks faster, like it's urging me to open up, but vulnerability has never been easy for me. The truth is, leaving the Heralds wasn't just an escape; it left behind a vacuum of love and belonging I haven't yet filled. Eben's warmth beside me is comforting, and when he squeezes my hand, I find a little courage.

"Well…" I take a long breath. "My grandma worked like a CIA agent to make sure I had a few secret Christmas memories as a kid, so I wouldn't feel left out, which to her was the worst thing you could do to a child. We celebrated quietly in her basement, and she broke all my parents' rules to make it happen. She used to say, 'Sometimes parents make dumb decisions.' I think that was her way of overruling my mom and dad without feeling bad about it."

"So now you're sentimental about both Christmas and old people?"

I laugh, grateful for his abridged summary of my life.

But the smile fades as something heavier washes over me.

"Sometimes I worry I'll never find that feeling of home again," I say, my voice barely more than a whisper. "Not like with my grandma on those secret Christmases. I can surround myself with shiny baubles and trees and lights, but the fear of never belonging is always lurking."

Inside his pocket, his hand traces my knuckles, back and forth. I flex my fingers in invitation, and he takes it, interlocking until our palms meet. All my awareness funnels to that point of contact. His broad hand stretches my tiny fingers wide. His thumb strokes the center of my palm. I close my eyes and ride the sensation of warmth and friction between us. My whole body tingles with how good it feels—our fingers twined together in his pocket. Somehow better than any sexual encounter I've ever had.

When I open my eyes, I can feel him watching me. I gather my courage and look up. The lights reflect in his gaze, but there's something else there too—the promise of more. Of belonging… with him. My heart skips.

"Melody," he murmurs. I see his breath; it ghosts across my face, my nose, my lips. "Can I kiss you?"

I swallow and nod, suddenly nervous. It's been a while since I've kissed anyone, and I want to get it right. I run my tongue over my lips, and Eben's eyes track the movement.

With his free hand, he tucks a strand of hair behind my ear, then traces my jaw from ear to chin. His thumb slides across my bottom lip, parting it as he leans in. The moment is perfect—until my cult-induced Spidey sense kicks in.

I yank away like I've been electrocuted.

"Melody?" Eben asks, but I can't answer. I can barely breathe.

Ten feet away, looking directly at me, is my family.

CHAPTER 14

$\mathcal{T}$he next few seconds feel like a decade in my body. The lump in my throat. The wide-eyed, horrified, painful expression. The sudden pull back from Eben like I'm committing the worst sin on earth—unmarried, in a compromised position with a man I barely know—while my mom, dad, and little brother stare at me blankly. We lock eyes for a full minute that feels like a century, and somehow they're looking at me and through me at the same time.

I scoot away from Eben, trying to put oceans between us. Thank God there's no cliff to impulsively shove him off, because if there were, he'd be at the bottom of a ravine. I'm angry, sad, mortified—and shocked by how much you can miss people who are less than ten feet away.

Eben cautiously touches my arm, and I yank it back, barely registering his confusion.

I tip my face to the sky, praying that whatever deity lives up there—God, Zeus, aliens, or nothing at all—will zap me into oblivion. When I look down again, part of my prayer has been answered.

My family has turned its back on me and is walking away. I

watch, overwhelmed by how odd it is to be strangers with the only people who've known me since birth. People who've seen me in both dirty diapers and acid-wash jeans. Who held my hand in the ER when I broke my arm, who razzed me for always leaving a nasty toothbrush in the sink. And Mom—who instinctively pressed her warm palm to my forehead at the first "I don't feel good." Who else knows I puked in a Dairy Queen parking lot after the first day of kindergarten?

Their absence is a hollow void inside my chest. But the pain of not being able to erase my life—wipe my memories *Men in Black*-style—is sharp and jagged, a feeling I haven't figured out how to be estranged from.

My little brother, only ten, turns around to get one last look at me, but Dad quickly guides him forward. I watch them recede while the lump in my throat grows.

Once they're out of sight, I come back to Earth and see Eben studying me carefully.

"Is that your family?" he asks, so softly, like a louder word might pierce my composure.

I let out a shaky sigh. "How'd you know?"

He takes my hand. "Everyone looked... in pain."

The way he says *it* knocks me back. I bite my bottom lip, stunned he thought we *all* looked in pain—not just me. I want to believe it, but it's hard to imagine they're feeling this, too, especially when the separation was their choice. Mostly.

"What would happen if you went up and said hello?" Eben asks, innocently, though the question strikes a match on an already defensive flame.

I suck in a deep breath and stare at the tulips again. Glittering, multicolored—the most secular of the secular display. They remind me of the *Wizard of Oz* (yes, I know those were poppies, not tulips). They are whimsical and beautiful— now suddenly laced with a poison I can't see.

I let a minute pass. "My parents would say hello. The way you say hello to someone crossing the street."

He nods and then tilts his head. "Do you know that for sure?" He can't imagine parents speaking to their daughter in the same tone they use for the UPS driver.

"Let's walk a little," I say, needing to move.

Eben slips my hand back into his coat pocket, like he's trying to warm my heart—not just my hands—after that chilly interaction.

"So," I say after a long silence, broken only by the crunch of snow-covered leaves under our feet. "There's a playbook."

His grip tightens. "Like… 'How to Cut Off Your Family 101'?"

"Basically. There are materials, pamphlets, and protocols. They script how to act, what to say—blah, blah, blah."

"That's cult shit," he says, stunned.

I can't help but laugh. "Uh, yeah. Turns out cults aren't just for Netflix documentaries."

He's quiet, shaking his head. I'm blowing this man's mind tonight—and not in the way I'd hoped. I'm not sure if Ally would be thoroughly amused or disappointed that my family just upstaged my sexy red dress and our smoking-hot chemistry.

He hasn't actually seen the dress yet, so there's still a chance for redemption.

"Hey, look," he says, pointing to a snow-dusted beech with a smooth trunk. At first, I didn't get it. It's out of the way, not part of any light display, tucked in a corner with rocks, dirt, and snow. Not exactly part of the spectacular secular extravaganza. Not even evergreen.

Up close, the bark is a palimpsest of hearts, arrows, and tangled initials. A lover's tree—with the occasional "so-and-so was here" from the self-admiring.

Eben crouches down to sift through the sticks until he finds a sharp one—ready to do some damage. The plant-lover in me jumps in front of him. "You'll kill the tree! No way that's allowed."

He scans the tree, the etchings barely worn despite countless seasons. He points at a half-buried plaque and brushes off the snow with the elbow of his coat. It declares this the park's official "arborglyph" tree—the one tree visitors are allowed to write on.

In other words: here's the one sacrificial lamb you're allowed to vandalize, you sentimental hooligans.

He offers me the stick. "What do you say?"

I take the stick, but I'm paralyzed—both on the health of the tree, and the fact that we're not actually lovers. Isn't he in love with someone else?

I feel his breath on the side of my face. "If it helps, I think this tree is really old—and the initials don't seem to hurt it."

It does help, but I still can't make the first cut—even if it's allowed. Plus, what would I write? What are his initials? Does he even know mine? I think back to the intake forms on Missy's desk.

While I'm busy spiraling, he's leaning in front of the tree, carving something I can't see. When he's done, he takes my hand and pulls me closer to admire his handiwork.

SC+MC

My brow furrows. Who the hell are these people?

Eben chuckles at my apparent confusion and bends to my ear, nuzzling with a warm mouth and a cold nose. "Santa Claus and Mrs. Claus," he whispers.

It's cheesy as hell, and I love it. My heart stops, my lungs forget to breathe, and somehow I survive the next few moments without air.

He pulls me in, our lips hovering—the heat between us melting me from the inside out. Before he can close the distance, I pull back.

"You don't want a throuple, right?"

Eben laughs, surprised. "What?"

"I'm just… not into that. Not that there's anything wrong with it. I'm a monogamy girl. I mean, I haven't been in a relationship in forever, but three people? I can barely handle one, and I—"

Eben steps forward and brackets my face in his hands. "What goes on inside that brain of yours?"

I sigh. "A lot."

"I can see that. Who are we in a throuple with?

"Your… girlfriend?"

His brows knit. "I don't have a girlfriend. Why do you think I have a girlfriend?"

"Oh, I don't know." (Because I eavesdropped on you and Missy, but let's not unpack that.) "Um, you don't have a wife either, do you?"

He drops his head in amused frustration. "Who hurt you?"

"Many people."

He smooths my hair back and meets my eyes. "Melody, I don't have a wife, a girlfriend, a boyfriend, or any combination of the above. I am an eligible bachelor. Is there a rose around here I can give you to convince you?"

"Maybe a light-up one?"

"Perfect. When we get to the gift shop, I will buy you one. A dozen, if you want them." His thumb traces my jaw, tipping my face up. Heat creeps into my cheeks. "Until then, will you settle for this?"

He tilts my chin and leans down to kiss me.

CHAPTER 15

$\mathcal{H}$is hands find my hips through my coat and pull me closer before sliding up to my waist. The kiss is perfectly chaste at first—just the gentle press of our mouths. Then his hand cups my chin, his thumb parts my lips. He tilts his head and deepens the kiss, his tongue dipping into my mouth, teeth tugging at my bottom lip. He tastes like hot chocolate and peppermint. A helpless groan rumbles out of me.

He pulls back, panting. "Is this okay?" he asks, resting his forehead against mine.

I bury my hands in his hair and taste him again. It's his turn to moan, and the sound does something to me. My body wakes up—suddenly, painfully aware of the last few celibate years. Heat rushes to my most sensitive places. All at once, I'm on fire. The hot, wet slide of our lips isn't enough.

All I can think about is the naked, sweaty slide of our hips.

"Get a room!" someone shouts in the distance.

Oh my God, I am in public.

I break the kiss and search for the heckler. There he is—my teen Christmas-plant arch-nemesis—waggling his brows as he lugs fresh cider jugs from the main building.

On instinct, I flip him off. He sticks out his tongue and speed-walks away. Pretty sure "taunting guests" isn't in the employee handbook, but I did bruise his ego with my superior knowledge of winter flora.

Eben glances down, amused. I can feel my face blazing—mortified by my inability to keep it in my pants, even in public. He laughs softly and smooths the back of his hand down my cheek.

"Come on." He laces our fingers. "Let's keep walking."

Ah, but the beast is awake.

I drift through the rest of the gardens in a daze. Heart racing. All I can think about is jumping this poor guy's bones. We pass a path of hanging Chinese lanterns. Eben says something about koi fish hibernating in winter, and I don't hear a word. I just stare vacantly at the various shades of orange under the ice.

"Are you okay?" he murmurs.

No. Absolutely not. I am a sex bomb, ready to explode.

"Hmmm?" is all I manage. My eyes can't stop drifting to Eben's mouth.

He grins, catching on, and dips to my ear. "You want to go?"

"Mmhmm," I nod. Heat flashes in his eyes. He squeezes my hand and steers us toward the exit. We bypass the gift shop (sacrilege for me, but hormones are driving). In the lot, his truck lights blink. It feels a mile away, even though it isn't.

He opens the door, and I start to jump up, but his hands grip my hips and lift me into the seat, pushing my coat higher as he steps between my legs. His lips meet mine in a delicious slide. There's that mint-chocolate scent again, and I realize that sometime between his hot chocolate and our makeout session, he slipped a mint. When he finally pulls back, I'm clinging to the lapels of his jacket for dear life.

"Hi," he says, wicked grin, eyes searching. "This better?"

"Yes," I say, breathless from our near-sprint to the car. A

chorus of kid-squeals ricochets nearby—we're still in public and I'm over it. "Can we go somewhere?"

"Your place or mine?" he whispers against my lips.

I picture the onslaught of Christmas he'll face at mine—garland, nutcrackers, trees on trees. My apartment looks like Buddy the Elf dropped acid, decided my living room was the North Pole, and went feral.

"Yours," I say, blushing.

EBEN DRIVES at least ten miles over the speed limit back to Cherryville. He hardly looks at me, just white knuckles the steering wheel and steps on the gas.

I realize I have no idea where he lives, but when he finally slows on the main road to turn, I spot the stone subdivision sign: Cherrywood Estates. One eyebrow twitches. These properties were in high demand when I was a kid: wooded paths, scenic little bridges over babbling brooks, and homes ranging from charming to full-on mansions.

We wind through the dark streets until he rounds a bend and pulls into the driveway of a half-stone, half-brick storybook cottage. I hop out and follow Eben to the double doors (not a wreath in sight).

Inside, I'm assaulted by an ultra-frilly, floral living room straight out of a '90s sitcom. I wasn't expecting Eben to have old-lady taste in décor, but here's hoping he just recently inherited this house from an aunt or a... Golden Girl.

"Can I take your coat?" he asks, shrugging out of his.

I fumble with my buttons, gaze snagging on a gallery wall of family photos: Eben between his parents—his mother, a petite, gorgeous blonde; his father, a tall, salt-and-pepper stud with a spray tan and an LED-white, troublemaker smile. Eben has his mom's eyes and face, as well as his dad's chiseled jaw and height.

Eventually, his dad vanishes from the photos. After that, his mom seems to shrink, her beauty fading year by year, until the pictures stop in Eben's late teens.

I slip my coat off, and he takes it. His eyes bug for a split second. I look down. Right: the fire-engine red dress Ally bought me—a little much for a first date.

He clears his throat and gazes toward the kitchen, trying to be a gentleman. "Do you want something to drink?" he asks, his voice a little hoarse.

My lady-boner is wilting by the minute in the presence of all these granny-chic florals and frills. For a split second, I consider asking Eben if he's got any Ensure. I settle on begging for alcohol instead. "You got any wine?" I ask, needing it.

"Beer?"

"That'll do." I follow him into a barren kitchen, where a few appliances and a tub of protein powder are the only items in sight. "Um, quick question—there's not a shriveled old woman tied up in an upstairs bedroom, is there?"

Both brows rocket up. "Wow. Dark."

I point at myself. "Raised in a cult."

"A cult that ties up old ladies?" He hands me a beer.

I roll my eyes. "No, but the brain goes to dark places."

"This is my mom's house," he says, nodding toward the woman in the photos.

"You live with your mom?" I take a swig of my much-needed beer.

He laughs, shaking his head. "God, no." He gestures to the yellow floral couch, and we make our way over. "This is my childhood home. She couldn't take care of it anymore, so she moved out, and now I live here." He glances around. "In my childhood home. That my mom decorated when I was four."

"Isn't that... weird?"

"Very weird," he says with a shrug. "I know I should sell and get a bachelor pad, but I can't bring myself to do it. She loved this house."

"Loved?" I say, raising my eyebrows. Why is he talking about her like she's gone?

He shrugs. "Loves."

"Or you could just redecorate," I offer.

"Easier," he admits, scooting closer until our knees touch. My cheeks flare. "Isn't that what you do?"

"Yep." I tip my emotional-support beer.

"Do you freelance?" he asks, leaning in.

I laugh. "Are you trying to hire me?"

"I trust you." He shrugs.

"You barely know me. For all you know, I'll turn this place into a boho bedlam. Animal prints, wicker furniture, color explosion."

He considers. "Kind of sounds nice."

I give him a look.

"Okay, fine. I'm more of a minimalist."

I roll my eyes. "All men think they are. Then I find the neon beer sign."

He shakes his head. "Not here, you won't."

I squint. "So if I snoop, I won't find a stash of anime porn somewhere?"

He screws up his face like I'm an idiot. "Who prints out their anime porn?"

"Aha!" I point at him, already feeling more relaxed. "I knew it. You're too pretty not to have kink skeletons in the closet."

He cocks an eyebrow. "And you don't?"

My brain flashes to my bedside drawer full of Christmas-themed dildos. Eben can never, ever know.

"I do not."

"So you've *never* looked up Santa Claus porn, not once?" He waggles his eyebrows.

I gasp, hand to my chest in mock outrage.. "I have *never—*"

"MROW."

I nearly hit the ceiling.

CHAPTER 16

$\mathcal{I}$ launch off the couch like a bottle rocket. I'm ninety-nine percent sure I've just flashed Eben my underwear. My beer goes flying—by some miracle, he catches it without spilling. I clutch my heart and whirl to face the creature that just detonated the most gravelly, demanding sound I've ever heard, right next to my ear.

And it's—the ugliest cat I have ever seen.

"Buster!" Eben scolds.

Buster is a fat, disheveled orange cat with crooked whiskers, slightly crossed eyes, and a mashed-in face. He looks up at me and meows again.

"What is that?" I croak. We hold eye contact. I'm terrified. Buster is... unfazed.

"Mrow."

"Sorry, he's hungry," Eben says. "Mind if I feed him?"

"Personally, I'm scared to see what happens if you don't."

He sets our beers down and heads to the kitchen. Buster shoots me a dirty look (I swear) and waddles after him. There's a cacophony of angry mrows, the crack of can, a spoon hitting a dish, and then—silence.

"You okay?" he asks when he returns.

"I'm not sure. Is that a cat?"

He laughs. "Mom used to say he was her Grandpa Bernie reincarnated, but yeah—mostly a cat."

"He's cute!" I lie, trying to be diplomatic.

"He's almost eighteen," Eben says. "My dad found him in a dumpster at the store and gave him to me. He thought a pet was a good consolation prize for not having a dad around. My mom *loved* that cat."

He's talking about his mom in the past tense again. My head tilts. "She couldn't take him with her where she is now?"

He hesitates, then shakes his head. "No. She's not allowed to have pets."

He doesn't elaborate, and I don't pry. When he wants to tell me, he will.

"I've never had a pet," I say.

His chest loosens, relieved by the subject change. "Never?"

"Well, unless you count my goldfish. Bert and Ernie."

One eyebrow lifts. "Bert and Ernie, huh?"

"Don't get it twisted," I say. "I adored those little fuckers."

He chuckles—deep and warm—and I melt a little. "Let me guess: school-carnival goldfish?"

"Shockingly, no. My grandma was pissed my mom wouldn't allow pets, considering her own puppy once ruined all of Grandma's carpets. It's practically family lore."

Eben laughs and sips. "So Bert and Ernie were Grandma's revenge?"

"Pretty much," I say, matching him, sip-for-sip.

"Was it effective?"

"Until the day I watched my dad flush them. One after the other. First Bert. Then Ernie. Talk about a core memory." I shudder just thinking about it.

"They were already dead, right?" Eben asks, eyebrow arched.

"What! Yes. My parents might be in a cult, but they're not

sociaths." I swat his arm. Good Lord, his arm is solid. Is he bench-pressing Mille and Edna simultaneously?

Somewhere along the way, one (or both) of us has been inching closer. Our knees touch. My skin burns where we meet. I want more.

We came here to hook up, but now I'm painfully shy. Eben's not making a move, and I'm not finding an in. My leg bounces with anxiety, and the whole couch shakes.

His hand covers my knee to still the movement. His eyes twinkle. "You sure you're okay?"

I gulp and nod. Eben's palm is scorching against my bare skin. Fire trails up my leg and pools low in my belly. I want to straddle him and run my hands down his chest. He's wearing a button-down, and I want to rip it open with my teeth.

My lady-boner is back.

"Your eyes are black," he says, grinning. Oh no—he's onto me and my horniness.

I tuck a strand of hair behind my ear. "Um. This has been great, but I really should get home. Early morning tomorrow!" My laugh comes out *ha ha ha*—the fakest sound ever produced by a human.

I start to stand, and he wraps a gentle hand around my wrist. I blink down at him, wide-eyed. "I'll take you home if you want. Are you sure that's what you want?"

I exhale a shaky sigh and sink back down. The truth is, I don't know what I want. Stay. Leave. Maybe throw up. All at once.

He catches me eyeing the cozy space between his chest and arm. "Here," he says, lifting it to make room.

I slide in and snuggle close. I don't look up, even though I can feel Eben's eyes on my face. I rest my head on his chest. His arm tightens around me, and I savor the steady rise and fall of his chest.

I thought I wanted sex, but this is definitely better—at least for right now. Eben's willingness to go slow, to sense what I need and not rush, is hotter than any one-night stand.

He traces lightly up and down my arm. I close my eyes. Is this the safest I've felt in two decades? I let myself dream: Is this the start of something real—or is it just deeply sad that a guy I've known for a handful of weeks makes me feel more secure than anyone has in twenty-eight years? I choose to hope for the first, so I don't ruin the moment with my usual neuroticism and self-doubt.

"So," he murmurs in my ear. A shiver climbs my spine. "What should we do with this room?"

For a second, I'm too busy thinking about what I'd like to be doing *in* this room. With him. "I'm thinking... rustic, cozy, lots of red and green, a dozen or so evergreens."

He chuckles softly, hand lowering to my hip with a light squeeze.

I expect an eye roll, a lecture, another grumbling reminder that he hates Christmas. Instead, he leans in and nips at my ear. Heat detonates in my core; the growl in my throat shocks me.

"Now, Mrs. Claus," he murmurs, breath ghosting my skin, "are you trying to turn my house into the North Pole?"

My breath hitches. Christmas innuendo shouldn't be hot, and yet. Coming from *him*—the man who hates Christmas? I turn to meet his eyes, glacier-blue and sparkling with mischief.

"Something like that," I say. The look he gives me makes me bold. I cup his cheek and turn into him. His hands cinch my waist and tug me closer. I tilt my mouth up; he meets me halfway. At first, the kiss is so soft and slow it almost hurts. He smells like good beer and that cinnamon-sandalwood I'm obsessed with. I can't tell if it's cologne or body wash—but I want to bathe in it. I'm already plotting to snoop in his bathroom until I find the bottle.

His hand finds my jaw and tilts my head so our mouths fit better. His fingers slide to my chin, easing my lips apart so he can deepen the kiss. My tongue moves first, slipping into his mouth to find his. He groans deep in his chest and leans forward, indulging me. My hand skims his neck, over his broad shoulder, and settles on his bicep. I squeeze, and the muscle flexes beneath my grip.

God, I want to bite it.

It's an intrusive thought, but the impulse is too strong to ignore. I break the kiss and dip my head, dragging my teeth lightly over his sleeve until I catch a pinch of skin.

His breath catches. He uses the opening to kiss and lick down my neck, his hands sliding from my waist down to my hips, fingertips flexing over my ass. He squeezes, thumbs flirting with the hem of my dress, teasing the skin of my thigh.

It's too much. It's not enough.

I swing a leg over his hip, dress sliding up as I straddle him. He leans back to find my mouth, his hands sweeping my hair from my face. Through his jeans, the hard length of him presses into my inner thigh. I roll my hips once, and his hands grip my hips, guiding me into friction.

His thumb slips under the hem of my dress. He looks up, a question in those beautiful, lust-hazed eyes. I nod once. He rewards me with a kiss as his hands skim my dress up over my hips. My thong is black lace; he groans and squeezes a handful of bare ass. His hands roam my bare hips and thighs while our mouths find a slow, relentless rhythm.

He breaks away, panting. I whimper at the loss. "I'm going to make you come, okay, Mrs. Claus?"

"Okay," I breathe, my voice an octave higher.

"And then we're going to save some for later," he whispers against my lips—his hand slips under the thin strip of lace at my hip.

I don't want to save anything for later. I want him to strip me bare and ruin me. But some wiser part of me knows that I'd panic later—and maybe he knows that, too.

His fingers find me, slick and hot. I buck and whimper. He groans as I soak his hand through the fabric.

"That's so hot," he murmurs.

"Touch me," I whisper.

"Say please." He nips my bottom lip.

I don't care. "Please," I beg.

He hooks a finger under the lace and slides beneath. He glides up and down until he finds exactly where I need him.

One finger enters. Then two. He breaks the kiss to watch me unravel. We're all alone except for the cat, no shared walls, so I don't hold back; sound spills out of me as my pleasure crescendoes. I grip his shoulders and ride his fingers. His other hand anchors my hip, thumb dipping into the tender hollow where thigh meets hip. He's rock-hard against my leg, and I angle myself to grind him through his jeans.

"Fuck, Melody," he grunts, tipping his head back. His thumb finds my clit while his fingers work. He leans in and sucks lightly at my neck, then breathes at my ear: "Next time, I'm going to unwrap you like a present."

The memory of my dream slams through me in bright, crackling flashes. I'm already so close.

"I'm going to lick you right here until you scream my name," he says—and it's the hottest thing anyone's ever said to me.

I cry out and fold into his chest, shaking through the most intense orgasm of my life. His hand slips free, and his arms cradle me while the aftershocks roll through. When I can finally lift my head, his blue eyes are heavy-lidded. He trails a hand over my hip and—oh my God—sucks his fingers clean, one by one, like a decadent dessert.

I gasp, heat flooding my cheeks.

He licks his lips, a gorgeous and wicked grin.

"Way better than milk and cookies."

CHAPTER 17

'm hot for him again. How could I not be after that soul-shaking finger lick?

I sink my hips into him, reveling in the friction—his hardness, my softness. I bite his bottom lip, signaling I'm ready to go again. His hands slide up my thighs and spread wide over my bare ass. He squeezes, then gives a gentle smack. I squeak in surprise.

"Naughty," he whispers, teeth grazing my neck before he slides my dress back down my legs.

Clearly, he's decided to make the Nice List this year.

So annoying.

I climb off of him, pouting. I want more. It's been too long, and it's never been this good.

And now here I am—sex-starved and practically foaming at the mouth for a romp on this floral granny couch. But Eben's going to make us both wait, and I guess I should be relieved that he's not a pump-and-dump guy.

He shifts into a more comfortable position, then settles me back against his chest. His fingers play in my hair; he plants tiny kisses at my temple, my ear, my cheek.

God, I like him so much.

"Ally was totally right about you," I say, drifting into drowsiness.

"About me?" he asks in my ear, nails tracing lightly down my arm, sending goosebumps everywhere.

"About Christmas being a kink for you."

"What? She said that?" He sits up a little.

I yawn and snuggle in. "Come on—you've met her. Are you shocked? Ally is not shy."

"I've only met her a few times."

"You do spend your free time playing Santa Claus." I can barely keep my eyes open.

"And the only reasonable explanation is that I have a Christmas kink?" His hand stills on my arm. I stare at his long fingers that were inside me five minutes ago. Heat crawls up my cheeks.

"Duh. What else could it be?" I shift my hips between his legs. He groans and stills me with his hands at my waist.

"Easy there, tiger," he growls in my ear.

"It can't be because you're altruistic," I say, matter-of-fact.

"What? Why not?" he asks.

"Because you're too... hot." I finally admit.

He lets out his biggest chuckle yet, then dips close. "I wasn't altruistic enough tonight for you?" His hand slides to my hip. A sigh, and my legs drift apart on their own. He kisses behind my ear, and a shudder ripples through me.

I think he's going to reach between my legs again—but he doesn't. Instead, he just pulls me tight, my back to his chest, arms banded around me like he can't tolerate even an inch of space. I tuck my leg under his, deepening my little-spoon sprawl until we're fused, my back fitting perfectly to his front. I close my eyes and match the rise and fall of his breathing. This moment is pure peace, and I never want to forget it.

. . .

125

"MROW."

What fresh hell—

A beam of sunlight nails me in the eye from an unfamiliar angle in an unfamiliar room. I blink—and the 1995 fever dream returns. I fell asleep at Eben's.

There's pressure on my chest. I look down and come face-to-face with a gremlin.

Okay, not a gremlin—Buster, a cat whose smushed face and twisted whiskers are rapidly growing on me.

"Hi, kitty," I say cautiously. "Please don't hurt me."

I swear, Buster rolls his eyes before hopping off my chest. I'm alone on the couch, but the holy smell of coffee drifts in from the kitchen. I check my phone. It's almost nine, and we're supposed to be at Forest Park in fifteen minutes.

I rocket upright and immediately make myself dizzy.

"Whoa there, tiger," Eben says with a soft smile—throwback to last night when my ass was pressed to his hips. His hair is adorably rumpled. He's holding two steaming mugs. I need one, desperately, but we're already so late.

He hands me one of the coffees; I start to chug. He stops me. "Relax, I called Missy and told her we're both running late."

I get exactly two blessed sips before anxiety ignites like a rocket booster and blasts me out of my seat.

"You called *who* and told her *what?*" My hand shakes; hot coffee splashes my thigh. "Ow. Fuck."

"Whoa, whoa—it's okay. Missy doesn't know anything." He takes my mug, sets it down, and fetches a cool, damp towel. He hands it over and sits close, concern in his eyes.

"But won't she wonder why Eben and Melody are both late in the morning—together?"

"I think she has other things on her mind," he says with a shrug.

"What did you tell her?" My voice is shrill; I try to drag it down an octave.

His eyes glint. "I told Missy I fucked your brains out all night, and now we're late."

He says it like he's telling the time. I know he's kidding, but —damn. Part of me is sorry it isn't entirely true.

My face must scream terror, because he pats my knee. "Hey, I'm joking."

"What did you tell her then?"

"Nothing. Just that we're running late."

"Oh, God—somehow no explanation is worse."

"You know grown adults are allowed to be late—especially when they're not getting paid," he says, patient with my irrational responsibility spiral.

"Yes, but colleagues aren't usually late in the morning— together, unless..." I trail off.

"Unless what?" he prods, grin derailing my panic.

"Unless they spent all night fucking your brains out," I mutter.

He laughs and reaches for my coffee.

"Hey! I'm not done." I grab for it. He blocks me, swaps it into a travel mug, seals the lid, and hands it back.

"You can finish it in the car. We're super late and ruining our reputations, remember?" He winks. I perish.

"We have to swing by my apartment for my Mrs. Claus' outfit!" Panic flares.

"No time," he says, tossing me a bag.

I peek inside. Oh, hell no.

"I LOOK RIDICULOUS," I grumble, smoothing the fabric of Eben's extra Santa suit. The pants were swimming on me, so I ditched them and belted the jacket—somehow too big and too short at once. We detoured to a drugstore so I could grab deodorant and a fresh pack of underwear. I'm not usually rockin' the "sexy drugstore undies," but last night's activities necessitated fresh drawers before volunteer hour.

I take a whore's bath in the bathroom, swapping my lace thong for the only option: white nylon granny panties tucked next to the diabetic socks. I lift my Mrs. Claus walk-of-shame getup to inspect the damage. God, let no one ever see me in these.

I collect side-eyes like coupons on my way out. Pretty sure "had sexy fun times last night" is stamped on my forehead. I curtain my face with my hair and beeline for Eben's idling truck.

"Let's get out of here," I hiss. The employee "rearranging" firewood is rubber-necking so hard I'm worried he might sprain something.

We pull up to Forest Park, and my anxiety rears up. I *know* it's absurd. I *know* we don't owe anyone an explanation. I *know* we are adults. But the trauma of being spied on in purity culture has a long half-life. The fear of moral judgment lights me up like a pack-a-day smoker—miraculously, I'm not one.

Eben notices. Hard not to—my knees are bouncing so hard the truck vibrates. He takes my hand.

"Hey. It's okay." He squeezes my hand. He's warm and steady. One by one, butterflies replace the swarm of bees in my gut.

"I'm sorry," I mumble, eyes down. "I think I'm having an allergic reaction to my past."

He pauses, choosing his words. (A desirable trait.) "I think you're having a normal reaction to being abused by a cult," he says. "Who sound like busybodies, by the way."

I smile—real, unforced. I can't believe Eben has now witnessed two cult-adjacent freakouts.

"I really am doing better," I say softly. "It sucks that you've seen a couple of bad moments. It doesn't happen that often, I just never know what will pop up or—"

"Who you'll run into," he finishes.

"Yes." I don't look at him. "And I haven't... gone out with anybody in a long time. Not that we're going *out*. I just mean being with you—last night and now—maybe it's bringing up old stuff."

Whew, that was painful to say. Color climbs my cheeks. I don't want to assume one not-so-innocent night means more to me than to him.

He doesn't let me hide; he tilts my chin. "You can't control the world. Considering what you've been through, you're doing great." His eyes are so soft, I melt.

My brows tilt up. Do I look like a scared puppy? "So you don't think I'm freaking out all the time?"

"No." He tucks a lock of my finger-combed hair behind my ear. "I mean, you're definitely a little neurotic—but who isn't?"

I smile and look away—half touched, half mortified. Heat pricks my eyes. I can't tell if it's anger or embarrassment or something else entirely, only that it's the kind of ache that rearranges your soul.

I don't have time to wade into the deep end of that thought. I look up at the building, and two familiar faces stare back from the window.

Millie and Edna have their noses smashed to the glass like Labrador retrievers, watching us in the car.

"I think we're being watched," he says, like we're in a Jurassic Park reboot, and someone let out the velociraptors.

"Oh, we are," I laugh, feeling a little dizzy as his hand squeezes the back of my neck.

I glance up again, and the olds have multiplied. At least ten of them are plastered to the window now. Roger's on tiptoe, trying to peer over Millie's bouffant.

"Is this super triggering?" Eben asks earnestly.

"No—this is hilarious. Nosy old people were never my problem."

"We'd better head in," he says.

We hop out; the seniors scatter like roaches.

Inside, Missy is waiting. She eyes us. "You two are better than The Young and the Restless reruns around here," she harrumphs, one brow arched.

Heat rushes to my face as we both glance at my bare legs under the walk-of-shame half-Santa suit. No wonder everyone at the pit stop was gawking; the jacket barely covers my hoo-ha. I tug it down, but Eben isn't letting anyone shame or speculate.

"Mel's car is in the shop, so I picked her up," he says coolly. The casual way he says *Mel* makes me shiver. "Sorry we're late."

Missy squints, then shrugs like she couldn't care less. "Your fan club awaits." She nods toward the community room. We turn—and my stomach drops.

The seniors pack the doorway. Some smirking. Some scowling. But one thing is clear:

They know exactly what's up.

CHAPTER 18

"*I* think I'm gonna be sick," I say.

"Act natural," Eben whispers in my ear.

But it's too late. The residents know. It's written all over their faces. They may have joint replacements, hearing aids, and pacemakers, but they were not born yesterday.

"Hi, boys and girls," Eben says, clearing his throat to deepen his voice. He adds a nervous little wave.

"Oh, cut the crap," Edna says. "We're on to you two."

"Yeah, they came together!" someone shouts.

"They sure did!" Millie fires back, and everyone laughs.

Oh my God, this is my worst nightmare. I was worried about Missy, not the geriatrics. I should have known this crowd would swan-dive straight into the gutter. Eben locks at me, lost for words—ridiculous and ridiculously cute in his wig, beard, and Santa hat, cheeks bright red.

"You know what, screw it," I say. I yank off Santa's wig and beard and pull the pillow out of his suit. In two seconds, he's transformed into Sexy Santa, and the nursing-home ladies swoon. Even Missy peeks out of her office.

Eben is hot on his own, but there's something about him in the suit without all the bells and whistles that is life-changing. I go for the belt. He leans down and murmurs, "What are you doing?"

"Roll with it," I grit, opening his coat to reveal an undershirt clinging to rippling pecs and toned abs.

"You really think I'm not going to tap that?" I say, chin-jutting at his perfect torso.

"You go, girl," a lady thumbs up.

"Santa *baby*!" another whistles.

"I'd hit it," a gruff man crows, raising his cane. Everyone stares. "What?"

"Listen, Bob is allowed to be still figuring some things out," I shrug.

Bob sniffs loudly.

"And so are we," I say, gesturing between me and Eben.

Eben gives me a smug grin. I want to die, but I chose the path of public thirst, and now I have to own it.

"Go strut your stuff, Mr. Claus," I say, and swat his ass. He flinches; okay, maybe I pushed the bit too far.

"Sorry," I mutter, cheeks hot.

His hand seizes my waist, and he murmurs in my ear, low enough only I hear. "You'll pay for that later."

His hand deliberately skims my ass before he struts into the community room. The old ladies squeal for their upgraded Stripper Santa. Good thing he's not bashful—these sex-crazed seniors are not exactly hands-off.

"Hey, ladies—hands to yourselves!" I call, marching in to play bouncer.

WE'RE NEARLY at the end of our hour, slouched in chairs, exhausted from entertaining at nine a.m. Half-empty pitchers of skim milk and OJ, trays of grocery-store cookies picked over in front of us. Missy starts rounding up everyone for a field trip to the YMCA for a water aerobics class. Edna hangs back, watching us with a glint in her eye.

"Psst," she says, thumping the button on her wheelchair to inch forward. She points at us with a bony, yet impeccably manicured finger. "If you two ever need some privacy, my room is available."

We jerk upright, eyes meeting. Eben turns away, covering his mouth to smother a laugh. I bite back my own smile and tip my head at her. "Uh, thank you, Edna. We're okay, but that's very kind."

"For twenty bucks," she adds with a heckler's grin.

"Oh, wow," I say, swallowing laughter. A sales pitch!

"It's a steal. You can't even get a motel room for that cheap anymore."

"You're right, you can't," I say, humoring her.

"And the sheets here? Three hundred thread count," Edna nods, like it's really something.

"That's, like, Hilton-level comfort," I say. Under the table, Eben grabs my knee, shaking with suppressed laughter.

"That's right," she says. Millie shuffles up, clearing her throat.

"Ed, what are you doing? We've got a bus to catch," Millie scolds, tugging weakly at the wheelchair handles.

"I'm coming, I'm coming!" Edna spins her chair around and zooms toward the door.

"We're gonna miss it," Millie huffs, hustling to keep up.

"Oh, no!" Edna deadpans. "We're gonna miss doing pool-noodle pushups in Speedos while teenagers point and laugh."

As they go, Eben and I fold over in laughter. "Oh my God," I wheeze, holding my sides.

"Can you imagine?" he asks. His red velvet knee brushes mine as our laughing ebbs. His gaze snags on the hem of my skirt. He looks away fast, pink creeping over his cheekbones. I glance down—my makeshift Santa dress has ridden up, flashing my nylon granny panties.

"Fuck," I yelp, snapping my knees together and yanking the fur trim down—not that it helps. "You didn't see that."

He presses his lips together, fighting a smile.

"I don't usually wear those," I blurt. "I—I was in a pinch."

He lifts both hands. "I'm not judging."

"You are! You're trying not to laugh!" I shove his shoulder.

He pinches thumb and forefinger. "Little bit," he admits, nose wrinkling.

I punch his arm—and notice a woman shuffling toward us, concerned. She's not much over sixty; I've seen her before. Quiet, lovely, keeps to herself. Her eyes are a piercing blue, familiar in a way that prickles my skin.

"Excuse me," she says softly to Eben. "Do I know you?"

Eben turns, eyes widening. He shoots to his feet. "Ah, you're going to be late for water aerobics," he says, guiding her toward the hall with a hand on her shoulder.

"I just feel like I know you from somewhere," she says, peering up at him.

He glances at me, then back at her. He's warring with himself. I want to help, but I have no idea what's going on—until she follows his gaze to me, and I see it: they have the same ice-blue eyes, hers still sharp beneath the haze of forgetting.

The heated conversation with Missy clicks into place.

As understanding hits me, he exhales, almost relieved. He bends to her eye level and takes both her hands.

"Hi, Mom," he says softly.

CHAPTER 19

"*M*om?" she says, eyebrows pinched.

He rolls his lips and strokes a thumb over her knuckles before saying, "I'm your son, Eben."

"My son?" she asks, still confused.

"Your one and only," he nods.

"Who did I have a son with?" she asks, tilting her head.

He sighs—deep and regretful. "Ronnie Golding."

Her eyes flash with anger. Her lips curl into a snarl. "Ronnie Golding? That rat bastard."

"And there it is," he says with a nervous laugh.

"Lying, cheating, no-good, piece-of-shit, son of a bitch—"

I blink. It's wild hearing so much venom pouring out of such a tiny, grandmotherly-looking woman. Her big, blue eyes—Eben's eyes—narrow into sharp little slits as she eviscerates the so-called King of Christmas. No wonder Eben hates the holidays. It's in his DNA.

"Where is he?" she demands at the end of her tirade, little fists balled up like she's ready to throw down. Eben wraps his big hands around both of hers.

"He's not here, Mom," he says softly.

"He's with that whore Rebecca, isn't he?" she says.

Ouch. I see spit fly when she says it.

"Nope—and we don't say that about women," Eben says. Then adds, almost to himself: "If anyone's the whore, it's Dad."

She scoffs, clearly not thrilled at being corrected, but not arguing either.

Eben clears his throat and steps aside. "Uh, Mom, this is Melody. She's my, uh, Mrs. Claus." He looks at me apologetically.

I step forward, unsure if I should shake her hand, hug her, or drop dead on the spot. Eben's mom gives me a look that could curdle eggnog.

"Honey, why are you dressed like that?" she says, her brow wrinkling in disapproval.

My face heats up faster than a mug of mulled wine. Eben touches my elbow, a gentle anchor in the awkwardness.

"Sorry," he whispers, "she doesn't have a filter anymore."

"What are you saying about me?" she snaps.

He sighs. I laugh, because what else can you do? "It's so nice to meet you..."

"Anne," he murmurs in my ear.

"Anne," I repeat. My brain, bless it, decides that instead of a standard greeting, I should curtsy. I actually curtsy.

Anne stares. "Oh," Anne says, then glances at Eben. "She's weird."

"Okay," Eben says, chuckling as he steers her toward the door. "They're going to leave without you."

"She's pretty, but weird," Anne adds. Eben throws me an apologetic look over his shoulder. I stand there, stunned, watching him guide her to the bus. The moment they're gone, I collapse into a chair, burying my face in my hands.

"Jesus Christ," I mutter into my palms.

A few minutes later, Eben returns.

"I'm so sorry," he says, yanking a chair toward me with his

foot and sitting so our knees touch. "I was going to tell you, but I was trying to find the right time."

I peek at him through my fingers. "I think I just made myself look like a giant moron in front of your poor mother."

He pries my hands away gently. "Don't worry," he says with a half-sad, half-teasing smile. "She won't remember."

I groan and drop my head between my knees. "That makes it worse."

He laughs. "Why?"

"Because I guarantee I'm going to make an idiot of myself every time I see her," I sigh.

He smiles, squeezing my knee. "And I guarantee she'll forget every time."

I look up and really see him: this man, comforting me after I made a fool of myself in front of his mother, is also losing a parent to dementia. I meet the sad glacier-blue eyes he shares with her.

"You do all this for her," I say, gesturing at the Santa suit.

"It's easier to pretend to be someone else," he admits quietly. "I can introduce myself as Santa Claus instead of the son she doesn't remember."

"She seemed to remember you today."

"She has moments of clarity." He leans back, stretching out his legs so they bracket mine. "But she never forgets Ronnie Golding."

That name again. It hangs in the air like a ghost of bad Christmases past.

"Your dad never comes to visit her?" I ask, doing my best not to stare at his chest through that criminally thin undershirt. Not the time to ogle a man baring his soul.

"Not once," he says with a shrug. "Which is probably for the best. My mom would definitely rip his dick off."

"Oh my God," I laugh, startled. "Your dad's... kind of problematic, huh?"

Eben winces. "Understatement of the century."

"Why do you work for him?" I ask.

He shrugs and leans forward, his fingertips fanning over my bare knee—slow and soft—I instantly forget my question.

"You ready to get out of here?"

It's a noticeable change of subject, but the half-smile on his face holds the promise of so much more—and yes, I'm very ready to leave. Maybe find a bed. Or a couch. Or the back of his truck. I'm not feeling picky.

"Not so fast," Missy says, sweeping in with a clipboard and shit-eating grin.

I jerk upright and tug my makeshift dress down as far as it will go. Eben leans back, and I mourn the loss of his hands on my skin.

"I've got a list of errands for the pageant," she says, passing him the clipboard.

He glances down and groans. I tilt it toward me to assess the damage.

"That's… kind of a long list," I say, already winded.

"And aggressively Christmassy," Eben adds with a grimace.

"Good thing you two are getting along so well," Missy says, with a glint in her eye, then pivots on her heel. I can practically hear the *ba-dum-tss* as she waves over her shoulder and marches out to chaperone the seniors to their field trip.

Eben and I sit in stunned silence, staring dumbly at the giant list: craft fair runs, hanging flyers, baking *hundreds* of cookies.

"Should we divide and conquer?" I ask, eyeing his frowny profile.

He whips toward me, scandalized—eyes wide, nostrils flaring. Real panic. "Oh, hell no. I'm not doing this Christmas shit by myself."

I suppress a grin. He'd rather suffer through this list with me than without me. As for me, I secretly swoon at the thought of running errands together.

"Fine." I sigh theatrically. "We should start with the cookies. They'll take at least three days."

"Three *days?*" he says, hating his life.

"If you do them right," I say smugly.

"Can't we just buy them?" I swear I hear a whimper.

"Better not pout, Mr. Claus," I sing-song, wagging a finger.

He mutters something that sounds suspiciously like he's still pouting. I press a finger to his lips to shut him up.

"Way ahead of you, Kris Kringle." I puff my chest dramatically. "It's time you were introduced to the—drumroll, please."

Eben blinks.

I clear my throat and plant my fist at my waist. "The Christmas Palace!"

"The Christmas Palace?" His eyebrows shoot up. He looks equal parts intrigued and terrified.

"For approximately eleven months a year, the Christmas Palace moonlights as a normal one-bedroom apartment belonging to a single woman who needs to muster up the guts to ask her boss for a raise. But in December, it's magically transformed into—"

"A place where Christmas obsession and cult trauma meet?" His eyes twinkle with mischief.

I glare. He's ruining my vibe.

"No, a place where all your Christmas dreams come true!"

His grin goes crooked. "All of them?"

My cheeks burn Santa-suit red. My mind flashes back to the night before. I shake it off. "Come on, Santa, we've got a lot to do."

As I march toward the door, I hear him sigh behind me. He's morphed from sexy-Santa stud muffin to pouty little kid in two seconds flat.

"Coming," he says at last, dragging his feet.

I finally have this man right where I want him—balls deep in Christmas shenanigans with no way out.

CHAPTER 20

Some families start baking cookies in October. My Italian Catholic grandmother was one of those bulk cookie-baking psychos—and now, six years after leaving the anti-holiday cult, so am I.

Baking and freezing: the rule of law for bulk batches. The last item on Missy's list is actually the first we need to tackle. "Bake assorted Christmas cookies" may seem like no big deal to some, but to do it right, it's akin to a military operation.

A short five-minute drive later, we stride into Cherry Mart still fully decked out as Mr. and Mrs. Claus. Cue more double-takes and craned necks. Maybe it's because now I'm on a mission, or maybe I'm just getting used to it, but the extra attention is starting to feel... normal.

Just inside the sliding doors, Eben reaches for a basket. I shake my head and point to a cart. "You don't storm the North Pole with a snowball," I say, my hands on my hips like I'm a general leading her troops into battle.

"More like General Claus," he says under his breath as he swaps out the basket for a cart.

"I heard that," I say, levelling a glare he ignores as he pushes a cart through the next set of sliding doors.

He slows and gazes wistfully at the bakery section, eyeing a tray of pre-frosted cookies.

"What are you looking at?" I swat his ass, playful. His eyes flick to mine, darker than before. My cheeks go pink. Too much?

"Nothing," he whistles innocently.

I clear my throat and steer us to the baking aisle—my natural habitat: flour, sugar, sprinkles, comfort.

"Unless you're a busy mom of four or recovering from surgery, store-bought cookies are a crime against humanity."

He grins. "General Claus has spoken."

I've been baking solo for years, so unlike some people, I don't need to spend hours scrolling Pinterest. I've got that sugary lineup on lock: my famous red-and-green M&M cookies, snowballs, Italian sprinkle cookies, lemon bars, and classic iced cutouts in the shape of the usual suspects—Santa, Rudolph, Frosty, and the whole North Pole gang.

I waltz down the aisle, tossing flour, sprinkles, sugar, and tubs of frosting into the cart. A red, green, and gold sugar explosion stacks up fast.

"How many cookies are we making?" Eben grimaces as another bag of flour hits the cart with a clang.

"Let's see—fifty-six residents, ten staff, and we should factor in like fifty more for friends, family, and the randoms... so, five hundred cookies?"

He pales whiter than Santa's beard. "F-five hundred?" he sputters.

"At least!" I chirp—just as a little wreath-shaped baking tin catches my eye. How is it that I don't own one of these yet?

I toss it in.

"What's that for?" he winces.

"Oh, nothing..." I say, all fake innocence.

He eyes the tin, then Missy's clipboard. "Wait, are we making a cake too? It's not even on the list!"

"It's wreath-shaped!" I bat my lashes like I'm not downright unhinged.

He runs a hand through his hair, deliciously tousled. Two teenage girls pass us with girly giggles and googly eyes. Eben doesn't notice.

"Are you quitting your job this week? Did you win the lottery? How do you have time to make five hundred cookies and a cake?"

I grin. "You mean, how do *we* have time?"

His eyes almost bug out of his head.

"Relax, it's easy," I say. "I've single-handedly kept the Beeman family in cookies for years."

"Who are the Beemans?" he asks, equal parts stressed and amused.

"Teddy's family," I explain. "I've spent Christmas with them every year since leaving the cult." I lob a bag of powdered sugar into the cart. "His mom's a piece of work, but she goes all in— matching pajamas, Christmas caroling, homemade eggnog, the whole nine yards. I know they're not my *real* family, but Christmas with the Beemans makes me feel like I get to participate in life. Real life. Full of joy and freedom. Not cult life, which is all fear and control."

I don't look at him, but I feel his eyes searching for a crack in the fortress. Nary a tear will slip through.

"What about you?" I ask him, feigning interest in a six-in-one sprinkle container I already own. "What do you do for Christmas, O Holly Jolly Hater?"

"Absolutely nothing," he says, crossing his arms and leaning on the cart handle. My eyes traitorously flick to his biceps flexing against the red velvet. "And it's glorious."

"Nothing? Nothing at all?"

"Beer, a rotisserie chicken, and football on Christmas Day," he shrugs. "As God intended it."

The joke makes me flinch—he notices.

"Sorry," he says, softer. "Bad joke."

I shake it off. "You don't even celebrate with your mom?"

"I try to visit almost every day—but it's just another day. I don't mention Christmas. She can handle me as Santa, but the last time I tried to give her a gift as Eben... it did not go well."

I bite the inside of my cheek. "That's really hard. I'm sorry."

He shrugs, suddenly fascinated by a set of Betty Crocker decorating tips.

I lean over the cart, mouth near his ear. "You really think I don't already own a sixty-piece set of stainless steel frosting tips?"

"Just the tips?" He turns, sadness swapped for mischief, one brow arched.

My jaw drops.

"Sorry—couldn't resist." He winks and plants a quick kiss on my cheek.

Butterflies take off in my stomach.

"Come on, General Claus," he says, steering the cart. "Let's get this over with."

EBEN HAULS six bags per arm up my stairs. I try to take one or two, but he doesn't let me.

"You could make more than one trip," I say.

He scoffs. "Real men don't make multiple trips. How dare you."

"Ever heard of toxic masculinity?"

"No, never," he says—and immediately starts doing bicep curls with the bags.

I roll my eyes and then come face to face with my arch nemesis: the deadbolt.

I hold my breath as I fumble with the keys. I've lived here five years, and it's still hit-or-miss if I can get this damn lock to cooperate. My fine motor skills tap out under pressure, and having an audience only exacerbates the issue. Not to mention I'm definitely having nerves about allowing this hot, holiday-hating man into my tinsel-torched apartment.

I try the lock once, twice, three times. On the fourth attempt, I'm seeing stars.

"Are you sure you live here?" Eben jokes. "Or are we breaking into some other Christmas nut's place?"

He tilts his head at the massive wreath on my door, framed with matching garland. Two poinsettias flank the welcome mat that reads *Oh What Fun!* between cartwheeling Santas.

His teasing smile falters when he notices the sweat bead at my brow. Without another word, he sets down the bags—a five-pound sack of sugar thudding to the concrete—takes my rhine-stone-studded snowflake keychain, slides my house key into the lock, and with a smooth twist: click.

"Thanks," I sigh. "You'd never guess I've lived here a million years."

He grabs the bags, and I shove the door open with all the dramatic flair I can muster.

"Welcome to the Christmas Palace," I announce in my best *Welcome to Jurassic Park* voice, flipping on the lights.

Cue the John Williams music.

"Whoa," Eben says in awe.

He steps across the threshold like he's entering another dimension—where a girl who can barely afford an oil change has single-handedly turned her apartment into a winter wonderland.

In the corner, my brand-new seven-foot tree twinkles like the night sky—hardly a speck of green peeks through the army of vintage ornaments and candy-cane ribbon. My coffee table is a full-blown Christmas village, complete with ice skaters and a tiny post office with a special mailbox just for Santa letters. Every flat surface is buried in garland. Even the couch is decorated with an assortment of red-and-white striped throw pillows and throws. Icicles hang from the ceiling, ready to impale me should Cherryville have a rare earthquake or someone slam the door.

Even my giant nutcracker levels me with judging eyes.

This is too much. You are too much.

Eben spins in a slow circle to take it all in. "This is..." He stops. "Something."

He looks dizzy. And a little green.

"Is it over the top?" I ask.

"Well, yeah," he says—like it's obvious. "But in the best way."

Warmth spreads across my chest. "Really?" I ask, hopeful now. Like maybe I'm not too much after all.

"You know how I feel about Christmas—and that hasn't changed." He steps toward the tree, arms still loaded with bags, an admiring twinkle in his eye. "But I can appreciate an artist when I see one at work."

I beam, ear to ear. Eben's looking at me like he likes me. Like, really likes me. Christmas-loving, cult-bruised little ol' me.

Then my phone buzzes in my pocket.

"Where should I...?" he asks, fingers starting to go purple.

"Oh—sorry! Kitchen's around that wall," I say, pointing past my dining table, drowning in garland and approximately one hundred red candles.

He disappears around the corner. I fish out my phone—expecting Ally, not Cassie. Again. Jesus H. Christ.

The warmth vanishes. My chest tightens.

Ignore.

"You need to take that?" Eben asks, poking his head back around the wall.

"Nope," I say too fast, shoving my phone back in my pocket hard enough to test the seams.

145

His smile fades. "Everything okay?"

"Spam," I lie, pressing a hand to my sternum to calm my racing heart.

"You sure?" he asks, taking a step closer.

No, I'm not okay. I need to sit down. Maybe lie down with a wet towel over my eyes. But these cookies aren't going to bake themselves.

"Let's get this dough on the road!" I chirp, forced cheer in every syllable.

CHAPTER 21

*I*t feels good to boss Eben around.

The kitchen is my domain, and Christmas cookies are my Mona Lisa, my Sistine Chapel. I'm the emperor of this Christmas Palace, and Eben is my humble, easily distracted servant.

I unload groceries like a general counting munitions—flours, sugars, sprinkles, candied toppings, nuts, and frosting. Eben tears open a bag of walnuts and nabs a handful. I smack his hand, grinning.

"Hey, those aren't for you."

"Oh, come on. I'm starving," Eben protests.

"We can order takeout once the first batch is in." I scorch my hands under near-boiling water because Mrs. Claus is nothing if not sanitary. Eben sighs dramatically and slides in beside me at the sink, warm shoulder to warm shoulder. Unhelpful. Distracting.

Adorable.

I try to shake him out of my head and dry my hands on my embroidered gingerbread village towels. I start flinging cabinets, rummaging in my chaotic pot-and-pan graveyard for a rolling pin and cookie cutters. A cascade of pot lids ambushes me, but I pop back up, victorious—and nearly collide with Eben.

He's wearing my Rudolph apron, the ridiculous red pom-pom nose perfectly centered on his chest.

"Reporting for cookie duty, Mrs. Claus," he says, saluting.

He's so cute, my heart pole vaults to the North Pole.

I tie on my own apron—a flirty, red-and-white striped number with a flared skirt. Eben's eyes crinkle as his fingertip grazes the ruffled strap.

"You're the sexiest little candy cane I've ever seen," he says.

Heat races up my neck. *Focus, Melody.*

"Preheat to four hundred," I order.

"Yes, ma'am." The wink should be illegal.

I'm whisking flour and baking soda when his arm hooks at my waist and tugs lightly at my apron string.

"What's next?" he asks, his breath warm against my ear.

Still all business, I shove the bowl and mixer into his hands. "Mix."

His fingers brush mine as he takes the bowl. I watch him stir —focused, taking my directions without protest. I stare at his hands as he mixes dutifully. Big. Just the right amount of calloused.

I wonder...

No. Don't think about it.

I kneel to retrieve my old recipe tin. The vintage Santa on the lid is faded and softened by time. After my grandma died, this was the one thing I asked to keep. All her magic lives in this little box.

When I stand, Eben is staring—and not at my face.

"Hey!" I scold, pointing at the bowl. "Focus."

He just grins and nods toward the tin. "What's that?"

"This was my grandmother's," I say, softening. "A wedding gift to commemorate their first Christmas. She kept every recipe in here." I flip the lid and thumb the cards, the paper edges worn soft with time.

"Go back one," he says, gently catching my wrist.

I flip back. The card is written in that familiar looping script that makes my heart ache.

Italian Lemon Drops.

I smile at the card, then up at him.

"My favorite."

His eyes meet mine, then drift down.

"You're supposed to be mixing," I murmur—but I lick my lips.

"Just a taste," he says, and kisses me.

He tastes like stolen chocolate (caught!) and he smells like cookie batter. Flour sticks to the stubble on his jaw, where I grab him roughly, but he doesn't seem to mind. I kiss him again, harder this time, my tongue tangling with his in a delicious swirl of sugar and heat.

It takes every ounce of willpower I have to pull away.

"You're distracting me," I whisper against his lips.

He brushes my chin with his mouth—one soft, devastating nip—and returns to the bowl with fake innocence. "I'll behave."

We fall into a rhythm. I call for sugar, zest, and eggs; Eben's an excellent sous-chef and an even better mixer when the batter gets too heavy for my tired arm. The timer ticks away. The kitchen smells like lemon, butter, and something reckless and masculine. *Him.*

While the first batch browns in the oven, I whip up the lemon frosting. I dip my finger in the bowl and scoop a dollop.

He seizes my wrist, eyes darkening.

"Hey now." That smug grin. "That's my job."

He sucks the sweetness from my finger, eyes locked on me. I watch, mesmerized, a slow, warm ache building deep in my stomach. My knees go weak. His hand steadies me. My body betrays me—I want him. I want him more than kids want toys at Christmas.

It's my time to shine. When it comes to tricks I have in the kitchen, there's one more I know he's not expecting.

"Actually, Mr. Claus," I murmur, setting the bowl aside, "I do have a very particular set of skills…"

My hands slide up his chest and loop around his neck.

"Oh?" His voice is rough, barely audible.

"Skills I have acquired over a very long career as an active member of Heaven's Heralds."

"Are you quoting Liam Nee—"

"Shhhh." I press a finger to his lips. He smirks against it.

"Skills that make me a fantasy for people like you."

He swallows, pupils blown wide.

My fingers tangle in his mess of dark blond hair, pulling him down until I can kiss his neck—soft at first, then with a teasing tug of my teeth that draws a low growl from his throat.

"According to that timer," I whisper in his ear, pressing closer, "we still have ten minutes."

I smile, slow and dangerous. He gulps.

I steer him backward, out of the bright kitchen and into the dim laundry room. A thin blade of winter light stripes his cheekbones. I pull his mouth down to mine, hungry.

I break the kiss to whisper in his ear. "Tell me if you want to stop."

"Don't," he says, immediate and certain.

"Good answer," I say, teeth grazing his ear.

He shudders, and my lips find his again, kissing deep and wild. I press into him. His breath stutters. My pulse sprints. Even through this ridiculous Rudolph apron, I can feel the hard length of him pressing against my low belly. My mouth waters. My thumb grazes him—just a tease.

"Mel—" His voice is breathy, my name tucked between deep, desperate moans that tell me I've got his full attention.

I drag my tongue down the side of his neck until I find the top of his collarbone. I bite gently. His hands squeeze my shoulders and then slide down my back until they settle on my waist.

My fingers trail down his t-shirt, lower, teasing him again through the apron. He sucks in a breath.

I'm literally cockblocked by Rudolph. But we can fix that.

I sink to my knees, running my hands down his torso, past his hips, using his legs to steady myself. I keep my eyes locked on his.

"Shit," he whispers, watching me through half-lidded eyes.

The word comes out husky. Panicked. Needy.

I lick my lips.

When you're raised in a cult obsessed with what young people are (or aren't) doing behind closed doors.

Purity culture. The shame of losing your virginity.

You get really (and I mean *really*) good at oral sex.

For some reason, blowjobs and getting eaten out didn't count as "sex." And you know horny and repressed young adults —we'll find *any* loophole to get some.

Not that the head honchos of the church would have agreed that BJ's were an acceptable purity "loophole."

Before he can ask me if I'm sure, I run my hands under the apron and unbuckle his belt—swift, one-handed. Very few things get me hotter than the metallic *clink* of a man's belt unbuckling.

"Where did you learn how to do that?" He's breathless. I smirk.

"There are a few perks of being raised in a cult," I say with a smug glimmer in my eye. "This is one of them."

Eben reaches behind him to untie his apron, and I stop him.

"Leave it," I whisper.

He doesn't argue. Just leans back helplessly against the wall.

I dip my head under the apron, and my eyes nearly bug out of my head. Even in the dim lighting of my laundry room, I can see through the velvet that he's *big* and already hard as a rock.

I stroke him once through the velvet, and his hips buck in response.

"Jesus," I hear him whisper. "Melody, I—"

"Is this okay?"

"Yes. God, yes," he pants.

I pop the button on his pants and tug the zipper down to reveal his tented boxer briefs. I can't help myself and run my tongue the length of his cock over the fabric.

His groan sends a shiver of pleasure through me. That sound is everything. I want to hear it again.

I peel his boxers over his hips and gasp.

I try to catch my breath as I admire the beauty of this man's cock. It's the perfect size—in both length and girth. I take a moment to admire the thickness, the hardness, how he's straining for me. I'm suddenly feeling smug—with lust, desire, control. For right now, he's mine, completely at my mercy.

I don't touch him. I don't kiss him or take him into my mouth. I just gently blow up and down the length of him.

I hear his gasp. My smile is wicked, even though he can't see it.

"You like that?" I ask.

His response is inaudible, but I don't need to hear him. I don't even need to see him. His body responds obediently by tightening; his cock swelling as I wrap my fingers around it.

I shift my weight from one knee to the other. One hand grips his thigh, my nails scratching lightly into his skin. While the other hand is wrapped firmly around his length. For a second, I don't move. I barely breathe. We're both still, quiet, panting.

There's no sound, no motion, no friction. He can't see me, I can't see him.

Eben is the first to break the silence.

"Are you—"

Before he can finish his sentence to ask me if I'm okay, I plunge my mouth around the length of him, taking all of him in one swift motion. I choke slightly as my mouth adjusts to accommodate all of him.

"Oh, fuck."

He moans, and I hear his hands grapple for the wall behind him.

His cock responds beautifully to the way my mouth tightens around him. I wrap my fingers around the base, gripping him firmly. I let the warm wetness of my mouth glide up and down the length of him in a steady rhythm. Occasionally, I switch it up by adding the pressure of soft sucking. It's the art of give and take, stimulus and response. One person can move only if the other sets the rhythm. He and I are in perfect sync. I let a whimper escape, a small release from the weight of needing him inside me.

My muffled whimper earns an equally needy response from him.

"Fuck, Melody. You're so good."

I nod, letting out a soft hum of acknowledgement. The vibration makes him jolt, his cock pulsing against my tongue. He picks up the pace—hips twitching, thrusting—fucking my mouth. But my hands on his hips restrain him. Steady him. Control him. A whimper indicates that he's desperate. Needy.

Ready for release.

"I'm so close—" One of his hands searches for me under the apron, finding my hair. "Melody, please. Can I see you?"

With his cock still in my mouth, I reach behind him for the apron string and tug it loose. The whole thing falls, and he pushes it to the side, letting it drop to the floor.

I look up at him, and he gazes down at me, a pink flush dusting his cheekbones. His eyes are hazy with desire.

He reaches down to tug the apron from around my neck,

and I pull away from him just long enough to slip out of it. And then I take it one step further. I undo the belt around my Santa jacket and shrug out of it, giving him a perfect view of my tits in the red lace bra I wore for him last night.

"Oh, God," he whispers. "You're so beautiful."

He reaches down to cup one of my breasts through the lace, swirling his thumb around my nipple. I lean forward and take him in my mouth again. He buries his hands in my hair, every inch of him trembling as he hurtles toward the edge.

"Melody, I'm going to—"

"It's okay," I whisper, swirling my tongue around the tip.

Before he can say anything else, I take him deep, all the way to the back of my throat and back again. I match the rhythm his body is begging for, moan softly, letting little whimpers vibrate across his cock.

"Holy fuck."

He tightens his grip on the back of my head—firmly, but with care. I let him have this last bit of control to take him over the edge.

One final thrust, and I feel his warmth fill the back of my throat. After one last kiss, I pull away.

I sit back on my heels and look up at him, smiling sweetly.

"Melody, that was—"

I gaze up proudly at Eben's hazy, blissed-out face. Before I can say anything smug about blowing his mind, the smoke alarm yanks us back to earth.

"Oh my God—the cookies!" I shriek, scrambling to my feet. Eben yanks his pants up, and we pinball off each other as we sprint to the kitchen.

"We forgot about the cookies!"

CHAPTER 22

*S*moke billows from the oven as I yank the tray of lemon cookies (who ordered them extra crispy?).

"Ow, ow, ow!"

The tray clatters to the stove, and I cradle my throbbing thumb.

Eben slides the scorched sheet pan of lemon hockey pucks aside and takes my hand. His touch is gentle, his face sweet and full of concern.

"Let me see it, baby."

The endearment knocks the air out of me. I can't remember the last time someone called me that, if ever. My seared thumb is suddenly forgotten; heat rushes to my cheeks instead.

"It's fine," I grumble, sheepish.

He ignores me, tests the tap, then guides my thumb beneath the stream. I wince, but don't complain. It's nice to be taken care of—even if I pretend it's not.

After a moment, he lifts my hand.

"That was a close one," he says, inspecting the burn, "but I think you'll keep it."

I laugh—unexpected and a little giddy. Who would have

thought the resident Grinch would turn out to be sweet, protective, and a natural caretaker?

Not on my bingo card, but I like it.

"Thank you, doctor," I say. "That was touch and go."

I take in the disaster zone: charred cookie remains, flour, sugar, and sprinkles dusting every surface like we shook a snow globe too hard. "Maybe you were right. We should've placed an order. This is... a lot."

He shakes his head. "No way. They deserve homemade. We just can't get—" His gaze drops, sweeping slowly over my barely-there lace bra and lingering near my hips. I follow his line of sight.

Oh, God.

Behold: my enormous white granny panties. Cotton. Waist-high. Unapologetically full coverage.

"...distracted," he finishes.

Heat detonates in my cheeks. "Oh. Wow."

This is mortifying.

"Wow is right, Mrs. Claus," Eben says, flashing me a grin that should require a permit.

Look, I'm a lingerie girl. I've dropped a pretty penny on lace thongs with silk bows, barely-there teddies, and satiny robes. Even though I don't have a boyfriend, I love to buy them and wear them around the house, just for me. Wearing sexy lingerie makes me feel confident in my skin—no man required.

But *these?*

These enormous knickers are *horrendous.* They make me feel one hundred years old. It's giving... GILF.

Kill me.

"Oh my God, I need to change out of these imme—" I start to turn away, but he wraps an arm around my bare waist and pulls me flush against him. I squeal in protest.

"Don't. You. Dare."

He growls low in my ear, fingers splaying wide and posses-sive across my ribs. My breath catches. My brain short-circuits.

"Now that you've given me the most mind-blowing orgasm of my life," he says. "I think it's only fair I return the favor. Don't you?"

I gulp. My face burns hotter than a tray of burnt-to-a-crisp Christmas cookies.

"Oh?" is all I manage to choke out.

"Mmhmm."

He flips me around to face him and presses his lips to mine. This kiss is filthy. Ravenous. His tongue licks into my mouth. His hands wrap around my waist, pulling me to him before sliding low over my ass—grabbing, squeezing, kneading the flesh. He toys with the edge of my enormous underwear, fingers curling under the seam.

He leans in, lips hovering just next to my ear. His breath is hot on my neck.

"You didn't think I was just going to let you show me up... did you, Mrs. Claus?"

The way he lingers on *Mrs. Claus* makes me sweat.

Eben leans over and wraps his hands around my thighs, hoisting me up. I squeal my legs instinctively wrapping around his waist. He pauses, looking into my eyes with an unspoken question, a moment stretching between us. "Still okay?" he whispers, his voice full of warmth and care. I nod, my fingers interlocking behind his neck as he carries me out of the kitchen, leaving our hardened molten lava rock cookies behind.

"That way," I breathe, pointing him in the right direction.

He carries me into my bedroom and gently lays me down on the bed. I stare longingly at my dresser, where hundreds of dollars' worth of lingerie are missing out on all the fun we haven't had in... well, years.

Eben looks around the room like I've brought him back to my padded room in the North Pole's psych ward. There's another small-ish Christmas tree in here, casting a soft glow, and more garland draped across every available surface.

"You are something else," he says, spreading my knees apart and climbing between them. His weight is exquisite. He braces himself on his forearms so I don't get crushed. His lips find mine, and he sucks on my bottom lip. I whimper as he starts to kiss down my body.

He kisses and licks down my neck until his teeth gently graze my collarbone. One hand finds my nipple through the lace of my bra and pinches—just enough to make me gasp and arch. He pushes the fabric aside and dips his head. His tongue circles and swirls with wet heat. I moan and close my eyes. He switches breasts, lavishing the same attention on the other.

My whole body is on fire as he continues his trail down my navel. His teeth find the top edge of my cotton panties and pull them down. He circles my belly button with his tongue, and I think I'm going to combust spontaneously.

He slips off the bed.

And it's his turn to sink to his knees.

He takes his time with me, kissing around my feet, up my ankles, and along my calves. His mouth licks, sucks, and gently bites the sensitive skin of my inner thighs. My hands grip the bed as he works his way up the length of my body, teasing every inch of me with soft, torturous kisses.

"Do you know what tastes better than cookies, Melody?" he says, as he wraps his hands around my hips and pulls me to the edge of the bed.

His fingers dip beneath the cotton. He somehow makes me feel like a Victoria's Secret model even in my drugstore underwear.

"No. I don't."

I gasp as he pulls my underwear down past my hip bones and gently scrapes his teeth over the jut of bone.

"Last night, I got just the tiniest taste," he says, his intense gaze never breaking mine. "Do you want to know what you taste like?"

"Yes," I breathe, barely holding in a whimper.

His head dips, and he licks a hot stripe over the cotton between my legs. The ache is unbearable. My hips lift towards him, almost involuntarily.

"You taste like peppermint," he says, his tongue teasing through the damp fabric. "And heat. And earth."

My breath catches.

"Like Christmas morning in the woods," he continues, voice reverent. "Cool and sweet at first... but there's this wild, earthy heat underneath. Fuck, it's addicting."

"That's my Candy Cane body wash," I say, grinning down at him proudly.

He laughs and looks up at me. "I don't know, I think it's *you*, Mel. I think you're my new favorite holiday treat."

His fingers dip underneath the fabric, parting me and playing with me. He finds my clit and circles it, slow and teasing. My breath comes out in ragged gasps as he traces figure eights through my slick heat.

"Oh my God," he groans. "Do you hear that?"

I arch back as one of his fingers dips inside me. Then two.

"Do you hear how wet you are for me?"

"Fuck, Eben," I say as his thumb circles my clit while two fingers pump in and out of me. I'm so turned on I could die. And we haven't even gotten to the good part yet.

"Please," I whimper.

"Please, what?" he murmurs, his voice velvet, his fingers working a steady rhythm. "Tell me."

I've always been shy with dirty talk, so I simply whisper, "Kiss me."

His grin is devilish as he pulls my cotton underwear down over my legs, discarding the hideous garment I fully intend to burn in the fireplace later.

I'm bare beneath him now, and his gaze rakes over me, slow and consuming. He pushes my knees up, spreading me wide open for him. His ice blue eyes find mine, and I can only imagine how desperate I must look. One side of his gorgeous mouth kicks up in the sexiest half-smile I've ever seen.

Then he lowers his head.

It's the same filthy kiss from earlier, only now it's between my legs instead of my mouth. Eben's fingers gently spread me apart so he can lick the center of me, his tongue applying pressure where I need it most. He drags a long, slow stripe down the length of me until he's teasing my entrance with the tip of his tongue. I grind on his face, desperate for more—more friction, more pressure, more of him filling more of me.

Almost like he can read my mind, he slips two fingers inside me. My wet heat grips him tight, and he lets out a ragged breath.

He sinks his fingers deeper, curling them until he finds that perfect spot. The one that makes my back arch and my toes curl. With his free hand, he pushes my legs back farther, opening me up completely.

He works me deeper, his fingers moving in a steady rhythm as his tongue swirls over my clit—circling and sucking. Relentless. He matches the rhythm and pulse of my body as I grind against his face, hands buried in his hair, moaning louder with every wave of pleasure.

The more I whimper, the deeper he goes.

Every sound I make is matched with a sexy, low growl of his own.

"Don't stop," I whimper. "Please."

He moans against me, his tongue swirling around my clit like I'm the best ice cream cone he's ever licked. He keeps going, the pressure building, soaring higher and higher until—

I cry out. I come apart. On Eben's hands. On his mouth. My entire body shudders with pleasure. Over and over again. It doesn't stop, and he doesn't let up until I am boneless. And even then, he keeps licking me like he likes the taste.

It's probably the most intense sexual experience of my life.

And if it didn't feel so fucking good, I might be a little self-conscious, but I'm too busy orgasming all over my sexy Santa's face to give a damn. I'm dripping sweat, I can't feel my legs, and I'm pretty sure we're not done yet.

As my breath slows, Eben strokes his hands up and down my legs and then stands and slips into bed next to me. I can see the outline of him through his pants. He's hard again, and the thought of having him inside me makes my stomach twist with anticipation.

"What did you *do* to me?" I ask him, breathless. "I thought *I* was the Blowjob Queen, but you…"

"I have a few tricks up my sleeve," he says, flashing that soul-stirring smile.

"Yeah," I say, dreamy and dazed. I can barely feel my limbs. My body is floating. Like I'm doing the backstroke in a cup of hot cocoa, on a marshmallow cloud of afterglow.

He traces lazy little swirls over my stomach.

"So… should we recommence with the cookie baking?" I ask, glancing at the clock. It's getting late.

He tilts his head, considering. "Depends… will you stay naked?"

"Eben!" I say, smacking him on the shoulder. "We're baking for the *masses!*"

"Hmmm. Good point." He actually looks disappointed.

"Tell you what," I say. "Once we finish and everything's safely tucked away inside the freezer, I'll make a batch just for us."

His eyes light up.

"In just my apron."

He leaps out of bed. "What are we waiting for?" He smacks my ass once, and I throw my head back in laughter.

"Let's get cracking."

CHAPTER 23

I swear, Eben and I are giving Santa's elves a run for their money with the sheer volume of cookies we've baked for this pageant.

After our sexy little detour, I take the world's fastest shower while Eben deals with the overdone batch (nearly breaking a tooth in the process). I throw on an off-the-shoulder sweater and jeans, pairing them with my finest matching bra and lace underwear set (phew), just in case things heat up again. I twist my hair in a clip to keep any fallout far from our batter.

Eben's eyes keep drifting to my collarbone as we stir and measure. Flour, sugar, and sticky dough cling to us both. We're careful not to touch—public cookies do not need any extra ingredients.

Cue the TikTok classic "you can't eat at everybody's house."

No, but really, we keep it G-rated with R-rated eye fucking. I consider it a win.

We prep tray after tray—Italian lemon, thumbprints, Mexican wedding or Italian snowball cookies (depending on who you ask). My fingers ache from rolling dough, and Eben's biting his lip so hard from focusing that he finally draws blood.

I'm used to baking alone. My grandma baked every year while she was still able, but I was never allowed to help. Ally's hopeless in the kitchen (though she's always happy to "assist" with the eating part), so it's usually just me: me and my cookies.

Today, it's me and Eben. And even though he allegedly hates Christmas, he's working his butt off to help me—which is... something.

Maybe a mutual love of Christmas isn't the dealbreaker I thought it was. Maybe he doesn't have to love it like I do— maybe he just has to be there while I love it. Maybe that's enough.

All afternoon, we've been a team. And for a split second, I can imagine myself... belonging. With him. Here, or anywhere. Making cookies and memories and sharing kisses and—

I'm getting ahead of myself. Our first official date was literally yesterday. We've known each other for a few weeks— nowhere near long enough to start ringing wedding bells.

God, Melody. Dial it down. *El desperado* vibes at a 10.

Must be the trauma.

"You okay?" he asks, nudging me with his elbow. I glance down—my cup of flour runneth over.

I dump it back in the bag and measure again. "Fine," I say, shaking it off. But when I meet Eben's eyes, the tenderness there makes my stomach do somersaults. I try not to read into it. My heart does anyway.

Bad heart. Bad. Heart.

We Tetris seven trays of sweets into my freezer after a "strategic purge," which means tossing anything that looks like it's been in there since the Ice Age. So... everything.

Eben opens a fossilized pizza box that's been in there since Thanksgiving. He gives it a cautious sniff and recoils. "How old is this?"

I snatch it from his hands and slam-dunk it into the trash. "Less judging, more cleaning."

Two trash bags later—full of rotted girl-dinner condiments and ancient takeout containers fermenting with Listeria—my tiny fridge miraculously has room for seven cookie trays.

"Whew," he says, wiping his brow. "I've worked construction sites less labor-intensive than cleaning out that fridge."

I cross my arms and scowl. His grin drops to my mouth, then—

"You've got a little powdered sugar," he says, tapping his own cheek.

"Where?"

Before I can touch mine, he catches my wrist and tips my chin. He leans in and—God help me—*licks* the sugar away.

He skims his tongue over his lip. "I'm not done with you yet."

I may not survive the night.

He lowers his mouth to my ear, fingers tracing the bare cut of my collarbones. "You wore this sweater just to torture me for three hours while I wasn't allowed to touch you."

"I did not," I protest, heart pounding. "I literally grabbed it off the floor."

He bends, teeth grazing the notch above my collarbone. My knees buckle.

"Whoa," he says, catching me at the waist.

The counter is a disaster—flour, sugar, a crime scene of sprinkles—but he lifts me anyway, sets me on the edge, and steps between my legs.

"Eben!" I yelp, half laughing, half warning.

He looks up through his lashes. His hands slide under my sweater, tracing slow circles on my skin. "Say the word, Mrs. Claus," he murmurs, mouth hovering over mine, "and I'll be very, very good."

My breath stutters. I nod, suddenly shy.

He tightens his grip. "Say it."

"Yes," I whisper—and that's all the permission he needs.

He kisses me—greedy, ravenous—like all that cookie baking

worked him up into an appetite. His hands slide higher beneath my sweater, cupping my breasts, fingertips grazing the stiff peaks of my nipples. I groan into his mouth, raw heat surging through me.

"More," I whisper. His grin is wicked against my lips. Now I'm the greedy one.

He flicks open my jeans with a sleight of hand—one second they're snug, the next they're peeled down past my hips. The chill of the counter on my bare skin makes me shiver.

He doesn't bother with my sweater. Not yet. Instead, his hands roam my thighs as he kisses me, licking deep. The hard length of him presses into my inner thigh. I brush him with the back of my hand, feel the heat and the damp through the fabric, and we both groan.

His hands cup my ass, and he freezes mid-kiss. "Damn," he breathes. "You're covered in sugar."

He lifts me by the hips, sets my feet down, and turns me, bending me over the countertop, palms braced on the faux marble.

"Can I have you like this, sweetheart?" he asks, sinking to his knees behind me.

Fire pools low in my belly, hotter than ever. He can have me any way he wants.

"Yes," slips out on a whimper.

I brace on my elbows, breathing hard, not sure what he'll do first.

Then I feel it—his tongue, hot and wet, licking sugar and flour from my skin like I'm some decadent, sugar-dusted beignet. The sensation is a dizzying mix of ticklish and sinful. My hips buck, but his hands steady me as he licks me clean. Each stroke is a slow torment, and my thighs part on instinct, aching for more.

"Where do you want me?" he murmurs, hands sliding up my

thighs and between them. He strokes me through the lace, and I whimper. "You want me here?"

"Please," I say, folding over the counter.

His fingers twist into the thin strip of lace between my cheeks and tug it aside. "This is in the way," he growls.

And then his mouth is on me again—flicking, licking, teasing my core. Something about being ass-up over the counter, half-naked and sticky-sweet, makes his tongue feel electric. I'm panting, squirming—trying not to scream. I don't need to scare the neighbors.

His tongue circles my clit, hands cupping my ass, holding me open. He sucks gently, and I nearly come apart.

"Fuck, Eben," I gasp as he licks a hot stripe from front to back.

"You still okay?" he asks, kissing the back of my thigh. A shudder rolls through me.

"More than okay," I pant. "But I need you."

He rises behind me, fingers sketching slow circles down my spine as he leans in, his erection pressing into my ass. Kisses trail along my neck to my ear. "Do you have condoms here?"

"I got some this morning." I nod toward the untouched pharmacy bag on a barstool, handles peeking over the counter.

"Good girl," he murmurs, patting my ass. He reaches for the bag; his hands shake as he fumbles the box. Good. I'm not the only one falling apart.

A belt clinks; foil rips. A heartbeat later, he's behind me again, the tip of his cock—hard and insistent—pressing at my entrance. My toes curl, and the tight squeeze reminds me *it's been a while.*

It was certainly worth the wait.

He eases in—inch by glorious inch—stretching me to take him. It's that perfect edge of pleasure and ache until, with one steady thrust, he's buried to the hilt and I'm breathless, pulsing around him.

My fingers curl around the edge of the counter, knuckles white as I grip for dear life. "I'm going to die," I rasp. "I'm actually going to die."

His lips brush my ear. "You okay?" Concern threads his voice.

I nod hard, hair tumbling from its clip. "Fine. Totally fine, just... fuck."

He sweeps my hair over one shoulder and kisses just behind my ear—a sweet, wordless promise.

A subtle shift of his hips and fresh sensation crashes through me. "Jesus," I moan, every nerve ending lighting up.

His hands slide under my sweater, nails skimming. He peels it over my head and tosses it aside. He reaches around to pinch my nipples through the lace, then returns to my hips for leverage. In and out, deeper and deeper—he finds a perfect, punishing rhythm that makes me see stars.

I fear I may never walk again.

Not mad about it.

"Can you come like this?" He asks, voice wrecked.

I nod, breath coming in ragged gasps. "But I don't want to—yet," I murmur between whimpers, desperate to make this moment last.

He pulls out slowly, turns me to face him so he can see my eyes. "Me neither," he says, kissing me. He lifts me easily, and I loop my arms around his neck as he guides my legs around his waist. He looks down, arranges us, and slides back into me. A few deliberate thrusts—and then I realize we're moving, leaving the kitchen for the bedroom, still joined.

I glance down—my bra is gone. My panties, too. I don't even remember when that happened.

"A little Christmas miracle," he murmurs, smiling into a kiss. He sits on the edge of my bed with me straddling his lap. His red velvet pants are somehow still on his lower half, even though I'm totally naked.

He notices me clocking his wrinkled Santa pants and arches a brow. "A new way to sit on Santa's lap, huh?" His eyes sparkle.

I giggle and push at his bare shoulders, fingers tracing hard muscle. I've never had this much fun during sex. The few men before Eben were predictable—silent grunts, zero creativity. But this? This is something else entirely.

Once will not be enough.

His hands return to my hips. He leans back and—

Oh God, that angle.

"Eben," I pant. "I want to come like this."

He nips at my bottom lip, smiling against it. "Your wish is my command, Mrs. Claus."

We find a perfect rhythm—our bodies in sync as he pumps into me while I grind down on him. I watch, mesmerized, as his muscles ripple and flex. His gaze is locked on my face, making sure I'm okay, waiting for me to fall. Color rises high on his cheekbones as I ride him. It's too much, it feels too good, and this time, I can't help it as raw, primal sounds escape my lips—to hell with the neighbors.

Pleasure roars through me like the Polar Express. I cry out, clenching around him as I come. His eyes squeeze shut, head tipping back. He groans, hips pressing into mine, hands stroking my sweat-slick sides as he shudders through his release.

He collapses back onto the bed, taking me with him. I pillow my cheek on his warm, glistening chest, both of us panting like we've just run a Holiday Half Marathon. His arms band my waist; he kisses the top of my head. Aftershocks ripple through us as our jelly-limbs remember how to be bones again. When I finally look up, his cheeks are flushed, and his eyes are heavy with quiet bliss.

"Damn, Melody," he rasps. "That—"

"Yeah," I breathe. "That."

We lie there a long while, just breathing, melting into each other. I could stay like this forever—weightless, warm, deliciously wrecked in the soft glow of after.

But he's a furnace, and eventually I roll off before I expire from a cuddle-induced heatstroke. He snags a stray towel from the floor and tidies up while I slip beneath the duvet, hoping he'll join me for some well-earned naked cuddling.

As always, he reads my mind. He shucks off his Santa pants. Somehow, he's still hard (should I be surprised my Mr. Claus is superhuman?), and for the first time, I get the full view of him, naked in the low light: post-sex glow, lean muscle, long everywhere. I want to lick him from head to toe.

"Come on, give us a spin," I say, twirling a finger.

His brows dip, amused. "What?"

"I've been naked twice tonight, and somehow you kept most of your clothes on. So." I motion again.

He sighs, resigned, and starts to turn.

"Wait—wait." I dive into the nightstand and produce a Santa hat. "In this," I say, tossing it.

He catches it against his chest, squinting. "You can't be serious."

"*Now*, Mr. Claus," I say, giving him the universal move-it-along gesture.

Another sigh. He plops the hat on—crooked—and does the slowest spin known to man.

Lo and behold... his perfect ass. I let out a theatrical sigh and lean forward to deliver a ceremonial smack.

"Hey!" he yelps, jolting. The hat tumbles off his head—

—and lands squarely on his dick, perfectly tented.

I lose it, laughing so hard I nearly roll off the bed.

"Oh, you think that's funny?" he says, flinging the hat aside.

I squeak and yank the duvet over my head. He climbs onto the bed, rips the covers back, and pins me—then tickles without mercy.

"Eben!" I squeal, writhing. "Stop!"

But then bodies graze in exciting ways—warm skin, hard muscle, hard... other things—and suddenly we're not laughing.

His hands slow. Mine stop trying to push him away. Our eyes lock.

We go still. The only sound is our breathing.

And then—

We're kissing again.

CHAPTER 24

*T*ime blurs, and I don't know what time we finally fall asleep—only that it's long after several slow, indulgent rounds of lovemaking, punctuated by lazy snuggles, sleepy chatter, and a midnight snack. It turns out Santa—aka Chef Eben—makes a mean grilled cheese.

We talk for hours. I learn that Eben hasn't been in a relationship since his mom was diagnosed with early-onset dementia in his early twenties. He's spent the last decade working and caring for her—no time to date and no real friends to speak of. He's quiet and shy and a bit of a loner.

I remember those awkward family photos on his wall—the lanky frame, the too-wide smile—and put two-and-two together: he's a late bloomer—one of those people who grew into their looks later in life. I skim a finger down his jaw as we lie shoulder to shoulder on my pillows, trying very hard not to drool.

He smiles again, and my heart just... stalls.

Puberty didn't do him any favors—but adulthood sure as hell did.

I tell him about Deb and Don, about my soul-sucking job

that barely covers rent. He tells me Golding Home hires designers all the time and promises to ask his dad if they have any openings. "Your living room alone could be a portfolio piece," he says.

The way his voice drops when he says it, the way I have to wrap my legs around his to keep from kicking my feet in giddy disbelief—

Yeah. That leads to a few more rounds of naughty list activities.

By the time I curl up on his chest, wrapped in his scent and steady heartbeat, I've never felt safer. Or more at home.

When sunlight streams through my window in the early-bird hours of Sunday morning, my eyes flutter open—and there he is. Already wide awake. And already... grinning?

"Morning, Mrs. Claus," he says, one arm tucked behind his head like a cocky bastard.

I roll over and realize my boobs are fully out. I yank the covers up.

"Hello," I say, squinting at him. "What's gotten into you?"

"I think you mean... what's gotten into *you?*" he says, waggling his brows as he holds up something *naughty.*

I gasp and bolt upright, suddenly wide awake.

"You went through my drawers?" I screech, lunging for it. He holds it just out of reach.

"I was just trying to put your Santa hat away—kind of weird that you keep it in your end table by the way—"

"Nightstand," I snap.

"Whatever," he shrugs. "Anyway, that's when I spotted some... very festive toys."

"I. Will. Kill. You."

"Aww, but Mrs. Claus..." He grins wickedly, brandishing the vibrator. "If you kill me, who's gonna fuck you with this Santa hat?"

"I am," I say, folding my arms. "Obviously."

"Come on," he waggles his brows and flicks it on. The hum curls through my belly. "Can I?"

Heat flashes up my neck. I'm sore, a little shy—but still, I can't resist him. I slide my knees apart and lift the duvet in invitation.

He smirks and disappears under the covers.

A breath later, the buzz skates up my spine. He eases it into me, angled just right. I melt into the pillows as he urges my thighs wider and lowers his mouth, tongue flicking over my clit.

It takes less than a minute for me to come undone.

He flips the toy, revealing the clit stimulator hidden beneath the white trim of Santa's hat, and moves it to my nipple. His tongue circles the other, and I whimper helplessly. His free hand begins a slow descent between us—

KNOCK KNOCK KNOCK.

We both freeze. Santa's "hat" drops and vanishes somewhere in the sheets.

"Jesus," Eben mutters, half sitting up. "Who the hell—"

He's sliding out of bed, still hard, and grabbing for his Santa pants. "They're knocking like you owe them money."

KNOCK. KNOCK.

I scramble for a T-shirt and a pair of leggings from a pile of clean laundry. One glance in the mirror confirms the rat's nest on top of my head. I'll deal with that later.

Eben follows me to the door, still yanking up his red velvet pants. It looks a little like I booked a private Santa Claus stripper just for me.

Oh, well. Time to give the mailman a show.

I peek through the peephole—only to see Ally pounding her ever-loving mind out on my door. I mutter a curse and fling it open.

"God, did you join the SWAT team recently, or—"

Ally storms past me—and immediately locks eyes with Eben.

His erection has thankfully deflated, but he's still shirtless, tousled, and wearing the unmistakable pants of a man who's had a *very* festive night.

Ally, somehow, seems too frazzled to register it.

"Oh my God, Melody, I've been calling you for hours—I thought you were dead."

I glance at my phone. Sure enough, in addition to three missed calls from Cassie, there are *twelve* from Ally.

"Okay, well... I'm *not*. I've just been—busy."

Ally gives Eben the once-over, eyes trailing from his messy hair down to his bare, muscled chest, finally landing on his red pants. Even though he's not hard anymore, the outline of him is still... visible.

Her eyebrows shoot up.

Oh God. I'm never going to live this down.

"Sorry, I see that," she says, flashing a sit-eating grin. "I'm just not used to you being so... preoccupied."

She takes a few steps in, glances around, and scrunches her nose.

"Did you guys have sex in here?"

"God, no. Ally, shut up."

"Cause it kind of—"

"Ally!" I cry, heat rushing to my face.

Ally throws up her hands. "Okay, okay, sorry. It's just that if you did, I was about to throw you a party. Like a first communion, but for someone who hasn't gotten laid in a thousand years."

Eben laughs. "Then I guess you'd better add my name to the cake."

Ally and I both turn to gape at him.

"No way. Hot Santa's celibate? Say it ain't so."

My face flushes, and so does his—probably thinking about all the *very* non-celibate things we just did all over my apartment.

He shrugs, a little sheepish. "I kind of... keep to myself."

Ally snorts. "Well, I'm glad you two reclusive freaks found each other."

She wanders over to the only burned trays of cookies that didn't make it to the trash and nibbles the lone semi-edible edge of a lemon hockey puck.

God love her—she'll eat anything that's even remotely edible and dusted with sugar.

"Other than not-so-secretly fucking and setting these cookies on fire—" She pauses, squinting at the tray. "Wait... are these for the old folks?"

She picks up a blackened lemon puck and whacks it against the side of the counter. It doesn't even crack. I'm pretty sure it dings the laminate.

"Because if so, you're about to owe the entire nursing home a new set of dentures."

"They were supposed to be," I say sheepishly.

Ally grins. "Oh, you were definitely having sex then—'cause you haven't burned a Christmas cookie in, like, seven years."

Flustered, I snatch the cookie from her and toss it back on the tray. Eben calmly slides it to the far end of the counter—out of her reach and, more importantly, out of my throwing range.

"I'm sorry, did you need something?" I ask, flustered but not actually mad.

Ally stares at me like I've grown a second head. "The Cherryville Flea Market? Did you forget?"

Eben and I exchange guilty glances—looks that say, *Yep, we absolutely forgot, but we were busy doing things that involved no clothes and a lot of powdered sugar.*

Ally rolls her eyes. "I see your sexcapades have officially fried your brains." She claps her hands together, switching into publicist mode. "Well, chop chop, children. We can't have those kids whispering their hopes and dreams to strange men in velvet suits without giving the forgotten generation five dollars first."

. . .

175

WE'VE GOT ABOUT HALF an hour before the flea market opens, so we swing by Eben's house on the way so he can freshen up (aka put on some underwear).

The second he steps out of the car, Ally lets out a low whistle.

"A butt that won't quit *and* a house in the Estates? Girl, put a ring on it." She tilts her head to one side, eyes gleaming. "Or maybe you already did," she adds with a wink, making an obscene jerking-off motion.

I reach back from the passenger seat to smack her hand. "*Ally!*"

She grins—but it doesn't quite reach her eyes.

In all my embarrassment over her nearly walking in on us, I fail to notice her puffy, red-rimmed eyes—like she's been crying.

She catches me playing mental CIA and immediately turns her head, pretending to admire Eben's mailbox.

"Ally, are you—"

"Are you spending Christmas with him?" she interrupts.

"What?" My brows knit. "What do you mean?"

"Are you and Mr. Claus going to spend the holiday weekend knocking boots or what?"

I blink. "I always spend Christmas with you—"

"I think Teddy and I are going away for the weekend."

My frown is immediate. "Oh."

"Yeah, sorry. It was a last-minute decision."

"Are you guys… okay? Where is he?"

"He's home with Tids. I think he ate part of a dead squirrel at the dog park and now he's got raging diarrhea." She chuckles. "Dumb dog."

Her voice cracks just slightly on the laugh.

I stare at her for a long beat. There's something she's not telling me.

If the roles were reversed, she'd hound me until I cracked. She'd poke and prod and force me to spill the beans.

But I'm not like her. She'll tell me when she's ready.

We sit in heavy silence until Eben returns to the truck, smelling like aftershave and sandalwood. He smiles, and I manage a weak smile back. My eyes flick back to Ally, but she's still facing the window.

I swear I see a tear slip down her cheek—

But the light shifts, and she swipes it away before I can be sure.

CHAPTER 25

*T*here's a line of about forty people outside Forest Park's Meet Santa booth.

And most of them are women.

Turns out someone took a video of Eben last week in his Santa Claus suit and posted it. The internet did what it does best—and dubbed him *Daddy Christmas*.

Now, women of all ages are lining up to "sit on Santa's lap."

I watch one woman squeeze his bicep, and the hair on the back of my neck prickles.

"Who knew we'd need security for this?" Ally says, shaking her head as she collects bill after bill.

The second we arrived and saw the line, she hiked the price of admission ten bucks—and added a new rule: no more actual lap sitting. You get to whisper one thing you want in his ear, give him a quick hug, and be on your merry way.

I watch another woman lean in and murmur something to him. Eben's eyes widen. His cheeks flush.

I roll up my sleeve like a cartoon character.

"Why I oughta—"

Ally grips my shoulder and yanks me back. "Chill, Popeye."

Four hours and two hundred people later, Forest Park is two thousand dollars richer for Christmas.

"Jesus," Ally says, finishing her count. "You're a cash cow, Daddy Christmas!"

Eben licks a snow cone as a group of middle-aged women pass by, giggling like schoolgirls.

I try not to pout.

I fail spectacularly.

He bumps my shoulder. "Cherry or blue raspberry?"

"I don't know," I grumble. "Cherry, I guess."

A second later, something cold brushes my lips.

I glance down—he's holding a spoonful of cherry ice to my mouth, grin lazy and infuriating. He hasn't done anything wrong, but I can't help it—*I still kind of want to kill him.*

"It's like thirty degrees out," I grumble.

"We're inside," he shoots back. "And they're blasting the heat like it's minus thirty."

I'm not usually the jealous type, but watching all those women fawn over him, touching him like they're auditioning for Santa's Naughty List?

Yeah. It did something to me.

I roll my eyes and part my lips, and he slides the spoon in. His eyes track my tongue as I lick the syrup from my lips.

He leans in and murmurs, "Nobody sits on Santa's lap like you, baby."

My cheeks blaze.

"*Christ*, I'm right fucking here!"

Ally's head swivels like she's in *The Exorcist*, glare sharp enough to cut down a Christmas tree.

He backs away slowly, snow cone and spoon raised in surrender.

Once Eben finishes his snow cone—and I'm (mostly) finished pouting—we tear down the Meet Santa setup and load everything into his truck. When we're finally settled, Ally pops her head between the front seats and pinches both our cheeks. "Okay, kids... what are we doing?"

I shoot a sheepish glance at Eben in the driver's seat. His mouth is stained from a red-blue sugar combo, and I've spent the last half hour imagining kissing the purple off his lips, preferably in front of his fan club.

I'm sure he's ready to go home. Maybe watch some football and mentally prep for Monday. We've been together almost two days straight. He has to be sick of me, right?

But when I look over, he's watching me—waiting for my cue. I bite my lip, still staring at his. He notices and grins.

"Because I'm third-wheeling so hard right now," Ally says, exasperated, "and I'd like to know if this is going to turn into a live sex show or a lunch run."

Eben's eyes sparkle. "What do you say, Melody? Lunch... or an early Christmas present for Ally?"

I'm going to die.

Ally claps her hands and squeals. "I like this guy. Can we keep him?"

I glance over at him, a little shy, warmth blooming in my chest. I'm happy—*thrilled*—that my favorite person in the world likes my... well, whatever Eben is becoming to me.

"So, golden boy, how do you feel about the golden arches?"

THREE LARGE FRIES (EXTRA SALT), and six cheeseburgers later— three for Ally—we're parked in the McDonald's lot, inhaling lunch in Eben's truck, heat blasting, the center console doing tray-table duty.

"Mmm. Tastes like bad morals," I say, shoving a delightfully wrinkly french fry into my mouth.

Ally sticks her tongue out at me. With her Cleveland Guardians cap pulled low over her eyes and a fry dangling from her mouth like a cigarette, I can't help but think that she looks so much like she did when we were in high school—tomboy charm, full of attitude and junk food.

Though now that I think about it, I can't remember the last time Ally asked for fast food. Usually, drive-thru runs are reserved for post-doctor visits, sick days, or when I'm bribing her.

I reach over to test her forehead for a fever. She swats me away like a mosquito.

"So tell me..." she says, slurping her Coke. "What's with the cookie-baking marathon?"

"Missy gave us a list of errands for the pageant," I say.

"What kind of errands?"

I hand her my phone so she can read the checklist I copied from Missy's clipboard.

Her eyes skim down the list. Her lips twist.

"Soooo... you're staging a Christmas fever dream for one *seriously* over-nogged nursing home administrator?"

"In her defense," Eben says, not looking up from his burger, "the nursing home's severely understaffed."

Ally groans, crumples her wrapper, and shoots it into the carryout bag like a basketball.

"Fiiiiine, I'll help."

"What? Ally, you don't have to—"

"Shhhh." She presses a fry-salted finger to my lips. "I want to. You need me." She dusts off her hands. "Besides, I'm the only one here with theater experience."

My brain flashes back to Ally's standing ovation as Beatrice in *Much Ado About Nothing,* our senior year. Onstage or off, nobody can verbally spar like Ally.

Still doesn't explain her sudden interest in our Christmas errands.

"Let me get this straight," I say, eyeing her with suspicion. "You *want* to help with Christmas errands?"

Ally has never—*not once*—offered to do any kind of

Christmas errands with me. She is the kind of holiday celebrator who shows up on the day. Maybe Christmas Eve, if
someone else is cooking and the booze is good.

Sure, she'll plan the fundraiser, organize the bake sale, and
boss the planning committee into tip-top shape. She lives for
logistics, not twinkle lights—a doer, not a dreamer.

Trinket shopping? Baking? Decorating?

She'd rather poke herself in the eye with a sharp stick.

She avoids my eyes when she says, "Yes. I love Christmas."

Eben groans. "Oh no. Not another one."

I glance between them. "Don't worry. Ally's just *okay* with
Christmas."

"It's like you don't even know me," she says, clutching her
chest in mock offense.

"I do know you," I say, rolling my eyes. "That's exactly the
problem."

She smirks. "Relax, Frosty. I don't have to *love* Christmas to
be good at it."

That's Ally in a nutshell—give her a clipboard and a cause,
and she'll run the North Pole like a Fortune 500.

Ally scrolls through Missy's list. "Okay, what's next?"

"Hmmm," I grumble, crossing my arms over my chest and
narrowing my eyes at her.

She ignores me and stops on a line that makes her snort.

"Feathered angel wings?" Ally eyes me like that shit is
bananas. She squints at the note again. "And make sure they're
real feathers?"

Her eyebrow shoots up. "Is this a shopping list or a scav-
enger hunt?"

I shrug, and it's my turn to avoid eye contact. "Yeah, Missy
is directing the seniors in a choir number before the pageant.
She has a vision. She also has a thing against synthetic
materials."

"God," Eben mutters. "Getting old is so humiliating."

I glance at him, lost in his own thoughts, and wonder just how loaded that statement is for him.

"Where the hell are you going to get real feathered angel wings? Heaven?" Ally asks.

There's a long pause. Then, simultaneously, we both look at Eben.

"What?" he asks, brow furrowing. Then, slowly, realization dawns. "Oh no. No, no, no, no."

Heaven, all right. And my freaking version of it.

My eyes widen. I squeal.

"Please, please, please." I clasp my hands, trying not to jump up and down and rock the truck.

"Come on, Mr. Scrooge," Ally adds, attempting a pout. It's not really her vibe—she mostly just looks like she smelled something weird.

"Where else can we get angel wings with real feathers?" I ask, hearts in my eyes.

"There's only one place I know," Ally says.

Eben lets out a long, defeated sigh.

WHEN WE ROLL up to Golding Home, excitement rushes through me like I just snorted a pound of crushed-up candy canes.

The parking lot's small, shared with a hardware store. I feel a twinge of guilt as Eben barely squeezes his truck into a spot and idles.

"All right, see you ladies soon."

"You're not coming in?" I ask. I know it's pushy. I've been inside Golding Home a million times—if they had a loyalty program, I'd have Platinum status (and my bank account would weep)—but I want him there.

I know things are strained with his dad, but selfishly, I still want to be introduced to him. I want to see the store through his eyes—not as the Christmas-obsessed menace I am, but as his home turf. The place he grew up. The place he works—the place he's paid for, in more ways than one, to keep running.

"You already know your way around," Eben says, eyeing the sweeping double doors wrapped in pre-lit garland, poinsettias, and more tinsel than a 1950s Christmas movie—like they're gussying up the gates of Hell.

Ally starts to fumble her way out of the truck, not caring one way or the other if Eben comes with us. To her, this is just another store. She's lived here her whole life and probably set foot inside twice.

I feel bad for dragging him here on his day off. But he *does* work here, so how bad could it be?

"Don't you work here, bud?" Ally asks, slugging his shoulder. There she goes, reading my mind again. "I work from home, mostly," Eben says.

He's clearly torn, eyes flicking between me and the tinsel-gilded gates of his own personal Hell. I can't help it—I hit him with the biggest puppy-dog eyes I can muster, plus a bonus lip tremble. He swallows and looks away, white-knuckling the steering wheel as if we might physically drag him out of the car (I won't rule it out).

"Melody can tell you the whole story," he says to the dashboard.

It's cute that he thinks I haven't already.

I inhale, ready to launch into my dramatic recap—like I didn't call Ally the second I found out about his mom—

But before I can breathe a word of my Oscar-winning performance, Eben lifts a hand.

"Later, please."

I nod and flick a quick, knowing look at Ally, who's currently half in, half out of the car.

Not that it matters. Because, as much as I feel for Eben—for everything his dad put him through—everyone has their weaknesses.

And my kryptonite? One-of-a-kind Christmas trinkets.

Ally and I slide out of the truck and start toward the entrance—when someone catches my hand.

I look down at our interlaced fingers, then up at Eben. His smile is weak, and he looks a little green around the gills, but he's doing it anyway.

My heart swells.

CHAPTER 26

The doors of Golding Home part the way I imagine the pearly gates would open—if I still believed in heaven. A puff of fake snow drifts down as trumpets blare overhead, welcoming each customer to a bougie North Pole wilderness of themed evergreens.

There's the classic Christmas—red, gold, and green ornaments, twinkling white lights, and glittering poinsettias. There's winter glam—a frosted fir dripping pearls, pink feathers, and gilded chandelier ornaments. And, of course, when the internet fell head-over-Instagram for grandma's blue-and-white chinoiserie, Golding Home delivered with a ginger-jar tree so elegant it could headline the holiday cover of *Traditional Home*.

Beneath each tree, wicker baskets overflow with ornate blown-glass ornaments in every color and shape. Elaborate Santa figurines ride snow-frosted sleighs pulled by Rudolph with a light-up nose. Pink champagne bottles sparkle in glitter "ice." Mini snow globes hold tiny ice skaters looping through a park.

It smells like cinnamon, pine, and the faintest hint of "you're about to max out your credit card."

I'm not much of a money girl (and the lack of zeroes in my bank account confirms it), but this place makes me want to become a millionaire just to fill a house with themed trees and obscenely sparkly ornaments. Maybe I should start playing the lottery.

And the crown jewels, the most magical touch of all—a miniature Polar Express that choo-choos around the entire store on tiny tracks embedded high above the shoppers. Every hour on the hour, a cheerful, old-timey conductor's voice crackles over the speakers: "All aboard the Polar Express!" I once told Ally I wanted one for my apartment. She looked me dead in the eyes and said I was already weird enough.

No matter how many times I come here (which, spoiler alert —is a lot), it always feels like the first time. There aren't many things that do, so I savor it.

"Mel, my fingers," Eben murmurs near my ear.

I glance down. Yikes, I'm crushing his hand.

"Oops. Sorry." I loosen my grip but don't let go.

When I look up, he's smiling at me with a softness that shakes my stomach like a snowglobe. His blue eyes catch the twinkle lights, and his smile is—dare I say it—adoring. I'm two seconds away from melting into a puddle of bliss—when a sing-song southern twang slices through the moment.

"Can I help y'all find something?"

I spin to find a bottle-blonde in her fifties—pleasantly plump, bright pink lipstick, mascara smudged into cakey concealer beneath her eyes. She's pretty, but maybe not convinced of it.

She spots Eben and her face contorts through a slideshow of emotions—first, a flash of unpleasant surprise. Then, instant horror at her first reaction. And finally, a megawatt smile so white it could outshine the snowcapped peaks of Everest.

"Oh my goodness. Eben!" she coos, a syrupy southern twang

that could say "bless your heart" and make you believe the organ had been personally sanctified.

"Hi, Mary Lou," Eben says, voice flat as a pancake.

Oh. Stepmom. Got it.

"Let me go get your father," she chirps, flashing a pageant smile and nose wrinkle flourish.

"That's not—" Eben starts, but she's already speed-walking toward the back. He sighs. "—necessary."

I try to temper my excitement, if only out of respect for the fact that Eben's relationship with his dad is fraught. But I've never met the Christmas King. And now that I know he's Eben's dad—

For fuck's sake, don't fangirl, Melody.

Ally pats Eben's shoulder, sympathetic.

"RIP to the good day you were having."

Ally peels off to lone-wolf shop. I hover at Eben's side, unsure what to do. He glances longingly at the sliding glass doors, clearly debating whether to bolt. Then his eyes sweep the store, like he's searching for a place to hide—maybe behind the life-size nutcrackers?

I squeeze his hand. His gaze finds mine, soft and vulnerable, like he's begging me to save him from the big, bad wolf.

And the man who appears is very big.

And very wolflike.

His voice booms across the store, ornaments rattling on their branches with every step.

"Look who the cat dragged in!"

Eben is tall, but this man somehow towers over him—at least six-foot-six of hulked-out muscle with a gut earned the old-fashioned way: time, beer, and zero remorse. His hair is gray-going-on-white, his beard and mustache more silver than snow.

He looks like Santa Claus—if Santa retired from pro wrestling and picked up Big & Tall modeling on the side.

Eben's mouth twitches, trying—and failing—to curl into a smile. His dad drags him into a bear hug like he's wringing twenty years of silence out of him. It wrings the life out instead. Eben goes pale as the Ghost of Christmas Past.

Then the Christmas King turns to me. He beams, showing off veneers as pristine as freshly fallen snow.

"This must be the cat."

He bows to kiss my hand. My cheeks go poinsettia red.

"Ronnie Golding," he says, straightening to full Santa-wrestler height. "The Christmas King. At your service—and forever in your debt for bringing my long-lost son back to me, just in time for my favorite holiday."

"M-Melody Whitaker," I stammer, sticking out my hand like a total idiot. "Big fan of your store, sir."

He shakes my hand and points at me with the other, already grinning like he's known me forever.

"You hear that, Ebby? She loves our Christmas store!"

He leans in, conspiratorial. "He's not being a big ol' Bah Humbug this year, is he?"

"Umm..." I glance at Eben. He isn't looking at his dad—or me. He's staring past us at a distant tree, like if he scowls hard enough, it might actually catch fire.

Ronnie's smile wobbles. For just a split second, something like regret flashes across his features. But then it's gone—buried deep beneath all that bluster and big-man jolliness. He claps a heavy hand on Eben's shoulder.

"I hope you'll stop by for Christmas this year, son."

Eben grunts.

"Bring this little sugarplum with you," Ronnie adds, winking at me. "Mary Lou over there makes four kinds of pie—at least two each."

He waves at Mary Lou, who's lingering at a safe distance, pretending to reorganize the ornament wall that already looks perfect.

"Best pie you ever tasted," he adds, patting his belly. "I gain ten pounds every Christmas. Had to buy winter pants."

Out of the corner of my eye, I notice Eben's hands ball into fists. Ronnie and I both look over. A muscle jumps in Eben's jaw.

"You used to say Mom made the best pie," Eben says, still not meeting his dad's eyes.

The air shifts. The store seems to go still, quiet, despite the music playing faintly overhead.

And then, as though the God I don't believe in has a sense of humor, the conductor's voice crackles over the loudspeaker.

"All aboard the Polar Express!"

Choo-choo.

Ronnie dips his head and sighs, pressing fists into his hips.

"Kid… that was a long time ago. Doesn't your generation do all that talk therapy? Journal it out, punch a few pillows?"

My jaw drops. Wow. How wildly dismissive—of Eben's pain, of the damage he caused. Like Eben should just get over it, so Ronnie doesn't have to face up to any of it.

No wonder things are strained between them.

Eben's lips flatten into a thin line. He gives a slight shake of his head—like he wants to say something, but can't quite bring himself to.

"It was nice meeting you, dollface," he says to me with a rueful smile, before heading back to what I'm assuming is an office. "See you on the Monday Zoom, kid."

And just like that, Ronnie is gone. Eben is still shaking his head when he mutters, "I'm gonna wait in the car."

He ducks out like the past chasing him. I watch him go, torn between going after him and giving him space.

My answer arrives with the sharp clink of an ornament shattering.

"Oh no. Oh, shoot," Mary Lou says, voice tight.

"I've got it." I hurry over. Her eyes are glassy; she dabs at the corner with her sleeve, trying to save the mascara.

"Can you grab me the broom, pumpkin?" she asks, not quite meeting my gaze. She motions behind the counter.

"Of course," I duck behind, fetch the broom and dustpan, and squat in front of her, holding the pan steady while she sweeps.

She has to stop every few sweeps to dab at her eyes.

"I'm sorry," she says softly.

"It's okay," I say. "I'm sorry about... that. About all of it."

Part of me wonders—is Eben overreacting? Ronnie seems like he loves his kid, even if Eben can't love him back. And Mary Lou clearly cares, even if he can't—or won't—see it. Yes, what Ronnie did to his mom was betrayal, but isn't there a point where you have to let go? Forgive? Let the past stay in the past and try to move forward together, even if it's messy?

I would give anything to have my family in my life—if they wanted to be there. But they don't. They haven't for a long time.

It's hard to imagine the roles reversed—to be the one who doesn't want them, the way Eben doesn't want his dad.

It hurts, even if the situations are entirely different.

Mary Lou pauses mid-sweep, watching me like she can hear the thoughts rattling around in my head.

"I can see it in your eyes," she says gently. "You think Eben's nutty as a fruitcake."

No judgment. Just understanding.

"No doubt about it—Ronnie's a charmer," she adds. "But he's not great with hard feelings. He likes to sweep things under the rug, let bygones be bygones."

She swallows. "Ebby's always been a sensitive boy. He took it real hard when Ronnie left—stayed loyal to his mom. I don't blame him for being mad at us. I really don't."

She tips the last shards into the trash and takes the dustpan from me with a sweet smile and a string of thank yous.

"Can you tell my friend when you see her that I'm in the car with Eben?"

"Of course, honey," she says, voice soft with sympathy.

I jog out to Eben's truck and climb into the passenger seat.

"Hi," I say quietly.

Eben's head rests against the headrest. He glances over and offers a weak smile. He's devastatingly handsome even when he's sad; I don't know how he does it.

"Hi," he says the word, but no sound comes out.

"Mary Lou seems nice."

"Yeah. She is, I guess." His eyes stay locked on the windshield.

"Your dad… seems like a piece of work."

He huffs a humorless laugh. "Understatement."

"Does he know your mom's…?"

"He knows," he cuts in. "Does he care? Different story."

I nod slowly, letting the silence stretch.

"I know what you're thinking," he says. "And yeah—I've done therapy. I journal. I meditate. I've read all the books about letting go and setting boundaries."

He exhales.

"But when my dad left, it was just me and my mom. She didn't have anyone else. Neither did I."

His voice tightens.

"Not long after that, she started forgetting little things. Where the bathroom was. How old I was. What year it was."

He swallows.

"One day, the police called. They found her barefoot a mile away from home, confused and scared. She went out for a walk and got lost. Couldn't remember her address."

He slumps lower in his seat, like the weight of the world is physically pressing him down.

"I was still in college, trying to figure out how to get round-the-clock care for my favorite person."

I reach for his hand.

"Your dad didn't help?"

He scoffs. "He's great when everything's easy. But in a crisis? He bails. After the incident with the police, I called him. He handed the phone straight to Mary Lou."

I squeeze his hand. He squeezes back.

"Sometimes I wonder if he saw it coming," he says. "And left before it got too hard."

I gasp. Eben shakes his head, softening.

"I don't think that was the reason. It was a few years before Mom got really bad. But I do think starting over is easier for people like him. New family. Clean slate."

"You're right about Mary Lou," he adds. "She's a good person. She always tried to include me—especially as I got older and my mom got sicker. But my half-brothers don't like me that much, and my dad..." He rolls his eyes. "He never misses a chance to make everything about him."

He rubs his thumb over my knuckles.

"Mary Lou helped me figure out Forest Park. At first, we thought it'd be temporary. Insurance covers the first hundred days. After that? You're on your own."

I blink. "You mean you pay...?"

"We drained everything from my mom's half of the divorce. To keep the house—and keep her at Forest Park—yeah, I pay."

"Out of pocket?" My eyes widen.

"About six grand a month. Goes up in January."

"Holy shit, Eben."

His laugh is dry, humorless.

"Hence why I work for my dad."

y jaw hits the floor.

"You pay all of that... by yourself?"

Considering that I can barely afford my rent—which is considerably less than six grand—I'm amazed he can still afford shampoo.

"The house is paid off, and my dad pays me almost six figures. None of his other kids work for him, so I get the nepo special."

"But... you hate the job?"

He shakes his head. "I don't, actually. I studied business. I like marketing, and I'm good at it. Working with 'the Christmas King'"—he throws up air quotes—"isn't my favorite, but he's mostly hands-off. Except when it's time for him to show up as the face of Golding Home for events and commercial shoots."

I hesitate. "I'm just surprised your dad lets you carry all that alone."

"He doesn't know," Eben says with a shrug. "And he's never asked."

I blink. "Wait—you never told your dad? Or Mary Lou? That most of your paycheck goes straight to Forest Park?"

He rolls his eyes. "Why bother? He'd probably tell me to sell the house and dump her somewhere crappy so Medicaid will cover it."

"You don't know that," I say gently. "You don't know that your dad wouldn't actually... show up for you. I'm sure Mary Lou would. She already has."

"I don't want to need him for anything," he snaps. "I'm tired of being let down all the damn time."

"You're already disappointed," I say. "What's one more letdown?"

"You don't know my dad," he mutters. "Nothing he does is out of the goodness of his heart. All good deeds come with strings attached—and a bow on top."

"Well, you're already paying the price for *not* giving him a chance," I say, folding my arms.

The air crackles between us.

The passenger door swings open, and Ally materializes, beaming, receipt in hand.

"You'll *never* guess how much they charged me for twenty-five real-feathered angel wings." She waves the receipt around like it's a Golden Ticket. "Zero. Fucking. Dollars! I told them it was for the nursing home, and they're hand-delivering our order this week."

"Wow," I say, sneaking a look at Eben. His face is unreadable.

"And guess what else?" Ally crows.

"What?" Eben says through gritted teeth, trying—and failing—not to sound annoyed.

"The Christmas King himself is making an appearance at the pageant!"

"What?" we say in unison. Eben visibly pales.

"Okay, technically his wife volunteered him," Ally amends. "But he's coming! And they're blasting it in this week's news-letter! Thousands of subscribers! Am I a PR genius or *what*?"

A little too good, Ally.

When neither of us answers, she adds, "I know I didn't *do* anything, per se, but it's the vibe I bring to the function."

She finally clocks Eben's stricken face and winces. "Sorry, man, I know things are... dicey with dear old Dad, but c'mon. What was I supposed to do—say no?"

Eben drops his forehead to the steering wheel. "My mom is going to *lose it* when she sees him."

"Relax," Ally says. "We'll suit him up in full Christmas King drag. She won't even recognize him."

I shoot her a look. She gulps.

"...I hope."

THE RIDE HOME IS QUIET, except for the classic rock station humming in the background. Led Zeppelin wails "Heartbreaker," which feels a little on the nose.

Eben doesn't say much. Neither do I.

When we pull up to my place, he barely puts the truck in park before muttering a quick "thanks" and unlocking the doors. No kiss. No hand squeeze. Not even a glance.

He waits for Ally to hop out, then peels out before I've even reached the bottom of the stairs.

There's a hollowness in my chest I didn't see coming. I know Eben has to go home eventually, but after everything—the baking, the sex, the *sharing*—it feels a little like the dreaded pump-and-dump.

I watch his truck until it's out of sight.

"Come on, let's go hang out in your apartment that smells like both cookies and sex," Ally says, marching up the steps. "We'll spray some air freshener first." When I don't immediately follow, she turns.

I meet her with big, watery eyes.

"Awwwww, babe! Melly-belly!" She pulls me into a hug.

"I think I fucked it up," I whisper. But what else is new?

"Boys are stupid—but also simple, thank *God*," she says, brushing my hair from my face. "He likes you, sweetie. A lot. He just hates his dad, and it's fucking with his head."

I sniffle, loud and snotty.

"Aww," she says—then makes a face. "Gross."

I laugh.

She grabs my wrist and tugs. "Come on, let's go raid the cum cookies you baked for the old fucks."

"We did not fuck near the food!"

"Ha! Got you to admit it."

I groan as she drags me up the stairs.

WE STEAL HALF a tray of cookies and collapse on the couch with the Hallmark Channel. Neither of us actually likes the sugary-sweet movies, but we indulge in the occasional hate-watch.

This one is called *Cowboy Claus*, about a big-city veterinarian who inherits her grandfather's reindeer farm, which doubles as a year-round Christmas-themed animal rescue.

"Mistletoe Ranch? You've gotta be kidding me." Ally bites into a frozen cookie. I swear her teeth are made of steel.

"Awwww, they're baking peppermint bark for that squirrel with anxiety."

"That's obscene," Ally says. "Everyone knows squirrels hate mint."

"I don't know, the man in the red-and-green flannel with the cowboy hat seems convinced it will help." I shrug.

When the couple tilts toward each other for Hallmark's signature almost-kiss—the painfully slow lean-in interrupted by a rogue child in reindeer pajamas—Ally hurls a cookie at the screen.

"Just bend her over already!"

"Ally!" I snatch the tray from her lap.

"Hey!"

197

"You're cut off."

She pouts. "Fine, but only if we order takeout."

I narrow my eyes. "Is Teddy coming over?"

Her expression shifts. She cocks her head to the side, too casual. "No. Why?"

I squint at her. "Since when do we hang out this much without Teddy joining us for at least one meal?"

"I'm spending time with my best friend. Is that a crime?"

"I didn't say it was a crime…" I study her. She won't meet my eyes. She's hiding something. I lean back and cross my arms. "What's with this last-minute decision to skip town for Christmas?"

She shrugs. "We just wanted to try something different this year."

"Why?"

She groans. "Ugh, can you just not be my incredibly perceptive best friend for once? Just sweep some shit under the rug!"

Ha. Got her.

"Teddy and I are going through a rough patch, okay? I just wanted to get away. Just the two of us. No Tidbit, even."

On my look, she adds: "Teddy's sister is gonna watch him."

My brows knit. "What's going on?"

"I promise I will tell you everything once we've sorted it, but for right now—can we just not talk about it?"

I nod. "Yeah, of course, Ally. For the record, you would waterboard the info out of me."

"You're not wrong," Ally says. "I'm a big hypocrite."

"As long as you're self-aware."

She rolls her eyes and opens a delivery app. "What do you want, bitch?"

We land on ramen. Forty-five minutes and roughly a million dollars later, I'm mid-bite—chopsticks poised—when my phone buzzes. My heart drops. I'm bracing for Cassie's name to light up the screen.

But it's Eben.

My stomach somersaults.

I glance at Ally. She rolls her eyes, but she's smiling. "Go talk to loverboy."

"I'll be right back."

I grab my phone and duck into my bedroom. "Hi," I say, trying not to sound too breathless.

"It occurred to me when I got home—I didn't even say goodbye."

"Oh." I laugh, awkward. "Bye?"

He chuckles. He sounds nervous, too. "I had fun this weekend."

"Me too."

"What time do you want to tackle that list tomorrow?"

My heart does another happy flip. "I get off work around five-ish?"

"It's a date," he says—and I can hear the grin. "And, Melody?"

"Mmhmm?"

"Pack a bag. Maybe a few stocking stuffers?"

I freeze for a hot second before I catch his meaning. Heat blooms low in my belly.

"Oh! Okay."

"And cancel anything that requires walking on Tuesday."

Click.

I sit down on my bed, heart racing, thighs clenched, brain buffering.

I hear Ally shout from the other room. "Do we need to go to the sex shop?"

"Shut up!"

I flop back on the mattress, grinning like a lunatic.

CHAPTER 28

*E*ben and I spend the whole week leading up to the pageant basically inseparable.

On Monday at five sharp, I jog out to his car in the shortest skirt and highest knee-highs I can excavate from the bottom of my closet, lugging an overstuffed bag of sexy goodies, toiletries, and a change of clothes. We squeeze in one Costco run for six poinsettias. We barely get them into the truck bed before his hands are all over me. We barely make the twenty-minute drive back to his place, making out at stoplights the whole way. Only one dirty look from an older woman in a Kia Sorento, so I'm counting it as discreet.

He pulls into the garage, yanks me onto his lap, pushes my panties aside, and sinks into me so deep I swear I can feel him in my ribs.

We already talked—I'm on the pill, we're both tested, neither of us is seeing anyone else—so condoms are off the agenda.

He keeps his promise: by Tuesday, I can barely walk. I work from his bed, take Zoom calls with wet hair and no pants, and spend my lunch break with Eben's head between my thighs (just until our Subway sandwiches arrive).

By Wednesday, we've finally worked enough lust out of our systems to focus on Missy's to-do list. We reserve a hot cocoa machine from a party rental shop, drop Mr. Simmons' Elvis Santa suit at the dry cleaner, and whip up the pageant program in Canva with a glittery gold template that I'm pretty sure gives Ally hives, all before our weekly check-in with Missy.

At the meeting, we break the news that only half the list is checked off. Missy gives us a look like we've personally set fire to Baby Jesus. Ally gives Missy a stern reminder that we're unpaid volunteers. That seems to shut her up.

Usually, I'd care about disappointing Missy. But with Eben's hand on my thigh under the table, inching higher and higher until I'm biting my lip to keep from climbing in his lap—I barely hear a word.

We must be more obvious than we think because Edna wheels up behind us and stage-whispers, "Twenty bucks. One hour." She points down a hallway and gives us an arthritic thumbs-up.

Eben and I trade a look, and Ally rolls her eyes. Missy is too busy spiraling over the news that *the* Christmas King is making an appearance Saturday to notice Edna trying to pimp out the supply closet.

On Thursday, I introduce Eben to my holiday lingerie collection, and I think I manage to sway him—just a little—on the whole anti-Christmas issue. He's especially fond of a red-and-green velvet "sexy elf" set I exhume from the bowels of my closet. I take a break from Mrs. Claus to be Santa's not-so-good little helper.

By Friday, the community rallies. Missy reports a flurry of festive donations: the Cherryville Elementary choir offers to perform, a nearby farm volunteers ponies in Christmas sweaters for rides out front, and the downtown bakery promises to drop off trays of cookies—freeing Eben and me for more... intimate acts of service.

A Christmas miracle, truly.

By Saturday, I'm so blissed out and sexually satisfied, I genuinely believe nothing can ruin my mood.

Cue the jingle bells of disaster.

"PLACES, PLACES, PLEASE!" Missy yells, but the nervous chatter drowns her out.

I'm anxious, standing "backstage"—which is just the medical hallway behind the main community room—wrangling the seniors for the opening number. My head splits with dance recital flashbacks, and it hits me: today I'm a dance mom for the over-eighty set. The seniors buzz like wizened bees whose hive just fell out of a tree. Everyone's looking for something: lipstick, a hairbrush, denture glue.

I bump into Edna, who's frantically rummaging through her purse (and any purse within reach).

"Lose something?"

"Just my marbles, honey."

Millie shuffles up behind her and scowls. "She can't find her scratch-offs."

"Oh." I exchange glances with Millie, who's exasperated that her friend wasn't ready for the performance at least half an hour early, like she was.

"We've got about ten minutes until showtime," I say. "Edna, why don't you go get your angel wings on, and I'll help you look for your tickets later."

"You're going to ruin all our hard work because of a gambling problem," Millie hisses. "She's trying to resell them to that big fat crowd out there."

"They're rich!" Edna snaps.

"If they're rich, they won't be buying lottery tickets you stash in your bra."

A lightbulb goes off. Edna reaches into her shirt, relieved, and pulls out a short stack of scratch-offs like a wad of Benjamins.

Millie groans. "She's a real alley cat, this one. And then wonders why her kid loves the ponies."

I watch, horrified, as Edna hikes up a leg in her chair like she's going to kick Millie in the shin. I step between them just as Missy appears with the dreaded rat-tail comb and starts fussing with their hair. They both protest like kids in a school play, and I back away like someone just pointed a gun at me.

The rising hum of collective voices from the community room catches my attention. I peek my head out the door.

What the hell?

It's standing room only. Every folding chair has a butt in it. The chatter is so loud that even Roger can hear it, and he dropped his hearing aids in Alka Seltzer last week.

Much to my delight, the first row (which Missy decided to sell at a premium rate for a "good cause") is packed with *Daddy Christmas* groupies. I hear one woman say she drove up from Florida. Florida? As if they don't have enough nursing homes to stalk down there.

Ally taps my shoulder, startling me out of my jealousy haze.

"Don't be one of those people."

I feign innocence, mostly to cover how embarrassing it is that I've gotten *this* possessive of "Daddy Christmas" in a matter of weeks.

About twenty-five residents are participating in today's pageantry—mostly those who are still fairly mobile, and not suffering from debilitating osteoporosis or severe cognitive decline. The rest sit in the reserved resident seating section along stage left. Those who know where they are are cheering on their friends. Mrs. Meyers—a tiny white-haired lady who refuses to sleep without curlers—made homemade signs from her grandkids' craft stash.

I spot Anne. Eben's mom. Sitting quietly in the crowd.

A sharp pang hits my gut. I find Eben across the room. He's nervous too, biting his nails like they've been dipped in butter.

He hovers near his mom in his Santa pants and a snug white tee that hugs his biceps—biceps that I know intimately now. He's sweating, eyes darting like he's had six shots of espresso.

He walks over to me and Ally. "Have you guys seen Ronnie yet?"

Ronnie. Wow. Even in absentia, the Christmas King can't get a "Dad" out of his firstborn son—brutal, baby.

He sees the gears turning in my brain—the way my parents would've locked me in the attic for casually calling them "Bill" or "Dianne." He lifts a brow.

"We work together. I'm used to calling my dad Ronnie."

"Makes sense," I say, cooler than intended.

He doesn't meet my eyes. Ally shoots me a stay-out-of-it look. It should be easy to keep my mouth shut—Ally's the meddling, opinionated one, not me—but I'm struggling. Other than Christmas, family stuff is my only hot-button issue. But this isn't my family, and Eben doesn't need a lecture on complicated fathers.

Not my circus. Not my monkeys.

I clear my throat. "No. Nobody's seen him. Missy was asking twenty minutes ago."

We're minutes from curtain, and I need my elderly angels winged-up and ready. The crowd already sounds rowdy and impatient, so we'd better start on time.

I peek through the doors again. The TikTok fans wave "Santa Baby" signs, and at least two women rock red bras with white fur trim—full SantaCon energy (aka see you on the evening news) at a family-friendly nursing home pageant. I'm a little shocked Missy let them in, but I guess she'll take anyone's money *for a good cause.*

Hey, at least they're giving the blue hairs something to talk about. I spot Roger ogling. I guess charity comes in all shapes, colors, and cup sizes.

"I'm just hoping my mom doesn't recognize him," Eben murmurs.

"How likely is that?"

He swallows. "Not very."

"What's the worst that could happen?" I ask. There's that familiar tug of guilt.

"Her nurse gave her a Lorazepam an hour ago," he says.

"And all Santa Clauses look alike."

He smirks. "No, we don't."

"Okay, fine. You Goldings are a special breed of Santa."

My gaze drifts over his Santa-clad torso, and his eyes darken as he takes me in just as hungrily. I've swapped my Mrs. Claus getup for something more formal: a long burgundy velvet dress with a high slit and a sweetheart neckline. It hugs all my curves in all the right places. Eben's family plight momentarily forgotten, as his hand finds my waist and tugs me flush against him. His icy-blue eyes melt into mine.

He ducks his head to my ear and whispers, "You look good enough to eat."

My lips part, my thighs clench, my hand skims up his chest, lingering on hard muscle beneath thin cotton—

—and that's when Missy *rudely* claps a clipboard right between us.

"What are you two doing? Where are my angels? Showtime is in five minutes!" she barks, giving me a flashback to my chain-smoking ballet teacher from third grade. If she says *pas de chat* with a hard H and accidentally spits on me, we might throw hands.

"The angels are in hell," Eben murmurs as Missy drags me away.

CHAPTER 29

*F*astening twenty-five sets of angel wings to the eighty-and-up crowd is about as easy as walking twenty-five kittens on leashes.

"Stand still!" I hear Ally yelling across the hall—volume ten being the only decibel range that registers around here.

As for me, I've pricked myself so many times with "safety" pins that it should qualify as a blood donation.

The crowd beyond the curtain is getting unruly—whooping it up for Daddy Christmas and, let's be honest, the kind of wholesome, thirst-driven philanthropy that looks *so* good on social media. You know, "the brand-sponsorship" kind of wholesome.

After Eben's viral moment, Missy tripled ticket prices and added a VIP tier: a photo with Daddy Christmas, plus a surprise appearance by the Christmas King himself (assuming he shows), and a 25% off coupon for Golding Home. I've already slipped at least ten of those into my purse.

Now the crowd—who've paid a premium for what is, essentially, a sixth-grade talent show, but for senior citizens—is buzzing like they're waiting for Gaga. Or Mariah, who, famously, keeps everyone waiting.

Missy rushes up behind me, scaring the shit out of me and causing me to stab my finger for what feels like the 450th time. I'm finishing the wings on Roger and Richard, both in fluffy bathrobes. We didn't have the budget for choir gowns, so Missy put everyone in mismatched white bathrobes. Angel wings and terrycloth—heaven meets Bed, Bath & Beyond. Thankfully, everyone was instructed to keep their clothes on underneath.

"Is everyone finally ready?" Missy huffs. "We're almost out of Coors Light."

Oh, right. We're selling beers for eight bucks a pop.

"You're all set," I tell Richard, patting his head—the former attorney scowls.

"Getting old is humiliating. Don't do it."

"Duly noted."

Ally appears beside me. "Okay, boss, I think we're good to go."

I glance at our seniors—winged, robed, radiant. Missy flashes a sociopathic grin.

"All right, it's showtime. "

ALLY and I file the seniors onto the "stage," which is just a curtain strung across some rafters. I don't love the setup—the residents aren't exactly steady on their feet—but Missy swears these were the lowest risers available that still allowed the audience to see the performers' faces.

It looks like a Netflix documentary waiting to happen.

We wheel Edna and the other motorized angels into the front row.

"All right," I whisper to Edna as I park her dead center. "You're the star of the show."

"Don't I know it," she smirks.

From the wings, I catch the tail end of Missy's emcee speech. She's thanking the local high school marching band for accompanying Betty Jo on piano. At seventy-two, Betty Jo's one of our younger residents—and a former music teacher. She waves at the teens like they're her prodigal students.

"And without further ado," Missy announces, dragging out the suspense, "may I present the Forest Park Assisted Living Christmas Angels!"

Cue thunderous applause. The curtain rises—literally, thanks to two janitors yanking ropes—and Betty Jo pounds out the opening notes. The tune sounds familiar, though I can't place it.

Then—

"GRANDMA GOT RUN OVER BY A REINDEER!"

Oh. My. God.

It's a collective, wheezy, tone-deaf shout. The audience gasps —then erupts into laughter and cheers. Flashes go off like it's a Rolling Stones concert. The seniors are bopping so hard I'm genuinely worried for their knees, but they are *thriving* up there —scream-singing louder with every verse, high on the crowd's reaction.

Missy is off to the side, clapping and singing along like a proud, unhinged stage mom. The musical lineup was all Missy and Betty Jo's idea—and I have to admit, their sense of humor is elite chaos.

Edna winks at a twenty-year-old influencer in the front row and mouths "call me" with her thumb up to her ear. Others attempt shuffly hokey-pokey dance moves—which make me nervous, considering these risers are basically death traps.

Ally catches my worried look and whispers, "Listen, it'd be better than going out on the toilet."

I whip my head toward her. "What?!"

She shrugs. "That's how a lot of people go, you know. On the john."

I roll my eyes and try not to laugh.

The musical numbers keep coming. The crowd roars when Roger nails a surprisingly animated hearing-aid gag during *Do You Hear What I Hear?*

"What?" he yells, cupping his ear.

The group sings again: "Do you hear when I hear?"

"Huh? Who said that?"

The audience loses it.

Missy beams and mouths, *That was his idea.*

But just as the final line—"Listen to what I say..."—echoes across the room, a shriek slices through the crowd.

"Dad! Cover up!"

We whip around. Somehow, in the one minute we looked away, Harold—one of the quiet seniors who wasn't even supposed to perform (primarily due to a sciatica flare-up)—has found a way to loosen both his joints *and* his robe.

And he's giving the VIP crowd a full-frontal show.

Judging by the dance moves, I'm not entirely sure it's accidental.

"Damn it, Harold. We can't have anything nice," Missy mutters, then screams, "CURTAIN! CURTAIN!!"

Of course, because the curtain has to be pulled by hand, Harold collects a few tips (no pun intended) before we can get the curtain—and his robe—to close.

Ally and I sprint toward him, but Harold's son vaults over rows of folding chairs like an Olympic hurdler and beats us there.

Every phone in the place is recording. Some people are waving dollar bills. Parents are covering kids' eyes and shoving cookies in their hands. Harold's son yanks the robe shut and throws up a hand to block the cameras.

"Come on, guys, he's eighty-two," he shouts.

Someone yells, "I'd still do him!"

Harold squints into the crowd, cupping a hand over his eyes. "Hey—who said that?"

Ally and I exchange a look.

It's going to be a long fucking talent show.

BY THE TIME Roger takes the stage to demonstrate a sourdough starter, the crowd has mellowed—and his presentation hits like a handful of sleeping pills chased with vodka. He's nervous, but a few TikTokers in the front row are genuinely into it. After he pets the dough for the 456th time, one of them tells him to start a cooking channel—and I don't think I've seen Roger smile that wide since his roommate finally kicked it and his double became a single.

Backstage, Eben cranes his neck, sweating bullets. The Christmas King *still* hadn't arrived, and I'm pretty sure Eben would sell his left nut to keep it that way.

Only five acts left: Maude's baton twirling, Millie's card tricks, and Edna, who refuses to tell us what dance she's going to do. Usually, that's a disqualifier, but when your talent pool is closer to playing poker with God than booking gigs on Earth… you let a few things slide.

Lazy clapping signals the end of Roger's sourdough siesta. Missy guides him offstage, brushing past me to hiss: "Where the hell is he?"

I shrug. "He'll be here." I check my watch and instantly doubt myself.

When we first told Missy the Christmas King would make an appearance, she was skeptical. Ronnie Golding brings equal parts charm and ego, and she wasn't convinced that having an egomaniac Santa in the program was good for *her* show (oh, the irony). She didn't want him stealing the spotlight from her seniors—or her. But then Golding Home offered to sponsor cash prizes, and ticket sales tripled with the combined star power of the Christmas King and his newly TikTok-famous son. It was an offer that jingled all the way to the bank.

A loud whoosh jostles me out of my daydream—followed by gasps, then startled applause.

I look up.

Flames shoot from each end of a silver-and-gold baton, held skyward by Maude. She's rocking an aggressively sequined leotard—cut low in the front, Jane Fonda high in the back—over shiny compression tights. Gotta keep circulation flowing, obviously.

Even the Floridians gasp. Maude doesn't flinch.

"This little firecracker won me the Miss Pear Blossom Pageant, 1959—in Boise!" she crows, fingers edging dangerously close to the flaming death stick.

Every eye is glued to the fire. Every pair of lungs holds its breath.

Forest Park residents aren't allowed so much as a tealight in their rooms. And here we are, tossing a literal torch around a room full of oxygen tanks. Super.

Maude hurls the baton high in the air. The audience holds its collective breath behind raised phones and half-covered faces. I inhale sharply—I know exactly how much Aqua Net we shellacked into Maude's platinum tower—a literal stairway to heaven.

Somehow, while the firestick is still airborne, Maude executes a full figure-eight spin with her 16-month-old hip replacement—then snatches it out of the sky in a blaze of glory.

The crowd goes wild.

I whirl to share a WTF look with Eben, but he's checked out. At this point, Maude could set him on fire, and he wouldn't notice.

Honestly, she seems hell-bent on setting *someone* on fire.

211

"Long live Miss Pear Blossom!" yells a curly-haired twenty-something in the front row—cute, in that 1850s Irish peasant way. Maude has a thing for hot gingers of all ages.

Missy and I lock eyes and lunge. Too late. Maude whips the flaming baton straight at Gingy. He shrieks and vaults back; the torch narrowly misses his waistband.

A whole new meaning to fire-crotch.

The baton hits the floor with a *forged-to-destroy-Hitler-not-softbois* thud. Maude is unimpressed. "What's wrong, kid? Can't handle a hot older woman?"

The crowd roars. They adore her.

Ally shakes her head in awe. "God, to have that kind of confidence."

Missy attempts to usher her offstage.

Maude grins. "Guess I'm too hot to handle for the Hot-Flash Honeys too."

Missy turns four shades of red. "Where's a cane with a hook when you need it?" she mutters. Missy steps up to the mic: "Let's hear it for *Miss Pear Blossom 1959!*"

Wild applause. Maude beams and bows as deep as her hips allow. She's got an encore in her, but Missy gently takes her arm to coax her offstage. Maude yanks free and spits: *"Hands off the fit."*

The room loses it. Poor Missy. This job is barely worth the bottom half of the $65K–$85K pay scale.

A few more acts fly by, and somehow the audience isn't bored—they're hooked. Our seniors aren't just old; they're vibrant, raunchy, hilarious, seasoned performers. It's an R-rated holiday spectacular (a few parents have already taken their kids outside).

We're down to the final act before Eben and his dad go on, and there's still no sign of the Christmas King. I'm pretty sure Missy and Eben are praying in opposite directions, like two lanes of highway traffic at night. And honestly? I don't know whose prayer is more likely to be answered.

The lights dim. A hush falls over the room. I check the clipboard—the Silver Belles are up.

A disco ball descends. (When did someone install *that*?) The projector flickers to life with a familiar movie scene. The music starts and—oh my God.

Edna's aide wheels her onstage. She's in a tight red Santa skirt, cleavage pushed to the North Pole. Three ladies sashay behind her in mini Santa dresses with fur trim. Compared to their "Santa Slut" lineup, my Mrs. Claus outfit looks Amish.

Barbara—platinum from a box—strokes her mic suggestively, and I realize we're closing on the GILF edition of *Mean Girls'* "Jingle Bell Rock."

Betty Jo hits the piano, and every Millennial in the audience lets out a delighted squeal. Edna's aide helps her to her feet. I brace myself for her to go ass-up and face-down, but no. She's steady. Standing, not dancing. Progress.

Barbara hands her the mic. Edna coos as the ladies roll their hips, nailing the *Mean Girls* choreography beat for beat.

I guess the new hips really *do* outperform the originals.

Ally and I can't help but dance along—this was *our* song. Our movie.

"Get it, Grandma!" a tipsy dude yells. I'm ready to hunt him down when Edna turns (with some assistance), spanks her own ass, and gives it a shimmy. She spots Millie offstage, sticks out her tongue, and smacks herself again.

"Told ya I could dance, bitch!"

"Yeah, but you're still broke!" Millie fires back. These two have been best friends for decades, and it shows.

They finish with a final roll of their slutty (artificial) hips. The audience stays on its feet for three straight minutes—whistling, cheering, hooting, and hollering. A Santa hat goes flying.

As the applause ebbs, a hush falls. Eben's gaze flicks to a single ornament trembling on a tree—like water rippling before the T. rex appears. Stillness thickens. Anticipation hangs heavy.

Then, like thunder rolling, a deep, booming voice cuts through the silence.

The Christmas King has arrived.

CHAPTER 30

*R*onnie towers onstage like Christmas King Kong, looking like he just benched 400 pounds just for fun on the way over. He plants a big, flirty kiss on Edna's cheek, and she practically swoons back into her wheelchair.

"Hiya, sweetheart," he purrs.

She giggles like a schoolgirl.

"I heard y'all were ready for Santa Claus," his voice ricochets.

The room explodes. Women and influencers scream like it's Timberlake circa 2001. You'd think we were on the Vegas strip —not across the street from a strip mall in Cherryville, Ohio.

If there's one thing Ronnie Golding knows, it's how to work a crowd. He waves, flashes those unnaturally perfect teeth, and within seconds, he owns the room.

Ronnie's eyes are a darker, harder blue than his son's. Eben has his mom's eyes—a soft, ethereal blue. His dad's are just... cold. Calculating.

But this crowd didn't come for warmth.

"Have you all been *goooooood* this year?" he drawls, stretching *good* like he's about to rip off his red velvet pants. (To be fair, they're already bursting at the seams—he wears them tight, leaving little to the imagination.)

The crowd shrieks in a chorus of yeses, and a slow smile spreads across his face. He's got them in the palm of his hand.

"I'm always good for you, Santa Baby!" someone slurs, her third Chardonnay talking.

Somewhere, Eben is having a coronary.

"Now I heard some of you met my son this year..."

Wolf whistles.

"Some of you saw him right here at the Cherry Bowl, taking pictures for a good cause, with Mrs. Claus by his side." He looks directly at me and waves.

My face turns cherry red. I scan for Eben—he's vanished.

The spotlight finds me.

Ronnie Golding and I couldn't be more different. While he lives for his small-pond, big-fish moments, I'd rather be a fish choking on air than be the center of attention.

Luckily, he doesn't share the spotlight for long. He's already eyeing one of the ho-ho-hos in the front row. The second marriage might not be the charm for Ronnie Golding.

I shudder.

"And some of you," he continues, squeezing suspense like he's auditioning for *The Bachelor*, "came from other states to meet—what do you all call him?"

The audience shouts it.

"Oh, that's right." His smile is for all the wrong reasons. "Daddy Christmas."

The room detonates. My blood boils.

Ally elbows me, balancing a plate of Christmas-themed snacks. "Change the record."

I grit my teeth. "Those are for the guests," I hiss, glaring at her plate.

"If I'm not getting paid, I *am* a guest." She pops a red-and-green Oreo.

Catcalls spike as the spotlight swings to the curtain.

"May I present... my protégé, my son, my *heir*—Daddy Eben Golding Christmas."

The room erupts like it's ancient Rome, and the crowd's about to watch a public mauling.

The look on Eben's face drains the blood from mine.

He walks onstage like an Anne Boleyn reenactment I once saw in a documentary—like he's about to meet his executioner. If I notice, no one else does. The second he steps beside Ronnie, the crowd combusts.

Daddy Christmas has arrived—and this is what they paid for.

What exactly they're *expecting*, I'm not sure. But judging by the panic in Eben's eyes, it'll be a surprise to *everyone*.

If it involves lap-sitting and whispering naughty requests, I'm going to need medical attention. Luckily, we're in the right building for that.

Ronnie throws a thick arm around him and utters the four fatal words:

"Like father, like son."

A single shriek pierces the air—frail but mighty, furious and heartbroken, all at once. The room stills. The sound hangs like a curse.

Apparently, the Christmas King knows that shriek.

His face pales like the ghost I fear he's about to become.

"No. He's. Not."

Three words. Sharp enough to restart time.

Anne Golding is on her feet. And by the look in her eyes, she's having one of her rare lucid moments.

Carrie-level lucid.

And for once—just a heartbeat—I swear, Ronnie looks guilty. Like maybe, deep down, he knows he deserves what's coming.

"My son. *My* son—do you hear me, you bastard—is nothing

like your motherfucking, lying, cheating, family-abandoning ass."

This. This is what Eben was afraid of.

And what Ronnie chose to ignore.

Until now.

Phones are everywhere. Flashes strobing. Recordings rolling.

Eben jumps off the stage toward his mom.

Ally nudges me. "Holy shit, we're going viral."

I elbow her.

But Anne doesn't want comfort. She wants revenge.

Her grief, her rage, her decades of unprocessed trauma snap her into complete clarity—free her, even momentarily, from the Alzheimer's prison she's been trapped in. For the moment, her mind is razor sharp.

"Mom," Eben whispers, rubbing her back. "Why don't you calm down?"

Ally pops another cookie into her mouth like it's popcorn. "Uh-oh. He said the magic words."

I elbow her harder, but even I can't help but wince.

I know he's desperate. I know he knows better. But you can't tell a woman—or any person, young or old—to calm down and expect peace. That's how you end up with your tires slashed and your soul rearranged.

The room is dead silent, aside from the soft clicks of phones.

In the age of TikTok and Instagram, this is primo content.

Anne stiffens, shrugs off her son's hands.

"No, Eben."

I gasp. Eben's mom remembers his name.

"I will *not* calm down. This is between me and your father. Go sit down."

Somewhere, someone whispers, "Oh shit."

Anne steps toward the stage. Not frail. Not right now. Every step is a reckoning. The crowd parts for her instinctively, like the Red Sea—it's almost Biblical.

A collective understanding settles in the air: a narcissist is about to get a long-overdue can of whoop-ass.

And naturally, phones stay up. If there's anything the internet loves, it's a narcissist getting called out on camera.

Ronnie swallows hard. And then lets out a shaky, forced laugh.

"Well, folks, it's time to introduce you to the *first* Mrs. Claus."

SMACK.

Anne's slap rings through the room—turns out faux beards don't protect against angry ex-wives. A gasp ripples across the audience.

I glance at Eben. His head is in his hands. He's clearly mortified, but looking around the room, he's not alone. It's as if all 200 of us were just zapped back to childhood, watching our parents fight in public.

I want to reach him, but the crowd is too dense, and barging through would only make this a bigger spectacle.

Ronnie touches his cheek. Not angry—just sad.

"I deserved that."

"You deserve so much more. Cheating on your wife for years, and then leaving her and your only son on Christmas Day."

Another collective gasp.

Anne faces the crowd. "Yeah. On Christmas. How do you like them fuckin' apples?"

My chest cracks open for Eben as a kid—abandoned by his father on what used to be his favorite holiday—while Ronnie parades around as the egomaniacal "Christmas King" for the whole town and his new side piece. My heart breaks for that little boy, and the words are out before I can stop them:

"And he leaves his son to pay the nursing home bills alone!"

I clap a hand over my mouth.

A hush sweeps the room. Eben's eyes snap to mine, flashing anger, hurt, betrayal—then ice. I mouth *I'm sorry*, but he looks away.

I'm going to barf.

Ronnie's face crumples in confusion. He clearly had no idea. He turns to Eben. I see someone zooming in on their phone. "Is that true?"

Eben blinks. Says nothing.

Anne's quiet now, too—her lucidity narrowing—but a mother's instincts don't fade. She knows that something is profoundly wrong, and her son is paying the price.

"Answer me," Ronnie booms. The sound rattles the room. We've all been grounded—collectively fifteen again.

That alpha-male bark is the match to Eben's fuse. His dad talking down to him like he's still a child—right here, in front of strangers and the goddamn internet—is too much.

Even across the room, when he steps forward, the floor seems to shift. Someone behind me mutters, "fuuuuuck," so I know I'm not the only one who feels it.

"I don't have to answer you," Eben growls. "In fact, it'd be better for you if I ignored you—but since you're demanding an answer? I've got one."

Ronnie arches a brow, but his shoulders sag, his confidence collapsing like a snowman in a heat wave.

"Someone had to step up. God knows it was never going to be you."

A ripple of approval moves through the crowd. Nothing the internet loves more than toxic masculinity falling flat on its impotent ass.

Ronnie opens his mouth, then shuts it when he sees Eben's isn't finished. He sneers at a too-close phone, "Can you turn that shit off?"

The influencer smirks. "Not a chance in hell."

Eben puffs his chest, fists balled tight. "If you left us then—

when things were good, when Mom was good—why the hell would I trust you to show up now?"

Now they're nose to nose—two Santa Clauses, squared off like rival silverbacks in a late-night nature doc.

Ronnie suddenly looks smaller than his son. The big red suit deflates.

"Can we talk about this..." He glances at the crowd. "Offline?"

Eben snorts. "I have nothing else to say to you."

He pivots to Anne, tears diamonding her lashes.

"Come on, Mom. Let's get you back to your room." He reaches for her hand, but she pulls away.

Missy slips in. "I've got her. Why don't you go get some air?"

Eben's eyes flick to me—blue ice—furious I aired private family business.

It's my turn to shrink.

"Sure. Thanks." His voice is void of emotion.

"Eben!" I call, desperate. He won't look at me. He won't look at anyone—he beelines for the exit.

The show's over.

The community room doors swing open, and I push through the stunned crowd after him. The women who came hoping to see Daddy Christmas shake his bells are too shocked to be disappointed.

I keep my eyes on Eben, weaving through the appalled audience, and slip out—just before the first cookie hits the Christmas King.

CHAPTER 31

"*E*ben! Eben!"
I call for him up and down the hallway—but the only voice that answers is my own echo, ricocheting with remorse. God, how could I be so fucking stupid? Ally's right. This situation was never any of my business. I should have stayed the hell out of it.

But noooooo, I had to go and open my big dumb mouth.

The worst part is, I know better. I grew up in a freaking cult. My whole life, I've been an iron fortress. I understand the importance of keeping other people's secrets confidential. I know how dangerous it is when someone you trust doesn't. It's not like me—meddling in another family's mess. I just like him so much, and I hate to see him suffer.

By the time I made it out of the community room, the crowd had revolted against the Christmas King. When I last saw him, he was spinning on one boot, taking cover from the barrage of Christmas-themed projectiles—cookies, candy canes, and a... jingly elf slipper? The front rows of influencers didn't get the heartwarming spectacle they came for, but they definitely got a spectacle.

Vaulting over the last folding chair, I caught sight of a few of them already swarming Anne—phones up like it was breaking news and not the messy fallout of a small-town pageant gone off the rails.

I would have jumped in, but Missy was already bulldozing through, swatting phones and steering Anne toward the exit like a bodyguard escorting a pop star offstage.

"Eben? Please. I'm sorry. Where are you?" I call again, softer, down the next corridor. And the next.

At last, I find him.

He's on the edge of his mom's narrow bed, tall frame folded in on itself like he's trying to disappear. My heart catapults to my throat. He looks up at me but says nothing.

I step into the room—and realize I've never actually been inside. It's humble, barely big enough for one person. On the wall opposite the bed hang photos of Anne and Eben from every stage of his life—T-ball, a trip to Disney World, homecoming, college graduation.

They're not there to cozy up the room. There's something precise about them, something almost utilitarian, like anchors. Like a lifeline lassoing in the parts of her life she's desperately trying not to lose—even as her disease violently claims more of it, piece by piece.

I hover in the doorway, heavy with shame. "Eben. I'm so sorry."

Only the HVAC hum answers.

I pace, sweating. "I care about you so much. Hearing what your dad did to you and your mom—out loud—while he stood there looking like a pompous ass? I lost it. I know I shouldn't have opened my big, stupid mouth, but it just came out. The injustice of it. I didn't mean to—"

A sob catches in my throat. Tears blur my vision. I almost miss the tiny gesture: he pats the space beside him on the bed.

"I know," he says, barely audible.

My heart drops as I sink onto the mattress beside him. Our thighs touch. He turns his palm up, and I lace my fingers through his. I squeeze. I don't breathe until he squeezes back.

After a long silence, he says, "He had that coming."

"Yeah." We sit in the stretch of quiet.

"Families are… complicated," I offer. It's the only thing I feel qualified to say. I can't stop replaying Ronnie's face—the shock when he realized that Eben had been paying the bills alone. The Christmas King might be emotionally stunted, but in that moment, he looked like a father. A father who cared, who didn't know his son was carrying this burden alone.

The pain radiates from Eben in waves. The adrenaline hasn't worn off, and I can feel it in his pulse, in the way his grip tightens and loosens. I squeeze his hand harder, trying to calm us both.

"Ouch," he says with a weak smile.

"Sorry. Just thinking."

A shadow crosses his face. He knows what I'm thinking—and hopes I'll keep it to myself.

If Ally were here, she'd kick me. Beg me to shut up, especially after what just happened. But I've been through too much to stay quiet. And anyway, turns out I can't.

Eben watches my face, bracing.

"I think you should give your dad a chance to make it right," I whisper—so soft I barely hear the words myself.

His hand goes slack. He inches away. "Melody—"

"No, listen. You shouldn't have to pay for this alone. Your dad clearly didn't know. Did you see his face—"

"You mean when you humiliated me in front of strangers and the entire internet? Yeah, I saw it."

Okay. That stings.

"He really didn't know, Eben—"

He shoots to his feet. "He didn't know because he doesn't

care. Mom and I didn't need him then—and we sure as shit don't need him now."

The tension in his voice coils like a cobra.

I stand too, heat rising for no good reason. "Yes, you do, Eben. You do need him."

"Melody, you don't know what I need. This isn't your family. Not your problem." He exhales, clipped. "And after you blew my confidence—slip-up or not—the least you can do is butt out."

My face burns. Eben has no idea how lucky he is—sure, Ronnie is a mess and nowhere near Dad of the Decade, but at least he wants to talk. At least there's a chance.

"Your dad is out there right now wanting to talk to you. Do you know how lucky you are? Did you even see the look on his face? He looked wrecked—"

Eben's expression empties. He looks past me like I'm a stranger.

"No, I didn't notice the sad look on Ronnie Golding's face. Maybe he was embarrassed. Maybe he felt nothing. I didn't see any phantom expressions, because they don't exist." His eyes cut to mine. "Instead of projecting some fantasy onto my family, maybe try fixing your own."

The words land like a slap. My eyes sting.

"You know I can't do that."

"And neither can I."

I inhale. I should let it go. Why can't I let it go?

"Okay, but maybe—on Christmas—we could stop by. Just for a minute—"

His hands curl into fists. His jaw locks. He's not looking at me anymore.

"I'm not going there on Christmas. Not now. Not ever."

I step back. "Okay. We don't have to. We can do something totally different."

He blinks at me. Stone silent.

"You already know I don't do Christmas."

I shake my head, confused. "But that was before... this." I gesture between us.

"This," he echoes, same gesture, "doesn't change how I feel about Christmas. Or who I am."

It's a dagger to my heart. I don't know why I thought he might see things differently now.

I swallow the lump in my throat. "So... you're not going to see me on Christmas?"

My voice comes out high and tight—like a deflating balloon. I sound like a mouse. A tiny, pathetic mouse begging for a scrap of cheese. Only in this case, the cheese is love. Love I can't seem to get from anyone—not from Eben, not from my family. Even Ally made other plans this year that don't include me.

"I didn't say I wouldn't see you," he replies. "I just—I don't do Christmas. I can't." He looks away. "I told you that."

"What are you going to do instead?" I ask, starting to spiral.

He keeps his eyes on the floor. "Same thing I do every year. Visit Mom. Get a rotisserie chicken. Watch football."

Indignation lights me up like a match. "You're going to spend Christmas with a *cooked chicken* instead of me?"

A long beat. When Eben finally looks up, his eyes are full of regret.

Oh my God. That's a yes.

Before the tears fall, before I say something else I'll regret—I bolt.

"Melody, wait—"

I don't look back.

I just run.

Out the door.

Down the hall.

I don't stop until I'm in my car.

. . .

AT HOME, I tear off my pageant dress like it's on fire. I crawl into bed in just my underwear, unable to stomach putting on Christmas pajamas—but too drained to wear anything else.

My phone buzzes and buzzes. I ignore Ally, ignore Eben, ignore unknown numbers. I'm finally facing the reality I've been dreading: I'm spending Christmas alone.

I just want to rot.

At some point, I fall asleep. Or dissociate. I think I hear a knock—soft, tentative—but my doorbell's been broken for years, so ignoring visitors is easy.

Eventually, my phone dies. Just like that, all contact with the outside world is severed.

Time goes fuzzy. I drift in and out of half-sleep for what feels like twelve hours. I lie in my bed like a corpse, heavy, motionless. Unable to feel anything but the weight of being utterly alone on Christmas.

Where did it all go wrong?

I know I should have minded my business, but it's not like Eben was planning on spending Christmas with me anyway. Ever since my family cut ties, there's been a bone-deep chill. A hollow where there was once community. A longing for something I lost—something I could only keep if I abandoned myself.

I've spent six years grieving the family that I could only have by being "perfect." Or at least, their version of it.

And now the old ache rolls over me in waves.

Something about this thing with Eben made me feel less alone. Less empty. Maybe that was an illusion—because even he doesn't care enough to embrace this one, simple joy. He won't let go of old wounds long enough to try something new—with me.

Or maybe it's me. Maybe I'm the one being obtuse about the whole Christmas thing. Maybe I should've let it go, shared the rotisserie chicken. Watched the football game. Sat beside the man I'm falling for and called it a successful holiday—because at least I wasn't alone.

But isn't that just the flip side of the same coin?

Betraying who I am just to keep someone else happy?

Morning light slips through the window. My eyes are crusted with sleep and dried tears. I didn't wash my face, so now my pillows are stained with mascara and regret.

I glance at the clock on my nightstand.

8:30 a.m.

December 24th.

Fucking Christmas Eve.

CHAPTER 32

CHRISTMAS EVE

I groan and roll out of bed, pop a few Motrin, and drag my ass to the shower. My body aches. My legs feel like they weigh a hundred pounds each.

The shower is surprisingly rejuvenating. I stand under the hot water until the steam turns the bathroom into a sauna—until my skin is practically burning. Until I feel—if not better, then at least clean.

When I finally get out, I wrap myself in a towel and shuffle back to my room. I sit down in front of my closet and sigh.

What does one wear for *Depressed Girl Christmas*?

Or maybe *Grieving Girl Christmas*—that one has some nice alliteration.

A Very Heartbroken Holiday.

You know what? Screw this D-list Hallmark movie. I might be alone, but that doesn't mean I have to be lonely. Christmas doesn't need fixing—I do. And I can make the best of this holiday, with or without a family, a best friend, or a man.

Besides, my sexy holiday drawer has never made me cry. Or feel unwanted.

I dig out my favorite holiday dress—a short satin slip with a cowl neck in holly-berry red. I shrug into it, slide on sheer black tights, and toe into my patent heels like I'm about to crash a Christmas party and take my heartbreak out on someone else's face under the mistletoe.

I give myself a blowout. Reapply makeup. Stare down my reflection like we're about to go to war.

In the kitchen, I wait for my phone to recharge just enough to order a huge holiday feast—tipping the shopper extra because it's Christmas-fucking-Eve.

It takes two hours, and when the groceries finally arrive, I discover that half of my order has been refunded. That's what I get for waiting until the last minute. I drag the bags inside and hoist the turkey onto the counter. I ordered a small one, but apparently everyone's spending Christmas alone—because all they had left was a twenty-pound bird.

Dear God.

I've never cooked a turkey before, but there's a first time for everything.

I panic-google and commit to the cold-water thaw. It's an excruciating process: ten hours of dunking and changing the water every thirty minutes. I forget about half the swaps, which I consider a win.

I make boxed stuffing with pantry scraps and mashed potatoes with margarine and 2% milk—because, of course, they were out of butter. The whole thing feels like a test I forgot to study for.

It's something like 5 p.m. before I give up on the thawing and decide it's time to season the turkey. A few sad shakes of salt, pepper, maybe paprika? I don't know. I'm guessing. Hoping. Praying. Doing the sign of the cross, even though I'm not Catholic (my grandmother was, so it counts, right?).

I wrestle the bird into the oven and set the time for five

hours, checking every twenty minutes like I'm waiting for it to start singing carols with me. Five hours turn to six. Then seven.

When I finally take it out and try to carve it, the damn thing is still raw.

I stare at it for a long moment before having a good, ugly cry. I hiccup, grab my phone, and dial up my favorite Chinese takeout. Thank God someone answers. I order nearly everything on the menu.

If I'm going to spend Christmas Eve alone, in my favorite party dress, with a ruined turkey and a heartbreak hangover, I might as well have fried rice.

I plop onto the couch in full formalwear and flip through channels until I land on the claymation *Rudolph*—the one I've probably watched dozens of times over the last six years.

It's mid-scene, right in the middle of "We're a Couple of Misfits." They're singing about how I feel exactly—*Why am I such a misfit? I'm not just a nitwit*—and usually that song would make me smile.

Tonight, it hits too close.

Because Rudolph the red-nosed reject and Hermey the elf who just wants to be a dentist? At least they have each other.

I keep flipping.

Eventually, I stop on the local news. There's an active crime scene at a bar across town. I kick off my heels and settle in.

It shouldn't make me feel better to know that someone out there is probably having an even worse Christmas than I am— but it does. Not a good look, I know. But right now, anything that dulls the ache of despair is a welcome distraction.

"Oh, wow," I mutter at the TV as the anchor cuts to a high-speed chase barreling down I-75. I lean forward, fully invested in the chaos.

A knock at the door interrupts my doomwatching.

Yay, food. That was fast—thank God, because I'm starving and emotionally unstable.

I drag myself to the door, undo the deadbolt, and open it with the joy of a woman greeting dumplings and spring rolls.

But it's not dumplings.

Before my brain can process, I slam the door shut again.

There's a pause. Then a muffled voice through the wood: "Melody, please. Open up. I need to talk to you."

I freeze.

It's too late to pretend I'm not home. She knows. And if I know her at all, she'll camp out in the hallway until I let her in. She was always the most stubborn of all of us.

I let out a long, exhausted sigh and crack the door open just enough to see her face.

"What do you want, Cassie?"

"I like your wreath," she says.

I slam the door shut again, heart pounding.

The wreath.

I forgot about the fucking wreath. Forgot she saw it—along with the string lights, the poinsettias, the cartwheeling Santa on my stupid doormat.

Then it hits me.

What did she just say?

I crack the door again. "What?"

"I said I like your wreath."

I swing it open wider, breathless, on the verge of a menty b —but what else is new? My brows knit in confusion. Is she mocking me? Pointing it out to shame me? But no—she's standing there, eyes glassy, lips trembling. Her hazel eyes—so much like mine—are wide and hopeful.

"Cassie," I whisper, voice catching. "What did you fucking say to me?"

She tucks a piece of her short, fluffy auburn hair behind her ear. Her hands shake. Tears spill over—hers and mine.

Still, I wait. I need to hear it again.

She draws a shaky breath. "I like—no. You know what?" Her voice cracks. "I fucking *love* your Christmas wreath, Melody."

And that's it.

I throw my arms around her.

CHAPTER 33

CHRISTMAS EVE

EBEN

I'm just a man and his rotisserie chicken.
On the couch. With a fork. A beer. College football on TV.

I don't even know who's playing. Don't care. I squint at the score ticker on ESPN. *Utah State vs. Florida International?* Who gives a shit?

Merry jolly fucking Christmas to me.

I tear off a hunk of chicken and shove it in my mouth. It tastes like sand. I wash it down with a swig of beer that tastes like piss.

I fucked up. Royally.

I've tried texting Melody half a dozen times. Called a few times, too. All left on "Read." No replies. No mercy.

Not that I deserve any.

But I don't want to be *that guy*—the clingy boyfriend—or psycho ex. Or, honestly, I don't even know what I am to her.

What I *was*.

We've only really known each other for a month and been sleeping together for, what, eight days? But somehow, in that time, she turned my whole world inside out. Like a snow globe shaken to hell.

Oh God, not me with the Christmas metaphors.

I spent my teens being a virgin and my twenties doing the hookup thing—bailing before anything got too serious. After what happened between my mom and my asshole dad, I figured it was safer to keep things light. Temporary. No one gets hurt if no one sticks around.

By thirty, even that had lost its shine. I stopped bothering altogether. Played it safe. Stayed solo.

And then along came Melody.

Messy. Gorgeous. Hilarious. Infuriating. The most chaotic person I've ever met, and the most caring. And brave. So fucking brave. She walked away from everything—her family, her church, her entire past—for a chance to be herself. No safety net. No one to catch her.

How many people could do that? How many would even try?

Still, she celebrates Christmas with wild abandon—smiling, decorating, volunteering. Wearing that ridiculous Mrs. Claus outfit to bring joy to people she doesn't even know.

Then she met me, and I dumped kerosene all over that joy and lit it on fire.

And still, she saw past all of it, reached through the wreckage of my past, skimmed my rough edges, and touched something in me no one else ever has.

I glance at my phone again—still nothing.

Buster finally jumps up on the couch, yowling for chicken. I reach over to scratch him behind the ears, but he dodges me, eyes locked on the rotisserie like, *No pets until I get snacks, idiot.*

"Fine," I mutter, flicking a piece to the floor. Buster hops down, sniffs it, and looks up like, *That's it?*

"You know what? Have at it." I drop the entire chicken on the ground. His eyes light up like Christmas trees, and he dives in face-first. Honestly, it's the happiest I've seen him in years.

I take a swig of my beer and start flipping channels—the remote snags on one of those creepy stop-motion Christmas movies. I don't know why these have always been nightmare fuel for me—maybe it's the jerky movements. The bullying. The way everyone gaslights Rudolph into thinking he's unlovable until he literally saves Christmas to earn basic respect.

I watch Santa shame Rudolph for all of ten seconds before muttering, "Motherfucker," and changing the channel.

Every narcissistic portrayal of Santa reminds me of my dad.

I land on the local news—apparently, two rival mall Santas went full North Pole Fight Club over "territory." Perfect.

I sink deeper into the couch and take another sip. The beer's starting to taste slightly less like piss.

The doorbell rings.

Buster grabs a chunk of chicken in his teeth and bolts upstairs like a raccoon on meth.

"What the fuck?"

My heart leaps—could it be her? Please, dear God, let it be her.

I scramble, nearly dumping my beer all over the coffee table —no time to clean it. I smooth my wrinkled shirt, rake my hair into something pretending to be a style, and bolt for the door.

I fling the door open—and my heart swan-dives off a cliff.

Not who I was hoping for. Not in the slightest.

Mary Lou stands there, sheepish, clutching what looks like a check.

I'm not gonna slam the door in her face. She's always been kind to me. Too kind, probably. But I can feel the heat rising up my neck as it slowly dawns on me why she's here.

Ever the intuitive stepmother, Mary Lou raises her hands like she's approaching a wounded animal.

"Honey," she says gently, "before you get mad—your daddy—*Ronnie* sent me. He thought maybe it wasn't a good idea to come himself."

"Damn right, it wasn't."

"Ebby, I know your dad hasn't always been the dad you needed. And I understand why you didn't ask for help with your mama—you figured he'd just let you down again." She blinks fast. "But I need you to know—he's all torn up about this. He wants you to have this."

She holds out the check. I glance at it. Ten thousand dollars. Made out to me.

"I don't want it," I say, handing it back. "I don't want his money. Now or ever."

She steps closer. "Honey, I want you to listen to me. This is not a gift. It's not charity. You *earned* this money. So did your mama. You take this check. And Ronnie told me he is going to cover your mama's expenses from now on—whatever she needs. It's a blank check for you and Anne. Got it?"

"We have the money. And I swear to you, you will never owe us a thing. Not a visit. Not a phone call. Nothing."

I stare down at the check. A lump rises in my throat.

"I don't know what to say."

"You don't have to say anything." She offers a small smile. "I just want you to know—if you'd like to join us for Christmas, you're always welcome—no pressure, of course. The door's always open."

There's a stretch of awkward silence before she adds: "And your little lady can come too—what's her name again?"

I sigh. "Melody."

"I've got presents for you and her waiting under the tree. If you'd like them. If not, I can mail them to you. Or donate them. Whatever you want me to do."

I don't say anything for a long time. Just stare at the check. Let it sink in. My dad's going to take over the bills for my mom.

The nightmare is over—assuming he follows through. But the look in Mary Lou's eyes, the look in my dad's eyes at the pageant... I think maybe he will.

A weight lifts off my chest—one I didn't know I was carrying until it slipped away.

"Okay, honey," she says softly, turning to go. "I'll see you later—"

"Mary Lou."

She freezes, turns back, eyes wide and hopeful. "Yeah?"

I swallow hard. "I think I messed up."

She glances past me into the house, spotting the half-empty beer on the table.

"You got another one of those?" she asks, nodding at it.

My throat tightens with something like relief. I step aside and hold the door.

"Yeah. Come on in."

CHAPTER 34

CHRISTMAS EVE

MELODY

*T*he silence stretches as Cassie and I sit on the couch. She takes in the room with wide eyes that linger on the tinsel, the tree, the garland—the whole Christmas explosion that is my apartment. The TV is off for now, but I'm itching to turn it on just for background noise.

"I wasn't expecting…" she trails off, her gaze landing on a throw pillow like she's afraid Santa might pop out of it and bite her. "All this."

I shrug, hugging a faux fur blanket to my chest. "Yeah. It's a lot."

She glances over. "No. It's… good."

That catches me off guard. "Really?"

Cassie nods slowly. "Yeah. I mean—it's weird. But good. It suits you."

A deep breath fills my lungs. I hadn't realized how tight my chest had gotten until now.

For a second, we just sit there—suspended in the quiet hum

of years lost and words unsaid. I want to ask a hundred things: *Are you safe? Are you out for good? Did you miss me?* But the questions tangle in my throat.

Instead, I reach for the tin on the coffee table. "Want a cookie?"

She eyes it warily. "Are they… normal?"

I grin. "Define normal."

Cassie cracks a smile, hesitant but genuine. "No poison or broken glass?"

"Only peppermint and butter."

She takes one.

I watch her lift it to her lips and nibble. She chews gingerly, nodding as the taste settles in. Her shoulders drop. She sits up a little straighter.

"These are really good. Did you make them?"

"From scratch, baby. Just like Grandma."

At the mention of our grandmother, Cassie's eyes lower. "You got more time with her than I did."

She's right. Cassie's six years younger. I was twelve when Grandma died—Cassie was only six. By then, the Heralds had caught on to our sneaky basement Christmases. Our parents got admonished. No more secret Santa sugar cookies. No more humming "Jingle Bells" while pretending it was a folk song. We still had a few cookies, but no Christmas shapes allowed.

"Why are you here, Cass?" I finally ask.

She freezes mid-bite, then lowers the hand holding her half-eaten cookie to her lap.

"I've been trying to call you," she says. "But you're very skilled at ignoring your phone."

"Damn right I am." I puff up my chest. "All those years ignoring Herald busybodies have made me an expert."

Her eyes flash with hurt. I bite my tongue.

"Courtney told me she saw you at the Christmas bar."

"Once a snitch, always a snitch."

"She left too."

"*Too?*"

Cassie nods, then takes a deep breath. She fiddles with her cookie, then shoves the rest into her mouth.

"You left?" I ask quietly.

She chews, swallows. "I did."

"Why?"

"I met someone," she says.

"Uh-oh," I say. "A non-Herald?"

She nods.

"That's amazing, Cass!" I cheer. Even my little sister is less alone than I am. I pop a cookie in my mouth. "I'm so happy for you! Tell me everything. What's he like?"

She hesitates. "She," she says softly.

I freeze, crumbs on my lip. "Oh. Oh! Cass, that's wonderful. What's she like?"

"She's great, but…" her eyes drop; her mouth pinches. She worries the hem of her sleeve. "Well, you can probably imagine."

I set the tin aside and scoot forward, wrapping her in a tight hug. She stiffens at first, but then relaxes into it, a hand settling on my elbow. Our foreheads touch.

"I'm so sorry I wasn't there for you."

"It's not like any of us were there for you."

I pull back. Cassie hangs her head in shame.

I tilt her chin up. "Hey. That's not fair. You were a kid."

"Old enough to know better."

"Sixteen's still a kid—especially when you're trapped in a cult."

She exhales, almost a laugh. "Kind of wild that we're more forgiving than the Heralds now, huh?"

"Wild," I smile. "How long have you been out?"

"Three months."

"Fresh deconstruction," I say, squeezing her shoulder. "You'll get used to it."

She nods, then glances toward the TV. "So… what do we do now? Watch Christmas movies or something?"

I follow her gaze and laugh. "Yeah, sure. We can put something on."

We settle into the couch as I flip on the TV.

"Hey, wait," I say. "Why aren't you with your girlfriend?"

"She's working tonight. I'm going to spend Christmas with her family tomorrow." Cassie pauses, tilting her head. "I wanted to spend it with mine today."

My throat tightens. I smile and cue up *Home Alone*.

"Let's ease you in," I say, tossing the blanket over both of us. "We've got a lot of catching up to do."

We don't talk much after that. Just curl up together, half-watching the screen and half-watching each other out of the corners of our eyes. My Chinese takeout arrives still piping hot, and we nosh on my lonely girl Christmas feast—not so alone anymore.

When one movie ends, we start another. *National Lampoon's Christmas Vacation, Elf, How the Grinch Stole Christmas*—as many of my favorite Christmas movies as I can cram into one night.

By the time the credits roll on *A Christmas Story*, we're both asleep—two sisters, snuggled up in a pile of faux fur, peppermint crumbs, and the kind of peace I never thought I'd get back.

When my phone buzzes to life for the first time in twenty-four hours, it startles me awake. I sit up, disoriented. The room is flooded with bright morning light.

Christmas Day.

Cassie's still out cold, drooling on one of my throw pillows. She looks cozy in a red-and-green plaid pajama set I let her borrow. I smile.

I got my sister back.

The best Christmas present ever.

My phone buzzes again—an unknown number.

Maybe: Forest Park Assisted Living.

What the hell?

Okay, sure—I kind of skipped out on the pageant early, but calling me on Christmas Day? Are they really that worried?

I answer, just in case. "Hello?"

"Melody, we need you to come here right away." It's Missy. Her voice is tight, urgent.

"What?" I sit up. "Right now?"

Cassie stirs beside me. She yawns and stretches, rubbing her eyes.

"Yes, we need you. It's… an emergency."

My stomach drops. "An emergency? Is someone hurt? Shouldn't you call 911 instead of me?"

"It's… Edna. She's asking for you."

I hear groaning in the background.

"Edna is *asking* for me?"

There's a rustling sound. Then Edna's gravelly voice cuts through: "Get your ass over here right now. I'm dying and I need you."

"You need me? For what?"

"Are you daft—"

More rustling. Missy's clearly wrestling the phone away.

"Please, Melody," Missy pleads. "We need you. It's for the olds."

Someone in the background shouts, "Who you callin' old!"

I exhale. "Okay. I'm coming."

"Thanks, Melody. We owe you one."

Another voice hollers, "I don't owe anyone *shit*!"

The line clicks dead.

I stare at my phone.

Cassie blinks at me, bleary-eyed. "Who was that?"

I sigh. "It's a long story. But I gotta go."

She checks her watch and nods. "I do too, actually."

"I—uh—what are you doing tomorrow?"

"Working, unfortunately."

"Right, okay." I look down, trying to hide my disappointment.

"But," she adds, "Rena's working on New Year's. She's a 911 operator, hence the weird hours. Do you want to hang out on New Year's Eve?"

I light up. "Really?"

She nods.

New Year's was another forbidden "pagan holiday" growing up. It's not one I've fully embraced—mostly because ringing in another year without my family always made me feel sad and alone. But now—

"I'd love that," I say, laughing as I pull her into another hug.

She hugs me back, just as tightly—quietly answering a question I hadn't dared to ask.

"I missed you so much," she whispers.

CHAPTER 35

CHRISTMAS DAY

MELODY

I get another frantic call from Missy before I've even had a chance to shut the door behind my sister. All I manage to do is yank a giant, ugly Christmas sweater over my pajamas and throw my hair into a messy ponytail. Then I bolt out the door.

Missy's already waiting in the parking lot when I pull in. I park haphazardly, even for me, and scramble out of the car, only to get yanked back by my seatbelt. I curse under my breath, unbuckle, and finally hop out.

She eyes me as I jog up, breathless. "Ope... I probably should have told you you had more time."

I glance down at myself—Christmas pajamas, clashing sweater, hair barely contained—and shrug. "What the hell is going on?"

"Never mind, honey—you look great!" she says, wrapping an arm around me like we're headed to brunch instead of a crisis.

I scrunch my nose. "Why do I need to look great for a nursing home emergency?"

She clears her throat and opens the door. "This way."

As soon as I step inside, I hear the faint sound of Frank Sinatra crooning *Santa Claus is Comin' to Town*—one of my favorites.

I glance at Missy, confused. She's wearing a strained smile, the kind that says *I'm keeping a secret and you're about to find out what it is.* A weird choice to blast Christmas music during an emergency, but okay.

We walk down the hallway toward the atrium. It's empty, but I can see all the way down to the residential wings. A few graying heads peek out from doorways, watching us like nosy neighbors.

My eyebrows knit together. "What's going on?"

Silence.

I whirl around.

Missy's gone.

"What the hell?" I whisper. Is this a bad dream?

Then I spot the community room.

Usually, it's filled with folding tables, mismatched chairs, and the seniors accusing each other of cheating at cards. One sad, half-decorated Christmas tree usually lurks by the window, like someone started decorating but got tired.

Not today.

Today, it's a forest.

Christmas trees—dozens of them—fill the space from wall to wall. All different sizes. All different styles. Traditional green, snow-flocked, frosted, fiber optic. It's like a showroom of holiday trends from the last decade.

I spot one strung with Edison bulbs—and freeze.

I know that tree.

I step closer, weaving between the branches. My heart starts to race.

I recognize *all* of them.

Mariah Care-tree, Buddy, Kris Pine, Noelle, Spruce Springsteen, Treeoncé, Blitzen, Holly Parton, Merry Tyler Moore—

These are my Christmas trees. From my storage unit. Each one I've collected over the years. Each one glowing, sparkling, twinkling like they've been waiting for this moment.

A carpet of fake snow forms a path between them.

I suck in a deep breath—and follow it.

The walk isn't long, but I savor it—glancing around in awe at all my babies, lit up and glittering for me. Together, in one room. My personal forest of joy.

A glittering ribbon catches my eye—and that's when I see it. Underneath every one of my precious trees are dozens and dozens of presents, wrapped in big gold, silver, and red bows— for all the seniors.

When I reach the window, the morning light pours through —and there he is.

Eben.

He stands in the center of it all, looking nervous and wearing a sweater so aggressively festive it stops me in my tracks. Garland is sewn in horizontal strips across his chest like he's been gift-wrapped by a tipsy elf. Red, gold, and silver metallic ornaments dangle from the knitted yarn, swaying with every breath like he's a walking, talking Christmas tree.

A full-blown holiday cheer explosion.

And somehow, he still looks like the most handsome thing I've ever seen in my life.

"Hi," I say, suddenly feeling sheepish.

"Hi," he replies, blowing out a shaky breath.

I glance around, overwhelmed, and gesture at the glowing forest. "How did you...?"

"A Christmas miracle," he says, then adds, "Also, Ally."

The magnitude of it hits me all at once—what he's done,

what she helped him do. My best friend. This man. It all starts to sink in.

My throat tightens. My eyes fill with tears.

"Melody," he murmurs, almost like he's grounding himself just by saying my name. He takes a breath. "I've spent two decades avoiding this holiday like the plague."

His hand brushes mine—just barely at first, like he's not sure if he has permission. When I don't pull away, he threads our fingers together.

My stomach does flip-flops.

"Christmas is supposed to celebrate love and connection," he says softly. "And the truth is... I didn't want it. Not after what happened between my parents. With my dad. To my mom, after he left. Everything felt splintered. Ugly. Painful. And for so long, this season was just noise and lights and fake smiles.

"But then you showed up. In that ridiculous Mrs. Claus outfit. With your garlands and your cookies and your eighty-seven Christmas trees."

He motions all around us, and I huff out a watery laugh.

"So when I was sitting there all by myself on Christmas Eve with my... fucking rotisserie chicken," he says with a crooked smile, "for the first time I felt alone. Really alone. Because all I could think about was how much I wanted to be with you."

My breath catches. The lights from my trees blur behind tears.

"And then my stepmom showed up—"

"Eben, wait," I squeak out. I swallow hard, shaking my head. "I want to say something."

His intense ice-blue eyes melt into mine. He nods, his pretty mouth clamping shut, waiting patiently.

"I shouldn't have pushed you to fix things with your dad. That's your family, not mine. I was projecting my own hurt, and that wasn't fair."

I hold his gaze, even though it's like staring into the sun. I want him to know I mean it.

"I'm sorry."

He exhales, the tension in his shoulders softening. "Okay," he says, a small smile lifting the corner of his mouth. "Thank you for saying that. But… you were right."

I blink. "I was?"

He grins, nods. "My dad was upset that I've been covering the cost of my mom's care. He sent Mary Lou to tell me he's taking over the bills."

"Wow." I'm in awe. "I don't know what to say."

"Say you'll stop by the Christmas King's house with me later."

I can't help it—my eyes light up brighter than all my Christmas trees combined. "Really?"

"Really, really."

I can't contain it anymore—I wrap my arms around his neck and kiss him. He pulls me in tight, his hands firm at my waist, kissing me like it's Christmas morning and I'm the only present he ever wanted.

And then, slowly, he pulls back.

A tiny whimper escapes my throat in protest.

"Now…" he murmurs, turning to grab something from the table behind him. "I found this," he says, pulling out a small, slightly worn tree topper wrapped in tissue paper. He unwraps it gently, like it's something sacred.

It's vintage. Hand-painted. A Santa Claus made of blown glass—delicate, beautiful, a little chipped at the edges.

"It belonged to my mom," he says. "My dad used to lift me to put it on the top of the tree, back before… Christmas got complicated."

He looks down at it for a moment, then back at me.

"I found it in the attic. I thought maybe… You should have it."

He holds it out, and I take it from him—carefully, reverently. I touch the side of Santa's face. More than just a trinket or a bauble—a symbol of healing. Eben's healing, and my own.

"I love it," I whisper, hugging it to my chest.

He smiles then—bright and beaming.

"I love you, Mrs. Claus," he says, eyes sparkling. "I mean… Melody."

He winks.

I laugh and roll my eyes, wrapping a hand around the back of his blond head and pulling him down to kiss me again.

"I love you, too, Mr. Claus."

He huffs a laugh against my lips. "So cheesy."

I growl and nip at his lips, playful. He gently takes the ornament from me, sets it back on the table behind him, then wraps both arms around me and kisses me again—deeper this time. He teases my mouth open with his tongue, tasting me. My arms tighten around him, fingers playing at the little hairs at the nape of his neck.

Low whistles sound from behind us.

We break apart reluctantly, and turn to see our favorite olds (and Missy) staring back at us through the faux forest, grinning like gremlins.

"Keep it PG, will ya?"

"Yeah, get a room!"

"They can have mine."

"I haven't seen this much action in years."

"What are you talking about? I saw you sneaking into Roberta's room last week!"

Finally, Edna scoots up, pushing them all out of the way to get to the presents, eyeing a large red package with her name on it.

"Move out of the way, Santa brought me a Nintendo!"

I laugh out loud as Missy hands Edna her gift and looks at Eben and me. "Thanks to you both, we raised triple what we were hoping to, which means every senior here got what they *really* wanted for Christmas." She winks at us, then turns to manage the present-starved seniors who are ready for Christmas to begin.

The bickering and catcalls are replaced by the joyous sounds of ripped wrapping paper, as Eben and I gaze into each other's eyes, surrounded by Christmas trees and geriatrics and twinkling lights and magic—all my favorite things.

"I like your sweater," I whisper, eyes raking over the bright green monstrosity in all its ugly-sweater glory.

"I knew you would," he says, eyes trailing over my oversized Christmas sweater and pajama ensemble like he can't wait to unwrap me later.

His head dips again, and I go back to kissing my very own sexy Santa-slash-human-Christmas tree.

Merry fuckin' Christmas to me.

CHAPTER 36

THE DAY AFTER CHRISTMAS

MELODY

*I*t's the day after Christmas, and all through the house, a creature is stirring, and it is… a cat.

Eben's cat, to be precise. Currently perched on my chest and making very intense eye contact.

Eben swears he's been fed, but I think he just wants me dead. So I do the only logical thing and declare war.

That's why Buster and I are currently locked in a high-stakes stare-off.

What the stakes are, I have no idea—nor do I want to find out.

"You're going to lose," Eben mutters, side-eyeing us from his side of the bed.

"Shhh." I wave him away. "I need to focus."

What's left of Buster's mangled old tail gives a twitch. His smushy face has a speck of food at the corner of his mouth. I zero in on it, eyes burning, forcing myself not to blink.

I'm only sixty percent sure Buster even knows we're in a

contest—but I'm one-hundred percent sure he's winning. My eyes sting—my vision blurs. Still, I persist.

I'm also one hundred percent sure the little demon is growing on me. Not sure the feeling's mutual.

Still ugly, though.

"He can go several days without blinking. I'm pretty sure," Eben says.

"Shut. Up." My eyes water, but I'm nothing if not resilient.

Come on. Just a little longer—

"HA! He blinked!" I swipe the tears from my cheeks and point triumphantly at the cat. "I win, you little fucker."

Buster MROWS, offended, and hops off the bed.

Eben is shirtless with delicious bedhead, a book in his lap. A *book*. I think it's about World War II, but whatever—it's reading. Just when I thought he couldn't get any hotter.

And here I am: naked in his bed, picking fights with his cat, not a book in sight.

Balance.

"You are deeply weird," Eben says.

"Hey!" I smack his bare shoulder. He grins and pats his chest. I smile big and cozy up under his arm. He returns to his book. I nip at his bicep, and he growls, fingers skimming up my ribs to my breast, circling my nipple lazily. I sigh dreamily.

We've been together ever since yesterday morning, when Eben declared his love for me in the middle of my very own Christmas tree forest. I heard from Missy and the seniors that he spent all night on Christmas Eve setting it up, taking his truck back and forth between my storage unit and the nursing home.

I spent all of Christmas Day showing him just how much I appreciated his magnificent declaration (and his magnificent... other things).

That reminds me—

"You said Ally let you into my storage unit"

His hand tightens on my ribs. He looks up from his book—but not at me. "She did."

I glance at my phone, realizing I have not heard from Ally since the pageant, despite her being very involved with Eben's grand gesture.

Highly suspicious.

"She was supposed to be away for Christmas with Teddy."

"Oh," he says, head tilting. "I don't know. Maybe they rescheduled."

He's hiding something.

"Eben…" I scooch away to look at him full-on.

"Hmmm?" he pretends to read, but his eyes don't move across the page.

"What are you hiding?"

"Nothing."

"You're lying."

"No, I'm not."

"Uh-huh." I smooth a hand over his brow. "Your eyebrow twitches when you lie."

He glances up, incredulous. "How could you possibly know that already?"

"I'm very observant. I was in a cult, remember?"

He sighs. "I remember."

"Did Ally and Teddy break up?" I ask suddenly.

Eben's eyes snap to mine. "Fuck, Melody—I promised I wouldn't say anything."

I'm already grabbing my phone and shoving my arms into the ruby satin robe I brought from home. "Are you kidding me? She told *you* and not me?"

"She didn't want to ruin your Christmas!"

"She's my *best friend on Planet Earth*! Who gives a fuck about my Christmas when she just broke up with the love of her life?"

I scroll to Ally's name—twenty-one missed calls from the night of the pageant. Oh my God, I thought she was calling about Eben, but what if she was calling about her breakup? What if she needed me? I hit Call.

She answers on the third ring. "Why are you calling me? You should be shacking up with your lover."

"Did you and Teddy break up?"

A pause. "That little shit."

"Don't blame him, I guessed. Also, why the fuck does my boyfriend know about Teddy before I do?"

"Oooh. *Boyfriend?*"

"You're trying to distract me."

"Fine. Yes, Teddy and I called it."

"Where are you? I'm coming over."

"No, you're not. You're going to spend the day with your legs in the air."

"You're at your parents' house, aren't you?"

She swears under her breath.

"Seriously, I'm coming over."

"If you do, I'll kick your ass."

"Fine, then you're coming over tomorrow. We'll eat leftover Christmas cookies, cry, and watch *The Notebook*."

"I hate *The Notebook*."

"I know. I didn't say we'd enjoy it."

A pause. "Okay."

"I love you, Al. I'm not going to tell you it's going to be okay. But I will help you bury a body if you need me to."

Her laugh is soft and wobbly. "I know you would."

I'm not used to hearing her like this. It breaks my heart. I don't know what happened between her and Teddy, but somewhere deep down, I can't help but feel like they'll find their way back to each other. Someday.

And no matter what, I know Ally will be okay. Eventually.

"We're going to die side by side in the nursing home, just like Noah and Allie."

"Who's Noah and Allie?"

"The toxic couple from *The Notebook*."

"Right. I hate them."

"Exactly why we're watching it tomorrow."

There's a pause on the other end. "Thanks, bestie."

I blink back tears. Her voice is so small. I want to fast-forward through the hurt and healing to the version of her forged by it. I want to skip ahead—to the day she sifts through the wreckage, gathers the broken pieces, and assembles them into someone new. Someone better.

But there's no speeding up time, and grief has no shortcuts.

I would know.

I swallow the lump rising in my throat. "Friends forever?"

"Forever and ever."

When we hang up, I pad back into the bedroom. Eben's pacing now, sweatpants on, worry in his eyes.

"Does she hate me?"

"What? No."

He doesn't look so sure.

I roll my eyes. "Relax—Ally forgives hot people very easily," I smirk, trailing a finger down his bare chest. "You're good."

He exhales in relief. "Thank God. I don't want to screw this up before we're even official."

"Wait." I squint. "We're *not* official?"

He grins. "Are we?"

"You told me you love me."

"I *am* in love with you."

"Doesn't that automatically escalate you to boyfriend status?"

"Does it?" His grin widens. "I didn't get the handbook."

"Fine," I say, turning toward the door. "If I'm not your girlfriend, then I'll just—"

He catches me and tackles me onto the bed, pinning me beneath him. "Melody Whitaker, will you be my girlfriend?"

"I don't know…"

He dips down and bites my nipple through the satin robe.

"Fine! Yes! I'll be your girlfriend."

"Good girl," he says, settling between my legs, spreading me wide. I'm already panting. "Only 364 days until next Christmas, and so far you're on the nice list."

"Gee, thanks, Santa," I tease.

He squeezes my ass. "Don't worry. There's still plenty of time to be naughty."

That brilliant grin flashes—and then he lowers his head and puts that pretty mouth to work.

We spend the rest of the day together, in bed and in love, already making plans for next Christmas.

And every Christmas after that.

EPILOGUE

ONE YEAR LATER

EBEN

*M*y eyes flutter open to find a pair of bright hazel eyes staring back at me, her chin resting on my chest, her long lashes fluttering like she's been waiting for me to wake up.

"Good morning, beautiful," I say, my voice still rough with sleep. I reach up to tuck a strand of her sleep-tangled, sex-mussed hair behind her ear.

"Merry Christmas," she says, flashing a big, dopey grin. She's already wide awake—of course she is. It's her favorite day of the year.

I stretch, slipping my hands under the covers. Melody is wearing my favorite thing—absolutely nothing. My fingers trace circles over her stomach, and she exhales the prettiest little sigh—still my favorite sound in the world.

I roll her gently onto her back and lean over her, pressing a kiss to her lips—careful of morning breath, but too in love to care much either way.

"Sleep okay?" I murmur, trailing one hand down the curve of her thigh.

"The best," she whispers, her legs parting in invitation.

I give her her first Christmas present of the day—three slow, deep orgasms. She gives me mine with those sweet pink lips wrapped around my, ahem, candy cane. Honestly, her gifted mouth is the best present I've ever received—second only to her kind heart and big, gorgeous brain.

Afterward, we tug on the matching Santa-themed robes she surprised me with last night—a nod to our Mr. and Mrs. Claus days. We wore them for about five minutes before peeling them off in front of the fire.

I finally convinced Melody to let go of her lease on that tiny apartment, and she moved in fully with me a month ago, right around Thanksgiving. She's spent every waking moment since turning my mom's house—now our house—into a full-blown Christmas explosion.

One year and two months ago, a Christmas tree in every room would have given me a full-blown apoplexy. Now? It just reminds me of her. Of her warmth. Her sparkle. That laugh that sounds like an angelic choir and feels like home.

Fuck, I'm in love.

I go downstairs to feed Buster and make us special Christmas coffees with whipped cream and cinnamon, bringing them up to her in bed. We sip and cuddle, enjoying the quiet of the morning, the cozy electric fireplace we installed last week flickering for maximum winter ambiance.

She glances out the window above our bed and squeals in delight.

"Eben—it's snowing!"

I look outside. A light dusting of snow has already covered the lawn and leaf-bare trees.

"Let's put on *White Christmas*!" she says, grabbing the remote and flipping on the TV above the fireplace.

"What time is Cassie coming?" I ask, settling in beside her.

"Cassie and Rena should be here around one. We're meeting your dad and Mary Lou at Forest Park at two."

Turns out if we dress Dad and Mary Lou like Mr. and Mrs. Claus, Mom lights right up. She still mutters a few profanities about Ronnie Golding under her breath, but my dad fully accepts that he deserves every last ounce of criticism. Mary Lou secretly loves it when Mom gives him the business, too. And the residents adore their yearly visit from the Christmas King.

LAST YEAR, we spent Christmas Day with Ronnie and Mary Lou, as well as my stepbrothers and their girlfriends. It was surprisingly pleasant. And everybody loves the hell out of Melody, which takes the pressure off me.

I've officially retired the Santa costume—and the Daddy Christmas gig (shudder)—for good. Well… who knows. I might pull it out one more time for a proposal.

Mel doesn't know it yet, but I already have the ring. Mary Lou and I picked it out last month. But I'm waiting—just a little longer. Moving in was already a significant step for her, and I want to ensure she's ready before we take the next one.

I plan to propose on her birthday in June—my new favorite holiday. Another day her family never celebrated.

Last year, Ally and I surprised her with a cake covered in twenty-nine candles. The look on her face—those wide, wonder-filled eyes, the way her cheeks turned bright pink—I'll never forget it.

I plan to spoil her on every birthday from now on, to make up for each and every one she missed.

It turns out, I don't hate holidays. Or Christmas.

I just needed the right person to share them with.

I watch her watching the movie, the glow from the tree in the corner of our room lighting up her eyes.

I lean in close and whisper, "I have a surprise for you."

She turns to me, eyes wide. "What is it?"

"It's downstairs," I murmur, pressing a kiss to the side of her head.

She doesn't waste a second—throws back the covers and takes off, running down the stairs like a little kid on Christmas morning. Buster stretches, yawns, and trots after her. I follow them both, coffee in hand.

I hear her reaction before I see it.

"HOLY SHIT, ARE YOU SERIOUS?!"

By the time I hit the bottom step, she's full-on jumping up and down.

In the center of the room stands a real Christmas tree. Strung with lights. Waiting to be decorated.

I lean against the banister, sip my coffee, and smile. "You like it?"

She launches herself at me, arms around my neck, kissing me a dozen times in rapid-fire. I try to protect my coffee, but a little dribbles out. She doesn't notice, and I don't say anything.

"I love it," she murmurs between kisses. "I love you."

I kiss her back, slowly, and whisper, "I love you more."

"Nuh-uh," she pouts, but quickly forgets we were mid-play-fight and turns back to the tree, eyes glittering.

"When did you do this?"

"Snuck it in last night after you fell asleep," I say. "The box next to it is from the attic. All the old ornaments from my childhood. Go to town."

She kisses me again, softer this time. It's meaningful and filled with promises of a future we haven't fully articulated yet. I smile against her lips, savoring the moment. The morning is chilly, but her warmth is all I need.

As she pulls back, her gaze lingers on the tree, eyes twinkling with possibilities.

"You like your Christmas gift?" I ask.

"Are you kidding? This is the best Christmas *ever.*"

Tears spring to her eyes. She drops to her knees in front of the tree, digging gently through the box of ornaments like she's unearthing buried treasure.

I stay where I am, watching her and taking a mental snapshot.

It really is the best Christmas ever. And I have a strong feeling they're only going to get better from here on out.

"Merry Christmas, sweetheart," I say.

ACKNOWLEDGMENTS

Turns out it's not easy to keep your Christmas tree up all year (who knew they got so dusty!?). But it did keep the holiday spirit alive through another hot Los Angeles summer—otherwise the vibes might've melted away along with our sanity.

To Najla, Jennifer, and the whole absurdly talented team at Qamber Designs & Media—thank you for bringing the artistic vision of SANTA CUTIE to life. The cover captured the essence of a "Cherryville" Christmas, and your dedication to getting every detail perfect shows on every inch!

Jessie at Book Blurb Magic—as a former copywriter, I loathe writing blurbs and bios (especially for my own projects). We literally gasped reading your take on our characters, the book, and us as authors and friends. Your words sparkle. Thank you!

To the wonderful Cara Lockwood at Edit My Novel—thank you for editing SANTA CUTIE with so much heart and for championing the book (and us as authors) right out of the gate. Your initial feedback put smiles on our faces for days. We're so grateful.

Danika Corrall, you design genius, you. You transformed our website—and us—into the vintage-holiday girlie pops we didn't even know we needed to be. You took our vision, said "hold my beer" and built a digital wonderland we're so proud to call our little corner of the internet.

JENNY

First and foremost, I want to thank the Alexandra half of Jenny Alexandra. In the past ten-plus years, there's never been a dull moment being your best friend. Some friends get crazy ideas— we get crazy ideas and actually do them. You're a hell of a human, writer, storyteller, and bestie, and watching you bring Melody, Eben, and their romance to life was nothing short of magical. To say you're a force would be the understatement of the century. You're getting FANTASTIC Christmas gifts this year! ILYSM.

To my mom, Mary Jane—thank you for always calling me a writer and for sharing the "Mrs. Buell" story, even when I was doing a million other things with my life. I know I didn't always want to write the thank-you cards or letters to the mayor or CEOs when there was a customer service "injustice" to tackle— but your belief that my words mattered has stayed with me more than you know.

To my Dad, Tim—thank you for your sparkle, quiet humor, and steady support at every stage of my life. I know what good men look like because of you.

Timmy and Olivia—thank you for cheering on whatever my next chapter is, even when Timmy thinks I'm nuts (and Olivia has my back). Olivia, thank you for letting me drop the spiciest parts of this book over Topgolf nachos on family golf night and for being a day-one cheerleader!

To Geo—for reading every awful thing I wrote between the ages of 18-22 and still telling me to keep going. You were probably the inspiration for my sadly lost teenage angst novel, *The Mind's Eye Lies*. You stubbornly called me a writer, even when I insisted I was busy doing capital-B Business. Your support spans decades, and I don't take a single one of those years for granted.

To Bill and Yolande—my amazing second parents. Thank

you for showing up full-force behind everything Alexandra and I tackle, and for taking me in as an honorary daughter. Yolande, there isn't a copyeditor with sharper word-and-grammar prowess. We're so lucky to have your eye on this book.

ALEX

For Moomah—always my biggest fan and first reader. Thank you for indulging every whimsical urge I ever had. I know I didn't finish all of them, but I sure did finish this one. Onto the next. ;)

For Daddy—thank you for always being a sucker for me, and for giving me the time, space, and encouragement to figure out who I am. You are the voice of reason in my head.

For Nick—you are my rock, my best friend, my love. Thanks for lending your abilities and assistance to everything I do. You never hesitate to help and support, and I don't know what I'd do without you.

For my friends and family—I always say you don't have to read my books, but many of you do anyway, and I'm so grateful. Even if you don't (and really, you don't have to), thank you for being plot points in my book of life. You inspire me.

For Jenny—my bestie, my ride-or-die, my soul sister. How lucky am I to do life, business, and now books with you? Thanks for asking me to grab coffee in that screenwriting class all those years ago—and sorry in advance for the one million books you're going to have to write before you die. :P

AND TO OUR DEAR READERS—as we write this, we don't know you yet, but we can't wait to meet you. We hope you'll stick around for future ships ;)

ABOUT THE AUTHOR

Alex and Jenny have been best friends, ever since a screenwriting class in Los Angeles turned two Ohio girls—one from Dayton, one from Cleveland—into inseparable partners-in-crime. Today, they run a PR agency by day and write spicy, sparkly rom-coms by night. Raised with lackluster (or banned) holidays, they now go all out at Christmas with adult money and zero restraint. When not plotting love stories, they're cooking, shopping, daydreaming, or globe-trotting together.

Join their Substack and get a (free! spicy!) bonus chapter of Eben and Melody's story: itsjennyalexandra.substack.com

Follow on Instagram, Threads, and TikTok: @itsjennyalexandra.

See what's coming next: itsjennyalexandra.com.

www.ingramcontent.com/pod-product-compliance
Lightning Source LLC
Chambersburg PA
CBHW071552110726

47908CB00007B/2068